POETRY BY QUAN BARRY

Loose Strife

Water Puppets

Controvertibles

Asylum

She Weeps Each Time You're Born

She Weeps Each Time You're Born

QUAN BARRY

Pantheon Books
New York

Copyright © 2014 by Quan Barry

All rights reserved. Published in the United States by Pantheon Books, a division of Random House LLC, New York, and distributed in Canada by Random House of Canada Limited, Toronto, Penguin Random House companies.

Pantheon Books and colophon are registered trademarks of Random House LLC.

Library of Congress Cataloging-in-Publication Data
Barry, Quan.
   She weeps each time you're born / Quan Barry.
      pages cm
   Includes bibliographical references.
   ISBN 978-0-307-91177-3 (hardcover : alk. paper).
ISBN 978-0-307-91178-0 (eBook).
   1. Families—Vietnam—Fiction.   2. Psychic ability—Fiction.   3. Vietnam—History—20th century—Fiction.
I. Title.
PS3602.A838S54 2014   813'.6—dc23   2014006309

www.pantheonbooks.com

Map illustration by Betty Lew
Jacket design by Joan Wong

Printed in the United States of America
First Edition

9   8   7   6   5   4   3   2   1

for TLB and MIB
with L&L

And then She saw them—*burn! burn!*
and simply the water was made as glass.

And She is the way when there is no way.
She weeps each time you're born.

Main Characters

Bà/Thuan

↓

Tu + Little Mother

↓

Rabbit

Huyen
OLD HONEY SELLER

↓

Qui
HUYEN'S GRANDDAUGHTER

An + Phuong, Hai, Duc

↓

Sang, Son

Glossary of Foreign Terms

Bà—grandmother

Ba—father

Em—a form of direct address used for children

Ong—grandfather

non la—a conical straw hat

ao dai—a traditional Vietnamese dress

VIETNAM

CHINA

HANOI

Mountain of the
Fragrant Traces

Epilogue [2001]

L A O S

THAILAND

South China Sea

CAMBODIA

HO CHI MINH
CITY

THE SAMPAN RIDE BACK DOWN THE SWALLOW BIRD RIVER IS uneventful, everywhere the dragonflies floating fat and red in the late-afternoon sun. The same oarswoman who rowed us out to the Mountain of the Fragrant Traces now methodically bears us away. We're all tired—even crazy Hung, his sunglasses firmly in place, seems to slump in his seat, a cigarette burning down between his fingers. The water is calm, the landscape lush and meditative, and when it comes time to leave the boat, the three of us remain sitting for a moment as if stunned, hardly believing the day is almost over.

On the back of Than's motorcycle I pass the same sights we saw on the way out. Everything looks familiar, like scenes from a previous life—the harvest still drying in the middle of the road, the people doubled over in the paddies in the fading light. I have spent the last week touring around the northern countryside with Hung and Than as my guides; after only a few days I trust them completely. Then Hung pulls up alongside one more time, his motorcycle splashed with mud. He looks at Than and makes a hand signal before taking off up the road. There one thing more, Than shouts over the roar of the engine. Because you are lucky, Amy Quan, yells Than, Hung thinks maybe she see us.

Ten minutes later we pull up out front. The simple wooden house is a perfect square, the boards splintery and gray, a ragged cloth hanging in the window in lieu of glass. In the yard, a hand-ful of chickens and pigs cluster in the shade of a tree, this late in the day the heat still invasive, all smothering. I can tell some-thing is different this time, something in the way Hung and Than keep glancing over their shoulders. Neither of them has lit up a cigarette. This not the house, whispers Than, we just park here. Up close a black crack weaves across one of his front teeth like a piece of string waiting to unravel. Than nods to Hung. Go with him, he says. For a moment he seems like he's about to say more, but he leaves it at that.

For the first time all day, Hung has taken off his sunglasses. Pale rings circle his eyes where the sun rarely touches his skin. Already there is a newfound earnestness in his demeanor. Hung the merry prankster. Hung who pretended to try to flip the sampan while we were gliding down the Swallow Bird River. I had caught a glimpse of this other Hung earlier at the Perfume Pagoda. The way he didn't know which of the two entrances to walk through, the Gate to Heaven or the Gate to Hell, and when he followed Than through the Gate to Heaven, how even with his sunglasses on, I could see the relief flooding his face.

The house is a quarter mile down the road. There are only four other houses in the area, each one also small and wooden, a rusty sheet of corrugated tin on the roof. Firelight flickers in the windows. As we walk, Hung keeps taking deep breaths in through his mouth. He moves with an air of quiet contempla-tion, head bowed as he leads me to this place he thinks I of all people need to be. In the silence his eyes glisten. Despite his con-stant clowning, at times I have sensed a deep sadness in him, as if his frequent jesting is keeping an inner darkness at bay. Beside me he treads like a man without hope. If I didn't know any bet-ter, I might think he is afraid of where we are going.

The moon teeters low on the horizon. I can hear crickets and frogs starting to call. Than and me, our families come from Saigon, Hung says in a low voice. The government doesn't trust southern people. No Hanoi business will hire us. So we're guides. He looks at me and I nod. Her name's Thỏ, he says. Rabbit. For Vietnam she gives up everything. His voice is barely a whisper as if he is really talking to himself. She will stay until every little one is heard. The northern and southern dead. Hung takes one more deep breath. He puts his hand on the gate. Now she's in house arrest, he whispers. No one is allowed, but out here . . . He nods around at the isolation of the landscape. A seedpod from a nearby tamarind falls on the metal roof, the clang echoing like a bell.

The gate swings open on its rusty hinges, the sound almost painful to the ears. Silently we enter the yard in the shadows as the full moon rises behind us with its long grayed face, and then someone opens the door and waves at the ground and I hear a voice which doesn't sound fully human calling *xin chao, xin chao.* Welcome. Welcome.

Later, back outside, the moon burns bright, the lights of Hanoi visible in the distance. Than turns the motorcycle off the rural road and onto the highway where we wait our turn to pay a toll. Around both wrists he wears a bracelet of prayer beads, each one inscribed with a tiny image of Quan Am, the Bodhisattva of Compassion, who Than says keeps him in Her sight as he wanders far from home. Now the street will turn to asphalt, the way smooth and clear. As we wait, I notice a young boy walking barefoot by the side of the road, a dirty piece of cloth wrapped around his waist. In the years to come I will make three more trips to Vietnam, the country of my birth, piecing together the story of Rabbit, of how she was born in the dirt and the sorrows to follow. I have spent the past six weeks touring Vietnam, this place where I was born in the same year as her, our lives diametrically opposite. I have seen everything the guide books speak of—Reunification Palace, the endless rubber plantations, tunnels running hundreds of miles under the earth. This is not a story of what is missing. Some things just have yet to be found.

As we wait in line to pay the toll, I watch the young boy walking barefoot along the shoulder. The highway before us is a long treeless strip of concrete miles from anywhere. Even now as I write this a decade later I wonder where the boy came from. I can still see him smiling to himself, holding something close to his chest that wriggles and flashes in the growing moonlight, the boy's ribs like a lattice. I stare harder. Slowly the cars inch forward, the drivers impatient, the bills ready in their hands, Than revving his engine. Then I see it—the boy is holding a live fish, the thing more than a foot long, his right hand lovingly stroking its pale iridescent belly, and he is walking down the side of a highway at night in Vietnam as though he has all the time in the world.

Along the Song Ma
[1972]

On this we do not agree. Some of us say she was made manifest in a muddy ditch on the way to the pineapple plantation. Others say it happened hunkered down in a piggery, the little ones with their wet snouts full of wonder at the strange bristleless being wriggling among them for milk. Either way we bow to you. Believe us when we say life is a wheel. There was no beginning. There is no end. But we will tell you the story as she believes it occurred under the full rabbit moon six feet below ground in a wooden box, her mother's hands cold as ice, overhead the bats of good fortune flitting through the dark.

WHEN LITTLE MOTHER TOOK OFF HER *NON LA* UNDER THE jackfruit tree, Lam knew what he had to do, and he knew what he wasn't capable of doing. All his long life he'd been the hand that shields the candle guttering in the storm. And now this young woman was standing in his yard underneath the jackfruit tree, the cuffs of her loose black pants dirty from paddy water. It was obviously the mosquito sickness, the kind that can eat twenty pounds off a grown man in under a week. Yes, it was definitely the mosquito sickness, but there was something else. He tried not to stare. Her pregnant stomach was stretched tight, her cheeks sunken, gums receding as if she had already died and nobody told her.

He was just coming back from gathering the wild peony root. With his cane, the errand took twice as long. The flower grew in a small grove along the road to the mountain. He had heard that on the other side of the mountain the landscape was bombed flat, empty C-rations and discarded magazines and clothes and everything the Americans no longer wanted strewn in the places where the butterfly bush used to flower.

He lifted his cane and motioned for her to follow him inside. A jackfruit fell from the tree and broke open, the smell instantly on the wind. Little Mother nodded and put her hat back on. Something shimmered at her feet. Lam blinked and rubbed his eyes. When he looked again, it was gone. He was an old man, older than Uncle Ho would have been were the old patriot still alive. He was old enough to remember the famines brought on by the Japanese army and their insatiable hunger for rice. Still, he knew what he'd seen shimmering at her feet—a ring of words shining in a perfect circle on the ground around her. Sông dài cá lội biệt tăm. *In the long river, fish swim off without a trace.* The sunlight streaming through the reeds in her hat.

Then Lam heard the sound of a door banging shut in the wind. His nearest neighbor was more than a mile away. This is what happens when you live in two worlds at once, he thought, but all he said to her was come.

His two rooms were just off the road along a bend in the Song Ma, the river an impenetrable red. No one was allowed on the other side of the Song Ma, the area declared a free-fire zone where anyone remaining could be shot without question. In the last year he had taken down the paper lanterns that hung from the branches of the jackfruit tree. Without the lanterns it was still obvious somebody lived there. Even on the eastern side of the river, it was best to be cautious, not attract attention. Sometimes when a convoy of trucks would rumble past, his house would shake, the planked boards rattling, the palm leaves thatching his roof rustling as if a strong wind were blowing.

Inside he offered Little Mother his only stool, turning it so the few stray pieces of reed sticking out of the warp were to the back. She bowed before taking his hand and easing herself onto it. He smiled at her humility. They say the Emperor has a throne of solid gold in his summer palace, he said. Can you imagine such a thing? She didn't answer. During the last war he had treated a Vietminh soldier with a blood infection who claimed his mother had worked as a cook at the palace. The soldier had said as a child he and his cousins would sometimes play in the many splendid rooms, the Emperor away for most of the year. The soldier didn't move when Lam stuck a needle in the top of his head, all of the soldier's joints swollen from the infection, his knuckles big as grapes. Once I sat on it when no one was looking, the soldier whispered. Sat on what, said Lam. The throne. The needle wouldn't stay in. A drop of blood appeared, beading on the scalp. What was it like, Lam said. The soldier gazed into the fire, the flames raging in his eyes. Finally the needle took, the metal ringing at an imperceptible frequency, vibrating like the wings of a housefly. The soldier didn't flinch as he answered Lam's question. Like sitting on a mountain of corpses.

Little Mother placed a hand on her swollen belly. In the firelight, shadows ravaged her face. In places her scalp was visible, her hair patchy as if moth-eaten. Child, Lam said. The word hung in the air. The time is late. The medicine will do for you what it can. He could hear the sound of flies buzzing among the overturned crates heaped with clutter in the other room where herbs and flowers hung from hooks. Rows of glass bottles lined dusty shelves. In each one floated insects, tiny birds, embryonic reptiles.

With his finger he began to draw a figure in the dirt. He made a star at the top of the head, a large X at the base of the spine. Then it was time, the flames the right shade of gold. Are you ready, he whispered. He could feel his heart ticking in his chest. Gently Little Mother reached out and took his hands, drawing them to her face. He uncurled his fingers to let her have a closer look.

In the center of each of his palms was a spot like a moldy thumbprint, the skin pitted with a deep green scar the size of a coin. When he was younger, he would sometimes chase small children playfully through the market, holding his open hands up in front of his face, the green scars like unblinking eyes. It's who I am, he said. She let go of his hands. The clock in his chest was pounding. We have to get the blood moving, he said. Let the light in. Little Mother nodded. I am an old man, he added. Please. Quietly she took off her shirt. The skin over her belly was stretched tight like an animal hide dried in the sun. He couldn't help but wince.

Even Lam is surprised by the steadiness of his hands, though there has always been a gentle knowingness in his touch. He lights a scrap of paper on fire and drops it inside a small bamboo jar, then places the mouth of the jar on Little Mother's bare shoulder. The jar tightens, the lip adhering to her skin as the fire burns up the air inside, creating a vacuum, the body's internal pathways invigorated as the darkness within is drawn out of the blood. After a while he lets go and the jar stays fixed where it is. Then he lights other slips of papers, drops them in other jars, attaching each one to a different spot on her body. The smell of burnt paper fills the room.

When he's done, he stands back. She looks arboreal, arms outstretched, her body wreathed with burls. Something in the way she holds her arms in the air reminds him of a tree. He imagines sitting under her boughs and opening his eyes as if for the first time on earth, her limbs bursting with white fist-sized flowers. Lam gasps, the memory of a long-ago afternoon suddenly flooding his heart. Life is a wheel. That love should summon him again through the curtain of all these years. There are times when one must prune the tree that bears the fruit. The new life has to come that day, that very night. He must do all he can. There is nothing and everything to lose. He lights one last strip of paper and drops it in a jar. Quickly he attaches this to the root chakra, the volatile door on the lower back.

The drawing of toxins to the surface of the skin. Like drawing light out of the darkness. Little Mother's body covered with mouths, each one breathing clean and fresh. Her eyes heavy-lidded, both open and closed. The seeing into a thousand rooms at once. An orchestra of doors and hinges, worlds opening, jaw-bones rattling in the wind. The body wheeling through room after room. Sometimes in the quest for health, one must pur-posely inflict damage. The tree pruned back so that the fruit will flower.

Will it come tonight, she whispers. Yes, he says, patting her shoulder, but he says it mostly to reassure himself.

Gradually the jars loosen and drop off one by one, and where each has been, a dark circle remains. Technically they are bruises, like kisses that bring the blood up to the surface of the skin, the blight patterning her body. The fire burning in the corner of the room begins to die out.

After her skin has cooled, he helps her to dress. For a moment he thinks he sees the skin of her belly trembling, but it is probably just a trick of the late-afternoon light. Together they walk out-side to the jackfruit tree. He has done all he can. He of all peo-ple should know that when the heart breaks, there is no salve. Around them the air hangs fetid with the wet heat that follows the southwest monsoon. On the ground the ants are already dis-mantling the ruined fruit.

Wait, Lam says. He hobbles back inside. He returns with a peony, its pink bud furled tight as a fist. Tell your mother-in-law Thuan I am her servant always, he says, pressing the flower into Little Mother's hand. He thinks of Thuan and her old-woman eyes as though rinsed with milk. If he were a younger man, he would run a needle through fire and take Thuan's face in his moldy old hands, carefully lifting the cloud from each of her eyes. He imagines that when he finished, Thuan would rise from the stool and behold him as he used to be, both their bodies once again young and flawless.

Little Mother nods and tucks the flower in the weft of her hat. She has never heard anyone call her mother-in-law by her given name. She knows Bà will be happy to get the peony, her milky eyes shining. For a second time Little Mother pats the flower with her fingertips, securing it in place. Everywhere the small bruises jewel her skin, each one the diameter of a child's wrist.

Three times Lam waves off the crumpled piastres she offers him. Please, she says, her eyes fixed on the ground, as each time he refuses. Finally she tucks the money back up in her conical hat. Grandfather, she says, turning to go. In the next life I will serve you. He places a fist in the scarred-green palm of his other hand and bows deeply. It isn't until she has fully disappeared around the bend in the road that he stands back up.

Sometimes things blow shut of their own accord. The way a door creaks on its splintery wooden hinges—pain in the very sound of it. How the pain comes fluttering up in the joints, the pain permanent like new teeth. This is a moment of thresholds. The sound of doors swinging wildly somewhere in the wind.

THE BRIDGE ACROSS THE SONG MA HAD LONG SINCE BEEN destroyed, but the little basket boat was still sitting on the near shore, bobbing in the current. There were no oars, just a series of guide ropes one could use to pull the bamboo boat back and forth. This was the last place she'd seen him. More than eight months had passed. Little Mother still remembered the shape of Tu's neck under his hat as he pulled himself across the water, the birthmark gleaming on the edge of his hairline. They had walked to the river hand in hand through the dusk, the bats just starting to stir. Something buzzed in her ear, but she didn't swat it, not wanting him to remember her as anything less than stoic, Little Mother eager to demonstrate that she would be all right in his absence. They both knew the time had come for him to disappear, the war changing the land around them. As he slipped across the Song Ma, Tu didn't look back. The sound of water lapped against the sides of the boat as he melted into the landscape, her heart slipping away from her body.

Little Mother studied the sky. There was an hour left until sundown. The old medicine man had said it would come that night. There was nothing else to do. On the far shore the rope was fastened around an iron hook set deep in a rock. She found the other end where she had left it tied up to the roots of a mangrove tree. Water sloshed in the bottom of the boat, the water hot around her ankles as she stepped in. Swiftly she pulled herself across the river, though it was mostly the current that carried her. The water coursed so dull red and matte she couldn't see anything in it, not even her own reflection.

On the other side of the river she stepped out of the boat and crawled hand over hand up the bank. Just five months ago there had been a cluster of families living on both sides of the Song Ma. The families had made their living fishing and ferrying people and goods across the river. For the past few months the charred remains of their huts dotted the shoreline. Over time the blackened heaps looked less and less like the remains of houses. It was hard to say who'd done it with any certainty. Little Mother took a deep breath and held it as she hurried past without looking. The patriarch had gone running back into one of the burning huts to find his granddaughter, the thatched roof like a woman with her hair on fire. Neither the old man nor the girl were ever seen again. Little Mother half remembered meeting the little girl from time to time, her hair done in two mismatched braids, one longer than the other, a space where her front tooth was missing, the head of the new tooth just starting to show. The grandfather had been a fisherman. He was known far and wide for fishing with a snow-white cormorant, the bird an albino, its eyes a bloody pink. Until the fire, most nights the grandfather and the bird could be seen together floating on a simple raft, the old man's long gray beard in stark contrast to his bald head. In the weekly market Little Mother had heard that the man and his granddaughter were somewhere still walking the earth. She imagined meeting the two of them, the blue flames of their spirits roaming restlessly through the dark. From the look of things, with the next good rain the last of the wreckage would wash down into the river, everything as if nobody had ever lived there.

A half mile down the road Little Mother came across the carcass of a wild sow. Its teats gleamed like big brown buttons up and down its bloated gut. Most likely the creature had eaten something poisonous. There was no noticeable trauma, though its mouth gaped, its yellowed tusks long as fingers where the gums had receded. Little Mother wondered if she herself looked like that—gums drawn so far back her teeth as if twice as long.

By the trunk of a black palm she stopped to rest. In the distance the Truong Son Mountains were hazy with ash. It happened often enough that she had learned to sleep through it, the nightly rumble of distant planes. Each time it started, the night sky would light up. The next morning ash would shower down, a black confetti floating as far as Qui Nhon on the coast.

The moon was just on the edge of the horizon as Little Mother rounded the final bend, the sugar apples coming into view in the yard. The one-room she shared with Bà was west of the Song Ma in the southern corner of the province. The first few months of her marriage things had been quiet. Then a small weapons cache was found buried in a field outside Hau Bon. The farmer said he hadn't worked the field in years, that he left it fallow as a place for the spirits of the rice to live, and that everyone for miles around knew it, but he was carted off to Pleiku anyway. After that, everything changed. Evenings she would see people floating through the hamlet she had never seen before, their accents hard to place. Across the Song Ma a village chief was killed. Someone draped a sign around his neck. PUPPET. Then one by one Tu and the other men of fighting age disappeared, some like Tu joining the Vietcong out in the jungle, others just slipping away. The bombings in the Truong Son Mountains began to physically change their topography, the peaks leveled, helicopters landing at all hours. And now the whole fifty square miles west of the river had been declared a free-fire zone. The Americans ordered everyone out. Tu said the Americans were trying to stamp out the Vietcong by banishing the local people. No people meant no food, no aid. In a free-fire zone the Americans could shoot without asking. Anyone remaining was assumed to be VC. Bà had begged Little Mother to stay, saying they would be all right because they were harmless, two women in the middle of nowhere, and besides, how else would Tu know where to find them when he returned from the jungle? Most of the other villagers had left for Cong Heo, the strategic hamlet in Binh Dinh Province, though Cong Heo had long since fallen into disuse. Little Mother had heard there was a wooden fence with razor wire running along the top, a ring of bamboo stakes all around the compound, the stakes gone soft with rot.

As she entered the yard, she could see the door was open. Inside, a fire was burning in the fire pit, but the room was empty except for their few possessions—some cooking utensils and a pair of rice bowls stacked on a small table, Bà's hammock strung up under the window. The tin bucket they used to collect water from the creek on the other side of the orchard was missing, a ring left in the dirt where the bucket usually sat. Little Mother picked up her sleeping mat and unrolled it on the floor. Slowly she eased herself down and took off her *non la*. The money was there, but the flower was gone, its little pink bud like a mouth. She took a deep breath and held the hat up to the fire, searching it with her eyes for the words Tu had paid for, had chosen just for her, and how the artist had painstakingly woven them through the lining. *In the long river, fish swim off without a trace.* How the local people believed that a girl who wore a conical hat laced with poetry would become milder, more gentle, the girl effectively domesticated. Like a water buffalo when the farmer takes her newborn—how in her mourning for her baby, the water buffalo will do anything the farmer asks.

Little Mother could feel the hole where her heart should be. The poem was gone, the writing rubbed out from sweat and the daily friction of her head. *Who tends the paddy / repairs the dike?* She considered going back out into the fading light, the mosquitoes beginning to swarm, maybe even going all the way to the river to look for the missing flower she had been entrusted with, but outside the visible world exploded and the first pain hit.

Bà tottered back into the hut carrying the tin bucket. Outside the sound of the burning sky roared overhead. She put the water down next to the fire and stood still for a moment taking in the scene with her remaining senses, her eyes gray with twilight. I knew the old man wouldn't disappoint us, she said. Quickly she hustled back outside to collect more firewood.

Left alone, Little Mother didn't cry out as her water sluiced down her legs and into the dirt. On all fours she made her way to the door. She wanted to see the mountains one last time. From the doorway they looked like a python after it has eaten a full-size animal. The dream was over, the heat of his hand on her leg. Already the memory of blue flames dancing on the mountainside was fading.

Their last night together she and Tu had sat staring off at the mountains. On the closest slope they could see a handful of blue lights twinkling. She'd sat back and waited. He was always telling her the most beautiful stories, transforming the world before her eyes. Tu cleared his throat. We all carry a light inside us, he said. He told her they were little blue fountains of flame where someone had died and gone unburied, the body's gases escaping into the air. In the distance she could make out four of them, the fires like indigo stars twinkling on the mountainside. Wandering ghosts, Tu said. Briefly he touched her knee. If you meet one, address it as *anh* or *chi,* he said. Brother Ghost. Sister Phantom. She nodded, her young face filled with seriousness.

Little Mother closed her eyes. Pain radiated through her body. She could still see the bright red birthmark on the edge of Tu's hairline, the mark shaped like a diamond. At times it seemed to change with his feelings, the color deepening as an emotion took hold of him. She would never see him again in this world. She crawled back to the fire and collapsed.

When she opened her eyes again, it was night, the air sulfurous and filled with thunder and lightning. Each time one hit, brightness like hell itself. She could feel the earth tremble, the one-room hut quivering as bits of dried thatch rained down from the roof, the splintery wooden boards rattling like teeth. On her mat in front of the fire pit she imagined what kind of world the planes came from, a land of fire and iron, liquid light, pain and the quiet that comes after. She tried to remember even the smallest scrap of her favorite dream, the heat of his hand on her leg, but all she could recollect was a cacophony of doors swinging wildly in a thrashing wind, the sound of their hinges like broken jaws. It was the only dream she ever had anymore.

There was a piece of rope and a knife and an old gunnysack laid out on the floor. Bà had the fire going strong, her eyes red in the light. The old woman lay smoking her pipe in her hammock by the window. The pipe was carved from an animal's thigh bone, the bowl itself the head of a dragon. Each time Bà inhaled, the creature's eyes burned as if alive. Little Mother knew that when the time came to act, Bà would fly into motion. They never talked about it, how Bà's eyes had soured in the last year, everything gone but light itself, though it didn't seem to slow her down any. The old woman was as she had always been. Up each morning before the sun's first rays, then doing the things that needed doing.

Bà tapped her ashes into a tin can. He will come, she said. The old woman had a way of knowing things she shouldn't know. Something hit the earth. A jar of *nuoc mam* fell off a shelf, the glass cracking on impact. It was the closest one they had ever felt, the thing as close as a mile away. The smell of fish drifted through the room. Even now he is on his way, said Bà, smoke shirring around her head.

Two rats came out of the darkness and stopped at the spot where the *nuoc mam* had fallen. Little Mother turned her head and watched them scratch at the dirt. Then another one hit, the power of a thousand tons lifting her body clean off the floor. One of the rats paused and looked at her. There was no fear in its eyes. Little Mother wondered if she were already among the dead. Finally the animal turned and along with the other scurried out of her line of sight.

In many ways the pain was just like the mosquito sickness, a burning all throughout her body. She would wake for a few minutes, a few brief images limned with each explosion—Bà stoking the flames, Bà fanning Little Mother with her straw hat, the night as if immolating itself, outside the sugar apples bursting on the bough—and then she would fall back into darkness. She could feel a door creaking open in her body. The circular bruises on her skin throbbed as if gasping for air.

A few hours past midnight they ran out of wood. There were hardly any rice husks left to burn. We need to save what we have, Bà told her. And so they sat in the dark, her body's doors opening at a glacial pace, like something fermenting. Outside the world going up in flame.

Toward morning Bà awoke when something landed on her face. The dawn was silent, no animal noises stirring in the growing light. The old woman was sitting in the doorway, her pipe cold in her hand. She could feel the first rays of the morning sun just coming over the mountain and struggling to break through the smoky haze.

Bà touched her cheek where the thing had landed soft as a moth. Another landed on her neck. It was coming down. She could hear it hitting the earth, each one alighting faint as paper. One landed in the middle of her forehead. She wiped it off and smelled her fingers. It was ash. The little round scar on her chest next to her heart began to grow hot. Little Mother, she said.

Later the sound of an engine coming through the orchard. Bà turns her head toward the noise. For the first time she is conscious of the gray lace glazing her eyes. She wipes her face with the backs of her hands. There is so much to do.

They were walking through the orchard. Judging from his smell, the first boy who arrived wasn't an American, his body as if wrapped in rotten leaves. Bà took another deep breath in through her nose. He wasn't Vietnamese either, not a northerner or a southerner, not even one of the ethnics from the mountains. She heard him call to the others, words like the barking of dogs. How many she didn't know, hundreds of thousands or just a handful, and all of them coming to where the first soldier had called them. Bà could hear the fatigue in their voices, the swinging of their heavy guns against their gaunt bodies. The sun trickled in from the east through the dark man-made clouds.

The first one was talking, saying words she knew were directed at her. Bà pointed into the hut. She could feel the soldier peering into the darkness, following the line of her finger. We must, she said. There's still time. Was he understanding? The scrim burned heavy on her eyes. She made motions with her hands as if breaking open a piece of fruit.

More words were said, then the boy was leading her through the orchard, away from the one-room shelter her son had built. In the crisp morning air she could smell the burnt fruit littering the ground. She remembered the day some months before when her neighbors had been relocated by the Americans, the sound of her childhood friend Hong Hanh's high-pitched keening as the soldiers carried her small body across the road to the waiting helicopter, loose grit whipping through the air, the whole hut shuddering as if it would simply lift off the earth, Hong Hanh's screams cutting in and out in the wash of the great blades. Mong Yen was a small hamlet of fewer than ten wooden huts. The Americans had cleared the area in under half an hour. Bà and Little Mother lived on the edge of Mong Yen. The day the Americans swept the hamlet, Bà and Little Mother had been curled up like sea horses in the small space Tu had hollowed under the floor during his last and final visit. The creatures of the earth crawling all over them as if they themselves were earth.

The day after her neighbors had been forcibly removed, Bà felt her way through the sugar-apple orchard to Hong Hanh's two rooms. The ancestors' bowls were still there on the shelf in the corner. A sheet of muslin lay in a heap in the dirt. Flies crawled over the hardened rice, a few of them drowned in the small dish filled with fish sauce.

For the first few days Bà picked her way through the orchard each afternoon while Little Mother was off working in the fields. Each day she would change the rice, recover the bowls with the muslin. Some days she would light a joss stick and clap her hands together as she bowed her head before fishing the dead flies out of the *nuoc mam*. By the end of the week none of her prayers had come true, but that wasn't the reason why she stopped taking care of the family altar of her childhood friend. All her life Bà's prayers had never come true. She didn't know anyone whose prayers did.

The final time Bà went next door she stood in front of the altar, the smell of sandalwood spicing the air. A breeze began to blow through the room, though outside the palm trees stood stone still. Then she saw it—a vision of her daughter-in-law lying in the dirt, the girl's stomach swollen and distended, her face as if dead. All week Bà had prayed for just the opposite. Not now. Please. Not in this world. The last time Tu had been with them, the sound of the couple's long nights of love filling the air which in a culture of one-room households it was taboo for anyone to acknowledge. For as many nights as it lasted Bà lay in her corner pretending not to hear the rhythmic noises and small groans coming from their mat but remembering her own nights of pleasure long ago in a world at war, hoping they were being careful but knowing that they weren't.

Later that day after Little Mother came home from the fields, Bà could feel her prayers had not been answered. The girl didn't even know. She was stirring the rice in a pot over the fire, the aura of the new life filling the room. There would no longer be enough rice to fill the bowl on the altar next door. Little Mother, said Bà for the first time. The scar just above her left breast throbbed. Now you must call me Bà.

And so it had come to pass. Little Mother lying in the dirt in the darkness of their one room, her stomach swollen and distended, her face all but dark. Outside Bà floating through the orchard on the arm of a foreigner.

Finally they arrived at a jeep. Among the soldiers there was more talk like the grunting of animals, the soldiers deferring to the boy who had led her there, the boy their leader. Already he was walking away. It had been years since Bà had ridden in a jeep, not since Terres Noires and the trees that cried white tears. For a moment she felt like a child again, she and her mother with their buckets full of sap.

She could hear the driver drumming on the steering wheel with his fingers. He had yet to start the car. Ash was still wafting through the air. From the backseat, she held her hand out and caught a black flake on the tip of her finger. She was glad to be with these foreigners. It was her own people who would've ruined everything. Most times the South Vietnamese soldiers would leave a body where they'd found it, not even caring enough to close the eyes.

Within minutes another soldier climbed in the front seat and slammed the door. The jeep fired up, and she was moving, the ash hitting her in the face. The soldiers were taking her to Cong Heo, the old strategic hamlet built by the Americans. The Americans didn't even know what Cong Heo meant. She had a way of knowing things she shouldn't know. The scar on her chest burned like a third eye. She hadn't crossed the river in years. She knew she wouldn't cross it now.

Wait. Bà held up her hand. The jeep came to a stop. Carefully she pointed at the house, gesturing that there was something she needed. The driver and the other soldier considered it, grunting among themselves. They were tired and didn't care, their resignation evident to Bà even as they spoke in their own tongue. *Oui,* she said, in the only other language she knew. She heard the car door swing open. The other soldier helped her out.

And if the glaze had momentarily lifted from her eyes, she would have seen two soldiers digging by the sugar-apple tree, a body bag lying on the ground, the body already in it. She would have seen another soldier hammering together a makeshift box made of splintery wooden boards from her own house. If Bà's eyes had been clean, she would have seen the boy-leader approach the long black bag, unzipping it partway, the boy reaching into the void and placing a single bright circle in the corpse's mouth as someone had done for his own mother years before on the island of Gye-do in the Korean Strait when she died giving birth to him, then sealing the bag up again.

Bà walked straight into the house, her hands at her sides. When she didn't come back after ten minutes, the driver stubbed out his cigarette and shot the other soldier a look. The soldier got out and ran up to the house, slipping on burnt sugar apples, the smell not unpleasant but for the tang of gasoline lingering in the air. After a minute he came back out shaking his head. The old woman was nowhere to be found. The driver glared at him, but the soldier just bowed and wiped a scorched apple off the bottom of his boot.

Please know that those among us who chewed the betel leaf say they did so for the sting of it. Blood ringing in the silvery chambers of the skull. A rush where normally there would only be inertia. The body's internal compass trained north even in the darkest dark.

EVER SINCE THE FIREBOMBING ACROSS THE RIVER THE OLD honey seller had been trying not to think about the future. The sun was almost behind the mountains. Her two nearest neighbors had packed up their few remaining chickens and pigs and left hours ago. The day before, the elderly village chief had said it was time. His women carried him down the road in his hammock, his feet never touching the ground. She had heard the routes through the jungle were cut, that the bombers had flattened everything in the free-fire zone for fifty square miles. One full day had passed, and when the wind was right, she could still see black smoke billowing up from across the river.

Huyen sat beside her hovel and spit out a long red stream into the dirt, her teeth the same bloody color as her spit. Inside their patchwork of sticks and canvas, Qui had fallen asleep on a ragged mat. Yesterday Huyen had kicked the girl awake and sent her out alone with an empty jar to check the hives down along the river. The girl didn't say a word as she took the jar and headed off. She never spoke anymore. The front of her black shirt was always damp and sour smelling, her long tangled hair falling all the way to the backs of her knees. Despite her wan complexion, there was a savage beauty in her face, bones chiseled like a deer's.

In the distance Huyen could see one last group of villagers slipping through the landscape, the sound of their wooden wheels rutting the earth. The whole village had emptied, her neighbors simply draining away. She knew they had left her and Qui behind on purpose. They didn't want to be around old Huyen and her sharp tongue and bloody teeth.

Toward dusk the leaf-nosed bats began to appear. Huyen opened her eyes. She didn't remember closing them. The moon was out. Qui was sitting beside her, the front of her black shirt damp as if she had spilled something on herself, a sourness wafting up off her chest. The girl was holding a jar of honey and tipping it from side to side, the honey rumbling back and forth.

Together they sat, grandmother and granddaughter, waiting for a sign as to what they should do, anything to spur them into action. *Em,* snarled Huyen, addressing Qui with the word meant for small children, though Qui was too old for it. Huyen cleared her throat and moved the lump of betel leaves she was chewing to the other side of her cheek. From time to time she would pose a question to her granddaughter in the hope of lulling the girl out of her silence. King, father, mother, child, went sailing in one boat, Huyen said, met a storm and sank. It was an old Confucian riddle. *Who would you save from drowning and in what order?*

Qui never took her eyes off the jar she was holding. The honey gleamed in the moonlight. On the ground her long black hair pooled like a hole. Through the empty village the sound of a door creaked painfully in the wind. As if to answer her grandmother, Qui put a hand on her belly, but Huyen reached over and swatted her hand away.

Dark clouds were racing overhead, the moon in and out of shadow when the woman arrived, the cuffs of her loose black pants caked with dirt. She looked as if she had been to the ends of the earth and back. There was no emotion in her eyes. Later, Huyen would recall that it had seemed as if she were floating, the stranger motionless in the moonlight. Overhead the leaf-nosed bats were spinning themselves into a frenzy.

The woman took off her hat. Her scalp gleamed through her patchy hair. Everywhere shadows massed on her face. Slowly, as if yawning, she opened her mouth and pulled something off her tongue. The object flashed in her fingers. She placed it in Huyen's wrinkled palm. It was a silver coin. Stamped on one side were two flowery dragons chasing each other's tails, on the other, a man with a Confucian-style beard. Grandmother, the woman said, her voice echoing inside Huyen's head as if the old honey seller were simply thinking the words to herself. In the next life I will serve you.

Then the woman turned her sunken eyes on Qui. The moon revealed itself from behind a cloud. The stranger bent down and kissed the ragged girl on the forehead. Lovingly she swept back the long black curtain of Qui's tangled hair and whispered in her ear. With her left hand the woman pressed her thumb and third finger together. The air filled with the sound of ringing, like a needle imperceptibly vibrating with human electricity, or a fly's wings beating to keep it aloft.

Under a nimbus of leaf-nosed bats, the woman held out her hand. There was nothing imploring in the gesture. Qui placed the jar of honey she'd been holding in the stranger's dirty palm. The woman tucked the jar in her shirt.

Huyen opened her eyes. Hadn't she just opened them? The woman with the hollow face was gone. Everywhere the sounds of the empty village echoed in the night. The old honey seller began to wonder if it had all been a dream. In the sky a few clouds shrouded the moon. She turned to her granddaughter. What did she say to you, Huyen demanded. The accusation in her voice masked a deeper fear.

Qui sat with her hands at her chest as if still holding the jar of honey and tipping it from side to side. Huyen wasn't expecting an answer. The girl hadn't spoken since the night Huyen had ruined her. When it came, she didn't even recognize her own granddaughter's voice.

Qui pressed the imaginary jar to her heart. She said *be her mother,* Qui whispered. Overhead a bat went spiraling through the night like a falling star. The old woman reached over and eased the imaginary jar out of her granddaughter's hands. It was the last thing Qui ever said.

In the morning Qui roused her grandmother. The girl moved with a newfound energy she hadn't shown in months. The front of her shirt was damp as if she had pressed two wet hands to her chest. Is it time, said Huyen. Qui nodded. Together they packed up their meager belongings and set out. Huyen followed without question. She had known this day was coming. After last night, the bats thronging in the air, she knew the moment had arrived. In some ways it felt good to hand over the burden of being the one in charge. Huyen smiled, her bloody teeth flashing. Maybe that was what had made her cruel. After everything she had done to Qui, it was only right that now she should serve her granddaughter. They were already in the next life.

Three things cannot be hidden long: the sun, the moon, and the truth. Thousands of candles can be lit from a single candle, and the life of the candle will not be shortened.

Tᴜ sᴀᴛ ᴜᴘ ɪɴ ᴛʜᴇ ᴛʀᴇᴇ ᴡʜᴇʀᴇ ʜᴇ ᴡᴀs ᴡᴀɪᴛɪɴɢ ᴀɴᴅ ʀᴏʟʟᴇᴅ up his pant leg. A small dark sack clung to his calf, the thing almost as big as a rambutan, but the skin was smooth and rubbery. He poked it with his finger and watched it toll like a bell. He was lucky. It was only the second one that day. It was almost done feeding and would drop off soon enough. He didn't have any salt, plus he didn't want to use up a match. In a way it was part of him. He stroked it with his finger. With his eyes closed it almost felt like a hot pearl or a young girl's innocence. For a moment he considered keeping it and somehow presenting it to her as a gift. This is my blood, he would say. When I am away from you, know that I am here. He laughed at the idea, knew it would be a twisted thing to do, to give your love a jungle leech bursting with your own blood, but he also knew if he did, she would nod solemnly in that way she had and hold out her cupped hand as if she were receiving the Buddha's unpolluted heart. She would treasure it until it was just a piece of shriveled skin. She would never throw it away.

Even lazing in the branches of a tamarind tree on the edge of the strategic hamlet, he was sweating. In the days and weeks after the monsoon, the humidity had emerged as if reestablishing its domain. From his perch on the edge of the jungle he could see the untended paddies, water buffalo wandering through the landscape at will. Yesterday he had watched an old man and a young woman having sex by the stream. As he watched, he made up a story in his mind, how the woman was actually the wife of the man's adult son but how she had fallen for the father because in her eyes he was the man the son should have been. Long after the man and woman had risen from the grass, Tu kept developing the plot, the son running off to join the northern army, then later killing his father in battle but only realizing what he'd done well after the fact.

Tu stretched himself to full length. There was nothing else

to do but dream. In Cong Heo there was no reason to work. Mostly the peasants sat around and drank a fermented rice wine dark as soy sauce. The Americans would provide everything, and why labor in the paddies when you might be relocated again at any moment? When someone could walk through the fields that you had planted by hand and with a flamethrower reduce all your work to ash in a matter of seconds?

Suddenly the leech dropped off his leg. He looked for it on the tree limb, but when he didn't find it, he realized it must have fallen all the way down to the ground, somewhere down there his blood pointlessly coating the grass. He tried not to see it as an omen, but there was no way his wife and mother could stay on in the free-fire zone, not after a full night of bombing. He could feel the birthmark on his face begin to smolder. Through the peasants in Cong Heo he had left word that if his family arrived, someone was to come find him. He would hug his mother and receive her blessing, then whisk his bride away deep into the jungle, maybe to the cave he had found by the falls. Afterward, they would wash each other in the thundering water. She would kiss the diamond red birthmark on the edge of his scalp, and then he would probably want her all over again.

He had learned about the baby from another man living in the jungle. He didn't know the man. There had been no joy in the telling. The man had simply said the women in the markets east of the Song Ma say you will be a father. When Tu had looked around in the darkness at the other faces climbing up into the trees for the night, all he had seen was fatigue. All night he lay in his hammock worrying he'd be shot—his face beaming, his happiness radiating outward like a beacon.

An hour after his small dinner of tapioca he could hear someone coming through the elephant grass toward the tamarind tree. A head popped up out of the brush. The sun's fading light reddened the landscape. It was a young girl, her hair in uneven braids. The girl pointed up at him. Uncle, she said, and smiled. Her front tooth was missing, the head of the new tooth just starting to break the skin. The time for daydreaming was long over, the birthmark on his face as if on fire. Tu shimmied down out of the tree and began to run.

From Cong Heo it was twenty miles to the river and then another two to the hamlet. It was the night of the full moon; he would be easy to spot regardless. He figured she was probably too big to move easily, though Vietnamese women had a way of working in the paddies right up until the moment arrived. The last time he'd seen her was by the Song Ma, her face still as a statue's and impossible to read. He wondered if she were angry. He had promised he'd be home well before this, and here it was almost three full seasons, more than eight months.

After only a few miles on the road, he saw an American convoy speeding his way. His first impulse when he saw the dust billowing up in the distance was to get off the road without being seen, but by then it was too late. He knew he'd been spotted. Running would only make him look suspicious. The first two trucks whooshed by. He had to close his eyes and cover his nose, the dust was so thick, so fortuitous.

It wasn't until a series of jeeps began to pass that one of them stopped. There was an American driver with an important-looking man sitting in the passenger seat, the man's silvery hair cropped close around his head, the cut so sharp Tu imagined it would draw blood if he touched it. The man didn't have on any of the colorful bars the American officers wore around their own bases, which made Tu realize how important he was—only those of high rank needed to hide who they were. In the back-seat, a Vietnamese soldier sat next to a haggard-looking Vietnamese man in the loose black clothing of a peasant, the man's hands tied together.

Ask him where he's going, said the driver. The Vietnamese soldier cleared his throat. In the fading light Tu could see there was something unbalanced about the soldier's eyes. The right one was brown, the left a pale blue. It was unsettling. Tu tried not to stare.

Grandfather. The soldier cleared his throat again. Where is the road taking you today? Tu wondered who the soldier was talking to. It wasn't until much later when he saw himself in the Song Ma that he realized he looked like an old man. His entire head of hair had been dusted white by the passing trucks.

Em, Tu said, as if he were the soldier's elder. The words came effortlessly to him. I am going to see the medicine man who lives by the Song Ma. I must have medicine for my heart. The soldier tried to hide his incredulousness. Grandfather, that's almost twenty miles. I must have it, repeated Tu. The soldier let out a long sigh and lowered his voice. Please ask him to say a prayer for all of us, he said, his blue eye gleaming like a marble. Tu looked at the prisoner. There was a thin red line of blood running from the corner of his mouth.

Tell him to be inside by nightfall, said the important-looking man in the passenger seat. The soldier coughed again. *Ong,* please be safely beside the fire before sundown. Tu nodded. Make sure he got that, the American added, but they were already driving away.

The sun had set, the air still humid. Tu was more than a mile down the road by the time the jeep came back, headlights off. This time it was the Vietnamese soldier driving by himself, in the darkness his blue eye reflective like a cat's. I will take you to the river, the soldier said, and nodded to the back. Tu climbed in. They didn't talk the entire way.

The full moon was just starting to rise. Tu could see the rabbit stamped on its face. In the backseat he put his hand down in a pool of something. He sniffed his fingers, then wiped the blood on his shirt.

The soldier pulled over at the edge of the river. Though he gripped the steering wheel attentively in his hands, he seemed tired, as if he'd had enough. Everywhere insects chirred in the tall grass. The soldier kept the jeep idling. Brother, he said as Tu climbed out. Please remember me in your prayers. Tu swung the door closed. Even in his weariness the soldier's blue eye burned bright. Then he turned the jeep around and headed back in the dark.

They were squatting by the river in the shadows of ash when he stumbled on them. They used to be houses, growled the old woman. Tu hadn't noticed her sitting there. In the moonlight he could see that her teeth were a deep red from chewing betel. Beside her was a young girl who looked to be barely in her teens. The girl was obviously demented but with a savage beauty Tu found startling. She raised a dirty arm and pointed, her long hair rippling over her shoulder. On the other side of the river he could see a boat bobbing in the current. Despite the girl's looks, he didn't feel any shame. Qui, hissed the old woman, but the girl didn't look away, her eyes shining as Tu took off his clothes.

When he was done undressing, he walked down the bank and into the water. Instantly his feet disappeared. For a moment he wondered why they called it the Song Ma, the River of Dreams. The water was a deep nut-red and warm on his skin, the river still swollen from the recent monsoons. Then something startled him, and he drew back. He looked again. Staring up at him from the surface of the Song Ma was an old man, hair dusted white as death. Then Tu saw the birthmark on the edge of the old man's hairline, the thing shining bright like a bloodstain. Feverishly he ran both hands through his hair before dipping his head in the muddied water as if his life depended on it.

He was across in less than ten minutes. He wasn't a strong swimmer, but the current seemed listless despite the water's swollen level. On the other side he crawled up onshore. Everywhere there was the smell of burning, the water like voices whispering. Quickly he got in the boat and began pulling himself back across to where the two women stood waiting. He didn't know where they were headed, but he couldn't leave them stranded. As he neared the other shore and gazed on the burned huts dotting the riverbank, he thought of the little girl and her grandfather, the fisherman who'd been killed in the fire. He wondered what happened to the silvery bird the man was always seen with, the bird as if carved from ice.

When he arrived back where he'd started, the women were still huddled in the shadows. There is nothing over there, he said to the old woman, nothing but death. At the word *death* the feral girl clamored into the boat. Tu was panting but not from exertion, the image of himself as an old man still in his mind. The old woman handed him his clothes and crawled in next to the girl. Even with the added weight the boat rode high in the water.

Crossing the river with the two women, Tu thought of hell and the childhood stories of the places that befell the body after life. He pulled the rope as hard as he could. If they capsized—he wouldn't let himself think of it. The underworld was said to be a festering blister, the darkness so cold it turned the skin blue. When he looked back across the river, he thought he could see someone standing on the shore they had just come from, the figure small like a child, its hair in braids.

On the other side they scrambled out one at a time. As he held the boat steady for the girl, Tu realized there was a smell coming from her. He didn't know what it could be. He imagined it had something to do with sorrow, though, despite the grimness of her physical appearance, the girl seemed animated and darkly beautiful, as if she were on her way to the happiest day of her life, her happiness in stark contrast to the landscape. Everywhere the world was charred. The bones of trees stood like primordial signposts warning of pestilence and death. In the moonlight the earth looked blackened like the skin of a fish.

The three of them walked single file without speaking. At one point they passed a burned shack with one of its walls caved in as if a car had driven into it. In spots the ground was still smoldering. Tu had to hold his hand up in front of his nose. It was obvious there were bodies inside.

A few hundred feet down the road something glimmered in the distance, but he couldn't be sure what it was. When they got closer, he could see it was a dead pig, the body completely charred, the long gleaming tusks exposed all the way up to the root where they were fused tight to the yellow jaw. The old woman picked up a stick and whacked it on the flank. From somewhere deep inside the animal Tu could hear things stirring. By the time he realized what was happening, they were already pouring out through the desiccated orifices of the face. A few streamed out of the shriveled ears. Bees. Honey bees. In the moonlight each one silvery like a coin. The sound of the bees' thrumming a dark electricity.

The air filled with the vibrating swarm, the bees pouring out, the pulsing mass coming on and on without end. Tu could feel their papery wings brushing against his face. It lasted only a minute, and yet it seemed like hours, their wings soft as wind. He had heard of such things happening in the land of the dead.

Quickly he touched the side of his neck to make sure his heart was still beating. He found it easily, his pulse hammering.

None of them were stung.

Finally there was the same bend in the road, the one he always remembered coming around on his way home from the fields. He thought of the last time he'd been there. How he had arrived at night, the darkness like a cloak, and how he found her sitting under a sugar-apple tree singing softly to herself. And here he was again. There was the same sugar apple she'd been sitting under and beside it a mound of fresh earth, an empty rice bowl propped in the dirt.

The simple wooden hut he'd built with his own two hands was torn apart. Two of the walls were dismantled, the splintery wooden boards missing. The truth began to present itself. Maybe he had always known. The girl rushed into the dark hut as if her heart were waiting for her, black hair streaming like a flag. What does she think is here, Tu asked, but the old woman just followed her granddaughter inside.

There was no reason to go in. The room was empty. No sign of his wife or mother. The ashes in the fire pit were long cold. A few pots and woven baskets hung on what was left of the walls. Underneath a shelf a broken jar lay empty. In a corner a tin bucket sat half full of water, his mother's empty hammock swinging in the breeze.

Tu sank down in the dirt. He waited for the tears to come, but nothing came. He and Bà had always been close. Somehow she had always sensed him, had always known what was happening to him even when they were apart, the scar on her chest often hot to the touch. The sugar-apple orchard was still smoldering, the orchard Bà's pride and joy. When the tears still wouldn't come, he sat back. A strange feeling of hopefulness fluttered in his stomach.

Then he heard a scratching, the sound of fingernails scraping on a door. He jumped up and ran through one of the missing walls, tapping on the floor with his foot. When he found the spot, he dropped to his knees and began moving the dirt with his hands. He lifted a board, the earth yawning open. The girl raced around and around the room, her hair flying, but when she saw who it was, her face dropped.

Bà rose out of the earth, her eyes completely white. *Mon chéri,* she said. Tu felt like a child as the tears wet his cheeks. Within minutes Bà had a fire going and some leftover rice boiling in a kettle.

And so they waited, each for their own reasons, each with their own thoughts. Bà sat with her dragon pipe clenched between her lips, the pipe's eyes burning as she scoured an old pot with sand, her face still grimy from her internment. Qui and Huyen were off in one of the remaining corners, the old woman untangling her granddaughter's hair. To Tu this was the makeshift vigil for his dead wife. He sat in what was left of the doorway looking off at the mountains. Even in the moonlight, ash still hung in the air. He thought of the first time he'd ever seen her. It was evening. She was riding her bicycle. In the road a small boy was driving three water buffalo to their night field. For a moment she stood up on her bicycle, pumping hard to pass the boy and his animals. Then her hat blew off as if plucked from her head by an invisible hand, her long black hair flying loose in the wind as she kept pedaling, the hat sailing behind her and landing in the road. He watched as the lead buffalo stepped on it. How she had gotten off her bicycle and walked back, picking up the smashed thing in her hands. Thinking she was all alone, she had cradled it in her arms. But he had been there, watching from a ditch by the roadside where he had been relieving himself. Her hair blowing loose as if she were standing on a cliff overlooking the sea. It had only been last year. She was sixteen.

Then somewhere in the long night a noise began. The sound of something banging, a door slamming shut over and over. At first the sound was faint, then the noise changed and filled the air. Tu looked to his mother, unsure of what he was hearing. Even Bà with the things she knew that she shouldn't know moved her head from side to side as if tracking a housefly and waiting for it to land. Outside, the night was filling with bats.

Qui was the first to locate the noise. She pulled herself up out of the dirt, moving like a woman out of balance, chest-heavy, her stained shirt glistening in the moonlight. In the doorway she stepped over Tu and walked outside to the mound of earth. At the foot of the sugar-apple tree she cocked her head and closed her eyes. She stood holding her hands in front of her chest as though cradling something until the two old women followed her out to the grave.

It was impossible, but finally Tu allowed himself to acknowledge what he was hearing. From the doorway he stood and watched the women massing in the yard. Something dove past his head. He turned and ripped a plank from one of the ragged walls and marched toward the grave. The women stepped back. He began shoveling the earth with the board. The fresh dirt moved easily. In less than ten minutes he hit something.

A box. Look closer and realize it has been hastily nailed together with sun-bleached planks from the one-room house where your mother lived with your grandmother, the old woman's eyes knitted with clouds. Wait until the top of the box has been lifted off, the body bag unzipped to fill your tiny lungs with the first clean air you have ever inhaled, breath sugary sweet. Know that the world doesn't always smell like this, ash and soot, though every time you smell it you will flash on the sudden feeling of lying on someone's stony breast. Let the man who is your father lift you out of the darkness and up into the moonlight. Look closely at his face, the birthmark on the edge of his scalp. You will not see him again for many years if at all.

See these four faces as they peer at you, one of the old women with tears in her ruined eyes. Wonder who all the other faces belong to who are crowding in to see your perfect form. Wonder why you have been chosen to speak for all of them, tens of hundreds of thousands of millions. In a country full of ghosts, begin learning how to distinguish between the voices of the bodied and the voices of the spectral.

Tu bent over to zipper the bag closed. He was careful not to look at the face of his beloved, her hair pooling like a dark star behind her head. Under the full rabbit moon he caught a glimpse of her hand gleaming in the moonlight. He touched her finger, a small bead glistening on the tip. He picked up her cold hand and put it to his lips. It was honey.

The Fall [1975]

VIETNAM

○ HANOI

CHINA

LAOS

THAILAND

South China Sea

Kontum
•

CAMBODIA

Buon Me
• Thuot

Nha Trang •

SAIGON
✧

In the beginning the words were all in her head along with memories of sulfurous clouds and leaf-nosed bats blessing her with their leathery wings. Perhaps we are the reason she didn't utter a single word for so long. The truth is during those first years of total silence, people hardly noticed. Why talk to the living when she had us? And if they had noticed her lack of speech, if they had wondered, what would they have seen? The way at dusk this baby girl would sometimes look at empty air, nothing there at all, and begin to weep?

S OMETHING WAS WRONG WITH THE LEFT SIDE OF BÀ'S BODY, and they were still hours from the coast. We should have left sooner, Huyen grumbled, eyeing the sun, her cheek packed with old betel leaves she'd already chewed. At this rate they wouldn't reach the highway by nightfall and would have to sleep outside again. Huyen wasn't even sure she wanted to reach the highway at all and now this—Bà with a sudden inclination to walk to the left, body listing like a boat. It was gradual. If the path were straight, within a few hundred yards she would be on the verge of walking off the trail as if headed into the muddy waters of the Serepok.

Huyen had first noticed a change days earlier as they packed up their belongings beside Lak Lake. Qui had been sitting under a palm tree plaiting her endless hair into two thick braids, the baby nested in her lap. In the distance a trio of elephants trundled across the shallows, their handlers nowhere to be seen. A canoe floated by carrying some of the local M'Nong people, the boat weighted down with housewares and livestock. It was then as Bà bustled around the yard loading the two-wheeled cart that Huyen noticed how the left side of her face appeared as if melting, the skin going slack. It's just age, Huyen thought, and put it from her mind.

In their two rooms by the shores of Lak Lake she and Bà had

argued about what to do if the central highlands fell. Would it be safer to be part of the fleeing millions pushing south all the way to Saigon on Highway 1, or should they stay clear of the masses and use forgotten trails like this? Bà had said it ran all the way from Cambodia to the coast in one form or another. From her girlhood she remembered new recruits arriving at the rubber plantation near Kontum, the people trudging in from a week's march on the trail, their faces haggard. How the overseer would immediately hand them each a tin bucket and send them out.

In the end Huyen decided they would go as far as they could on small trails following the Serepok east until it hit the Song Cai. From the highlands it was seventy-five miles to the coast. Nights they would sleep in what remained of the brush. In the coastal city of Nha Trang they would join the masses on Highway 1 and push south. Secretly Huyen feared the highway. She had seen mass exoduses before. The lawlessness, the air like tinder. The population realigning itself because somewhere far away somebody had drawn a line on a map, the population fleeing because everyone else was fleeing.

Huyen surveyed the trail ahead of them, the terrain jungly and overgrown. From the looks of it the journey would only get tougher. If you put in the work to sharpen steel, eventually it will turn into needles, she growled, but the adage didn't lift her spirits. Silently they trudged forward, the only sound the cart's wheels rutting the earth as Qui pulled it along.

Their fourth day on the trail was hot, but they were used to it. The elephant grass scratched their necks. Small brown burrs stuck in their hair, the sound of the Serepok always in the distance. The full face of the lidless sun shadowed them on their way. Each day their skin grew darker, except for Qui, who stayed the same ghostly hue as she pulled the cart along using a wooden bar built for an animal. The baby sat in the cart along with Huyen and some bamboo mats, a few utensils including a rusty cleaver which they used on chicken they were able to catch on the outskirts of abandoned villages. On the second night of their journey, outside the hamlet of Son Trinh, Bà had brandished the cleaver when they heard something rustling in the elephant grass. Who goes there, Bà whispered, but nothing appeared. As a precaution she had taken to sleeping with the cleaver under her head. Already if she lay down without it she couldn't sleep.

Mornings she blamed her dreams on it. Ever since her eyes had soured, her dreams had dissolved into fuzzy splotches of color. But since sleeping with the cleaver under her head, Ba's dreams had taken on a new brilliance, images clear as day. An orange spider the size of a crab lurking in the trees. A white horse grazing under a colony of bats. The French Foreign Legion officer coming toward her with his cold gray eyes, the tip of his burning cigarette that already smelled of scorched skin. Each night, dreams like a river of memories bearing her away in the current.

It was almost noon. Tomorrow they would reach the coast. Qui stopped for a moment and wiped her forehead. She could feel the ends of her braids tickling the backs of her calves. Her breasts hurt. The baby was taking less and less, but her body was producing more and more. Evenings the milk ran silver in the light of the fire as it leaked from her nipples. Along with her ghostly white skin it was her one miracle. Her chest burned day and night. Mornings the ground was damp where she'd slept.

Already the baby was no longer a baby. She was four in the ancient system of reckoning, the months counted in which the unborn are forming in the dark caves of their mothers. Traditionally it was said babies arrived fully one year old with their little old-man faces wrinkled and red, their old souls hardening in new vessels.

When he had first pulled her from the body bag buried in the ground, Tu had held her up in the light of the full rabbit moon. Love, he whispered. *Ai*. The air glittered with soot. He held her high above his head, letting the silver light bathe every inch of her. The goddess be praised, said Bà, bowing her head and clapping her hands in prayer. Huyen and Qui stood silent. Ash drifted through the sky, sparkling as if sprinkled with mica, then going leaden as it hit the earth.

When Tu brought the baby down out of the moonlight, she was completely clean. No blood or waxy yellow slick coated her skin, everything just soft and shining, her small cap of black hair fragrant as honey.

That night standing by the grave Huyen had spit a long dark stream in the dirt. Love, she growled. She reached over and took the baby from Tu, then handed it roughly to Qui. You name your child Love and the gods will be jealous, she said. The way she looked at him, the heavy furrows gathering between her eyes. As if to say, don't you know anything?

Tu didn't argue. His true love lay cold and dead in a make-shift wooden box at his dirty feet, her head resting in the bowl of her hat. A piece of ash blew into his ear. Frantically he tipped his head. As he pawed at his ear, he didn't see the ring of white words beaming up into the night, the poem he had paid for long ago in its entirety. *In the long river, fish swim off without a trace / Fated in love, we can wait a thousand years / Who tends the paddy, repairs its dike / Whoever has true love shall meet / But when?*

Tu looked to his mother, her gray eyes shining. She had a way of knowing things she shouldn't know. Already the baby was cooing in Qui's arms. A piece of ash landed on the baby's forehead. Bà nodded. It was settled. No one would ever call the child Love.

Qui swooped down and picked up the pale blue rice bowl half buried in the dirt and turned back to the hut. The baby suckled on her nipple. The young girl's face went rapt, the feeling as if a ray of light were being drawn out of her body. For the moment the memory of the thing her grandmother had done to her was forgotten.

Huyen watched her granddaughter walk back into the hut. Already the girl was cutting a path through the world like a mother bear, already her appearance less deranged. Huyen grunted, satisfied. She was the oldest among them, older even than Bà by some years. It was right for the others to defer to her. It was how she negotiated the world, how she'd lasted. If you showed any attachment to things, you risked the gods' wrath. It was best to act as if the objects closest to you were of no consequence. Indifference kept the pain from shattering you when ordinarily you should have shattered.

And so the night of the child's arrival passed like a dream. Inside the dismantled hut, the fire burned down in the fire pit. In the distance no blue flames danced on the broken mountain. In less than a week Tu was gone, back to his days in the jungle passing messages and parts of heavy artillery along the network.

Even during the few days he was with them, watching Qui handle the baby out of the corner of his eye, they had begun calling her Rabbit, naming her for the full moon that had licked her clean. The rabbit with its innocence, its youthfulness, its long bright ears that hear everything in the realms of both the living and the dead. Rabbit because the world is full of rabbits. Rabbit because by sheer force of numbers, the rabbit walks among us unnoticed but pandemic.

And even now on the trail east to the highway that will take them south, the baby sits in the lap of the old honey seller, the woman like a second grandmother to her. On Rabbit's face is a smattering of freckles across the bridge of her nose and cheeks as if someone has dusted her with flecks of cinnamon. From time to time across the highlands she will rub her ears as if trying to clear them of something. She can hear the old honey seller's heart beating, the sound filling her small head though no one else hears it, not even the heart itself.

By mid-afternoon they reached the Song Cai. It wasn't as glorious as the Serepok, but it would take them to where they were going. They could feel the earth beginning to descend. Three times Qui took the cleaver to the brush before giving up. They were less than thirty miles from the coast. The forests this side of the mountains hadn't been sprayed with defoliant, but the landscape was rapidly changing, the greenness giving way to aridness. When the wind was right, you could smell the salt. Sometimes Qui thought she could hear the sound of voices carrying on the wind—the sound high and raw like lamentation.

For the past few years they had been working their way down the coast. Shortly after Rabbit's birth, the Americans began withdrawing from the country. Even with the Americans leaving, the war dragged on, the rice harvests left rotting in the paddies or never planted in the first place. In Cong Heo the people ate rats and frogs, whatever the countryside had to offer. When the rats and frogs ran out, Bà with her turbid eyes led the four of them down to Lak Lake in the central highlands, the highlands once the stronghold of the ethnic tribes who had sided with the Americans. They lived beside the lake for two years while the Americans slowly exited. Now that the tribes had been abandoned, everyone was left to fight for themselves, the mountains steeped in blood. It was all a mystery no one could explain. Why a foreign power would come all this way and then just disappear.

Overhead the scavengers were circling on the currents. Despite her cloudy eyes, Bà could feel the vultures' cold gaze.

The birds were in their season. For them it was a time of plenty. All outcomes were possible. How many hours had Bà spent trying to calculate what might happen? Tu's years working the Ho Chi Minh Trail as a foot soldier for the VC should be enough. Theirs was a family of heroes—Bà with a burn between her breasts where the Frenchman had stubbed out his cigarette. But she couldn't be sure their years of service would save them in the eyes of the new government. There was talk of an impending bloodbath. Some said if your family hadn't left for the north during the Great Partitioning of '54, you were an enemy of the people. Bà didn't know what to believe. Only one thing was certain. A great unknown was bearing down on them. Overhead the scavengers circling like a storm.

Baby, sleep well, so Mother can go to the market to buy you a spoonful of honey. If she goes to the east, she will bring you the lychee soft as an eye. If she goes to the western market on the edge of everything, she will buy you the sleep from which one never awakens, fingers sticky sweet. Baby, sleep well, so Mother can go to the market.

THERE WAS AN HOUR'S WORTH OF DAYLIGHT LEFT. THE EMPTY
sky was washed of color. The scavengers had landed somewhere
long ago to clean some poor creature of its flesh. Finally it was
time. There was no moon, the sky overcast. Huyen took out an
old flashlight. She hit it a few times before the weak light winked
on. In the darkness Bà took charge despite her crookedness, her
unblinking scar guiding her through the shadows. With her one
good hand she took out their mats and the iron kettle with the
remaining rice in it. They had just enough left for two more
days. They had cooked the rest of it the day before, figuring it
would keep until the end. They were all too tired to look for
stray brush to build a fire. They lay down right in the middle
of the trail. Qui took Rabbit up in her arms and sat down on
a mat, opened her shirt. Bà handed her a rice bowl. It was the
bowl from the grave of Little Mother, the bowl light blue and
chipped along the edge. Sometimes when Rabbit held it, she
would move her lips and prattle on as if talking to someone.

Qui jostled Rabbit on her thigh, but the child kept squirm-
ing. She forced Rabbit's mouth onto her breast, but the child
turned her head away. Qui sighed. She put Rabbit down on the
mat and rubbed her hands together until they were warm. Then
she leaned forward and began massaging one of her breasts with
her bare hands, moving from the base of the breast all the way
to the tip. After a while she began to squeeze the area around
the nipple with her thumb and index finger. At first the milk
came hissing out. After a few more squeezes it shot out in a thin
stream, dribbling uselessly into the dirt. When she finished, she
switched breasts, milking the other one until it was bearable.
Slowly the last light drained from the sky.

As Qui emptied herself, Rabbit lay on her back on the bamboo mat, her legs and arms rigid. She had a way of crying without moving, only her tiny chest expanding as she gulped the air,
refilling her lungs, then the silent scream that turned her face

red. Even after Qui finished, Rabbit kept crying as she furiously rubbed her ears.

Bà and Huyen ate their rice cold, Bà's mouth awkwardly hitching up and down like a puppet with a broken string, one side of her face frozen. When Qui was done, Bà came forward with the mosquito net and laid it over the girl and the fussing toddler, the two of them as if trapped. Once long ago on the rubber plantation, Bà had seen a Frenchwoman get married, the young woman the niece of the *propriétaire*. The way the woman floated from the front door of the villa to the shiny black limousine, her veil trailing on the ground, her whole being as if swaddled in netting.

They lay in the darkness, Bà on a mat by the cart wondering where her pipe was, if her dead hand had dropped it somewhere in the brush. She could feel the cold metal of the cleaver tucked safely under her head. In the early part of the night, she dreamed of a wedding party walking through a minefield. The bride was the first to step on one. The noise of the explosion sent a cloud of white doves rocketing up out of the dead trees. The guests froze in place except for the flower girl, who continued to swing her tin bucket as she skipped along through the elephant grass. The child dipping her fingers in the milky white sap, then flicking the droplets into the air.

Qui woke up after midnight. Her braids lay in coils on the ground. Beside her the child was still awake, Rabbit's eyes focused on something remote. Qui looked off to where she was staring. After a moment she too could see it, a light dancing in the distance. It quivered like fire but was the wrong color, the flame a steely blue.

Gently Qui put a hand on Rabbit's face and closed her eyes. After a while they stayed shut. The old women were asleep.

Qui was mindful not to wake them. She slipped the cleaver out from beneath Bà's head, careful not to pull her hair, then moved toward the flame. It was farther off than she'd thought, the little blue light always winking just up ahead.

When she arrived, Qui could smell something cooking. Her stomach rumbled. It smelled like catfish and lemongrass. They looked up. None of them were surprised that she should be coming out of the forest—a young girl carrying a cleaver, her hair snaking down her back, her exquisite face as if carved from moonlight. The man in the group said something she didn't understand. He tried again in broken Vietnamese. You VC? She shook her head. He pointed to a spot next to where the fish was cooking over a small blue flame. She sat.

There were more than ten of them, a family of Bana. The women wore the traditional skirts, each one long and black with a panel of colorful red embroidery around the middle. The man was shirtless, his loose pants made of the same dark material. They talked in their own language. She couldn't be sure which ones were his wives, which his sisters.

The fire was starting to wind down. A woman sat shaping a lump of clay into a small gray ball. When it was good enough, she tossed it into the flames and for a moment the fire sparked a pale blue as the ball ignited and began to burn. Qui could feel her mouth watering.

The man said they had crossed a bridge made from the bodies of the dead, corpses strung together to make a way. Two days ago Buon Me Thuot falls, he said in broken Vietnamese. Route 7 is a river of despair. Do you know what this means, he asked. Qui nodded, but he said it anyway. It means we are dead.

The front of Qui's shirt suddenly went wet in the blue light. She could feel the hot milk dribbling down her stomach. One of the women noticed. Without a word she got up from her seat and disappeared into the darkness. The woman came back carrying a sleeping child. His face seemed older than Rabbit's, almost wizened, but his body was smaller, less than what it should have been.

Qui lifted her shirt. Instinctually the sleeping child took her breast in his mouth. His lips were dry and chafed her nipple. Qui tried to stifle a sigh. The rapture of a foreign mouth on her body, a hunger she could satisfy.

In the light of day if the little Bana boy could have described his dreams to his mother and aunts, he would have told them fabulous tales of leaf-nosed bats and the long white tongue of the full rabbit moon. He would have told them about a dead woman glowing six feet below ground with a pearl gripped tight in her hands, all through the air the scent of honey. He took as much as he wanted, and still there was more. Soon the milk spilled from the corners of his mouth. In the days and weeks to come, his face shone with a new glory. His form filled out, skin radiant and supple, soft as down. After his midnight suckling at the stranger's teat, he was never sick a single day for the rest of his natural life.

In the morning the world was dewy and bright. Qui lay on the mat next to Rabbit in the middle of the trail where they had gone to sleep. The cart still stood where they'd left it loaded with their possessions, condensation glistening on the jars. The cleaver was back under Bà's head.

Qui sat up and stretched. The old women were already awake. They had slept on top of a hill. Through the dead trees she could see down to where the Serepok had run dry. If she turned east she could just make out a wide horizon where the world seemed to come to an end. She picked Rabbit up and walked to the edge of the hill and lifted her shirt, the baby's face flushed from a restless night. Qui closed her eyes, then the familiar feeling of light issuing out of the body. Water rushing downhill to find itself.

Overhead scavengers were already circling for the scent of

rot. Huyen watched the birds sail in rings on the wind. All that was left to do was pack up. They had another long day before them. One by one the old woman picked up their bamboo mats. Under Qui and Rabbit's there was something in the ground. Huyen brushed back the dirt with her foot. She didn't blanch when she saw what it was.

It was a face, the eyes still open. For a moment she considered digging further to see if she could find a gun. What is it, said Bà, her heart gone cold, but already Huyen was covering it back up.

They traveled all day over the highlands toward Nha Trang on the coast. Bà lay in the cart with her useless body, the baby nestled in her lap. Huyen hobbled forward on foot. The smell of salt sharpened in the air, the land leveling down. On this side of the mountain the populace lived on the ocean, the people fishermen and their business the business of fishing. Qui thought of the Bana family she had met in the woods. We are dead, the man had said, the man with his stories of crossing the Song Den on the backs of corpses. Like stepping on logs only softer, he'd added. Qui kept walking, the blisters on her hands starting to bleed. One of the women had described how you could feel the soft dents growing on the backs of the dead, like bruises on fruit. Spots where the bodies had been stepped on repeatedly.

Years ago in Cong Heo, Qui had heard stories about the NVA using peasants to ford streams. How the Americans would send fighter jets to bomb an area, houses and roads and animals all destroyed for the sake of a single bridge. Little did they know that by nightfall the rivers were again being crossed. By the light of the moon the peasants would stand shoulder to shoulder in the muddy waters, then bend over, their backs like wooden planks. Entire villages were lined up, even the elderly, each becoming a single stone in the human road. Then the NVA would roll a series of bicycles over the living bridge, bicycles loaded with rice and ammunition and medicine.

For the third day in a row Huyen was chewing the same betel leaves, the leaves long stripped of their punch. She looked up into the blue sky. A white bird floated in the air. It was a seabird. She could tell by the wide yellow feet and the fact that the bird stayed close to earth. In the distance a haze hung over the far horizon, the line indistinct between the sky and the South China Sea. Everywhere flocks of the little white birds with the wide yellow feet swirled in the air.

From the back of the cart Bà grunted and lifted her right hand. By the side of the trail there was a dragon-fruit tree growing in a ditch, each prickly arm green and spidery. They were succulents, a kind of cactus, the fruit itself magenta though the flesh was white and speckled with small black seeds. Huyen walked over and picked one. She peeled back the thick pink petals and bit into it, chewing a little before spitting the mush back out into her hand and offering it to Bà.

Bà turned her head away so Huyen offered her the fruit directly. Painfully Bà lifted her head and took a bite. At the familiar sweetness, the seeds crunching between her teeth, she remembered the first time she'd ever eaten dragon fruit, the tree with its green arms armed with spikes.

It had happened at Terres Noires. The black earth. Bà's breasts newly blossomed. She is standing behind the old wooden shed where the tin buckets are stored, each one rinsed out at the end of the day, the old women and children peeling the white residue from the sides and collecting the sticky peelings in a heap, which in turn will be measured and added to the day's take. Thirty feet off someone is being beaten in the water station again, the sound of the victim's voice familiar, something almost pleasurable in the man's cries, though she cannot place it. The way his breath catches in his throat, the man gasping. An inexplicable burning grows in her loins as she listens to his agony.

Then she sees them. A pile of bright pink oblongs gleam on a table underneath a white tent. Everywhere there are acres of plates and silverware. She isn't supposed to be standing here behind the shed where the tin buckets are stored when not in use. Her mother is out working the twelfth sector, bringing in her thirty pounds a day, which is easy in the twelfth sector because the trees are the ideal age. The white sap pouring out of them like tears.

And where is she now? A long communal building, a barracks. Things cluttered in the corners. Personal effects. Pots for cooking. Mats. It has been a long time since she has set foot in this world. Even with everyone out working in the sectors, the lingering smell of hundreds of unwashed bodies. He is sitting on a stool with his shirt off, a series of fresh welts running the length of his back. Is she still a child or was she ever a child? The man is older than her by whole lifetimes. Yet there is something about him that draws her to him. Perhaps it is the beauty of his hands, the skin of his palms like milk. Where is she and how did she come to this place? A room where she finds herself all alone with a shirtless man and his shredded body. But the man is winking at her. On the floor the sunlight pools in a yellow swatch. He is smiling as he reaches down inside his pants and pulls it out. She moves toward him. *Pour vous,* he says. Even when they had been beating him, he had managed to keep it tucked between his legs. The stolen fruit bright as a jewel.

Qui and Huyen stood and watched Bà toss in the cart. Together we unpeeled it, says Bà. The hunger of our hands, the black seeds crunching between my teeth. He takes his perfect milky palm and wipes the juice from my chin. Then he kisses me, our mouths full of dragon fruit.

Huyen could feel the headache stalling at the back of her brain. She had spit out the old leaves miles ago. Qui looked at her grandmother. I don't know what she's saying, Huyen said. It's gibberish. They stood watching as the juice rolled down Bà's chin. Finally she lay still. She's dying, Huyen added. Qui didn't even nod. Overhead a few of the small white seabirds floated in the blue, each one like a V in the sky. All right, Huyen said. Let's go.

From the last hill leading into Nha Trang they could see a mass of boats in the port. People were in the water holding what looked like bundles over their heads, a small fleet already making their way out to sea. Later, Huyen would hear a rumor about an American battleship ten miles off the coast, and that if you could reach it, it would take you with them.

Late afternoon they came to a neighborhood. The highway was still another few miles east. They walked through deserted streets. Some of the houses had been dismantled, names and markings taken down, signs blacked out. Trash littered the ground. An old dog lay in an alleyway. As they wheeled by, it lifted its head and sniffed but didn't get up. Something in the eyes—an animal weariness, as if it had seen this all before.

We should make the highway by sundown, said Huyen. She nodded toward the cart. People will help us. Somewhere she had picked up a large stick and was using it to make her way. Qui wondered where her grandmother had come into this newfound hope, this belief in people. Qui knew what would happen. She had seen it in the eyes of one of the Bana women when the man had offered Qui some of the fish. Overnight a thousand-year culture of hospitality had been reduced to every man for himself. The milky hollow in Qui's chest was on fire. Who would help them? If things were different, she wasn't even sure if she would help.

They walked on. A car shot past headed toward the highway, a sea of heads visible in the window, furniture and suitcases tied to the roof. As it sped by, Qui saw someone training a gun on them out the passenger-side window. It was a child, a young boy sitting in a woman's lap, the boy's face hard, his arm steady. The car continued on its way. Before the car reached wherever its destination was, Qui knew the boy would shoot somebody.

A man was standing in a doorway. It looked like it had been a shop of some kind. Through the window Qui could see the empty shelves. The man wasn't wearing a shirt as he stood coolly smoking a cigarette. A handmade flag was tacked just above a window, the flag red with a single yellow star in the middle. It was probably something his wife had stitched up from rags. Qui wasn't sure which one was prettier. The north's solid red with the one yellow star or the southern flag of the Republic of Vietnam, three red stripes running horizontally in a field of yellow.

There were other people making their way to the highway. Many of them were traveling with carts and bicycles loaded with possessions. Occasionally a motorbike would speed past, or just as often someone would be pushing one, either out of gas or trying to conserve it. Everyone looked dirty and hungry but energized just the same. Qui tried to imagine what had happened in these streets in the first minutes when news of Buon Me Thuot hit, that the central highlands were falling. Qui knew that for many it was the beginning of a road without an end.

It took a while for her to notice that not everyone was fleeing. Qui saw a woman carrying a burlap sack of rice on her back. Two teenaged girls walked beside her, one with a proprietary hand on the sack. Both of the girls carried large sticks. They were walking the wrong way back up the street. The woman looked tired. Maybe she wasn't ready to abandon her ancestors. Maybe in her mind she told herself she had nothing to fear, that she had never uttered a single word against the north, but her eyes said something else.

At the end of the street, Qui stopped and put down the cart. They had arrived at the boulevard that would take them to the highway. On one side of the street there were open-faced shops and small buildings, on the other side endless white sands and the aquamarine waters of paradise. Huyen looked at Qui. What, she said. Qui shook her head and picked up the cart again. Her hands were bleeding, the skin blistered and peeling. It would take too long to explain. Clouds of the small white birds sailed on the winds. She had never seen the ocean before.

It's not too late, said Huyen. We could stop here. It was true. The world was fleeing without knowing exactly where, people pushing south as if just the word *south* could save them. Huyen traced the horizon with her eyes. The four of them could simply walk off the road, find an abandoned house, build a fire. In the early morning before sunup, she would take Qui out to the ocean, teach her to wade into the surf at low tide, throw a net. They were mountain people, but they could learn. Qui wiped her brow with a bloody hand.

A man and a woman meet in a barren landscape. The man is a dragon, the woman a fairy. Why they love each other we cannot say. What their congress looks like we do not know. In time the woman lays one hundred eggs, each one the soft pale color of mercy. There is joy and happiness followed by much sorrow as often occurs with pairings of this kind. Eventually the man and woman accept that they can no longer be together, their love poxed by the stars. The man is of earth, the woman water. She takes fifty of their children to the sea, he takes the others to the mountains. Such are the origins of the Vietnamese people.

AND NOW THEY WERE STOPPING. EVERYWHERE PEOPLE MADE camp in the road. It was well past midnight, the noise of a million displaced voices and the full moon like an eye over the world. Huyen massaged the back of her skull with her fingers. If she kept her eyes focused in the middle distance, the headache was bearable. All over the highway campfires blazed like the fires of an army. Some of the travelers looked as if they had been on the road their whole lives. She wondered if, when the time came, they would know how to stop.

Qui piled their bamboo mats one on top of another and laid Bà out, folding the mosquito net on top of her. She picked up the baby and opened her shirt. A young boy in a group on the edge of the road sat watching, his eyes black as holes. Qui wasn't sure if it was hunger or curiosity or something darker that made him stare.

Huyen spit some chewed rice into her palm. She tried to feed it to Bà, but the old woman wouldn't open her mouth, her eyes snowy. A man was picking his way up the road carrying an armful of dried brush. He stopped and stared at Qui before peering at Bà lying in the moonlight. She'll be dead by morning, he said, without any inflection. Huyen had thought he might offer some of the brush to build a fire, but he didn't.

Hours later she nudged Qui. Most of the fires along the highway had burned out. It's time, she said. She lifted Rabbit up off of Qui's stomach where the baby had been sleeping and put her down next to Bà. Say goodbye.

Overhead something fluttered through the darkness. Rabbit rubbed her ears. The world went black like the moment before a curtain lifts. Gingerly she put her tiny hands on her grandmother's face. Through the fabric of the old woman's shirt she brushed the spot with her lips where Bà's scar gleamed next to her heart. A dog barked in the distance and then a flash and then everything, Bà's life spooling into her granddaughter in the span of a human kiss.

Lady, your face is growing wet. A light mist slicks your cheeks, but it's not rain, the sun peeking through the haze. Lightly you run a finger over your forehead and stick it in your mouth. Salt. Spindrift. You begin to recognize the soft sting in your nostrils, the world listing at five degrees. Then you realize it's not music filling the air so much as the cries of seabirds.

A sudden splash. A body hits the water, then another before a gun is fired into the air. In the sky the line of little white birds riding the winds parts for just the briefest of moments before re-forming. You watch as the man with the gun takes aim at two dark shapes in the water, the shapes paddling furiously. Another few shots and they stop moving and sink below the surface. For the rest of the short journey south nobody else jumps overboard even though the ship never leaves sight of land.

The day began on a quay, an interminable line slugging forward. People standing in the hot sun waiting for their turn to make their mark on a piece of paper, lines organized by place of origin. Ha Nam. Nam Dinh. Ninh Binh. At the head of each line there is an agent and a doctor from the company who looks at both sides of the hands and pries the mouth open, searching for signs of fever because, aside from fever, everything else is acceptable.

A recruiter walks among the lines saying it will be the easiest three years of your life. He is missing his left index finger all the way down to the knuckle. You notice this and everything there is to see. Your eyes are clear as gems. You try not to stare as he says something about free medicine, thirty pounds of rice a month, eight-hour work shifts, and the company will pay to bring you right back here, repatriate you in the land of your ancestors with money in your pocket.

All over the quay large men stand around holding rattan canes as if the foot-long sticks were nothing more than fancy pointers used to direct traffic. Some of the men are foreign, ex-members of the French Foreign Legion, their faces etched by sun and swifter sharper things. Some of them stare openly at the women. One scratches the black stubble of his chin with his cane as if that's all he ever does with it. Already you are learning that order is something the company must maintain at all times, and that it is the job of these men to do so at any cost.

Two hours and then you're up. How old, says the agent. Your mother looks at you as if he's asked for your weight, something she needs to consider. She reaches over and brushes a strand of hair from your face. Thuan is fourteen, your mother says, her voice smoothing over the lie. The truth is you were born in 1930, and you will be ten in the fall, your eyes clear as water, but as you are learning, women are mercurial. Tell a man what he wants to hear and he will see whatever you tell him. The agent plunks down a contract. Sign here, he says. You take up the plume and dip it in the inkwell, draw the small square with the two lines that partition it like a rice paddy, the symbol of your clan. Your mother looks on. There isn't even hope in her eyes, just resignation. A mother and a daughter, their hunger like a bond between them.

What your mother doesn't know. The agent doesn't care how old you are. He gets paid three *xu* for every signature he collects.

It's a good place for a family, the agent says. The company will look after you. Your mother wonders why, now that he has your signatures, the agent keeps spinning his lies. Everyone else from Nam Dinh headed south years ago, and none of them have come back, though everyone in Nam Dinh knows what happens down on the plantations. They went for the same reason your mother has decided to make the move. There is simply nowhere else to go. Even the rats in Nam Dinh are scarce. War is settling on all the continents of the known world, and rubber is the dark currency that makes it all possible.

Another three hours and the processing is done. One of the company's men moves from line to line collecting the contracts, filing them in a brown binder that you will never see again. Each person who signed was promised ten *dong* just for signing, though the workers from Ha Nam have the lowest rates of literacy. Even before boarding *Le Cheval,* which will take you all south into hell, the people from Ha Nam will be swindled out of four *dong,* a fact they will come to find out in the days ahead, though there is nothing they can do about it.

On board you are given a shabby mat and told in French to find space on deck. The sailor who tells you this speaks like a native, but his skin is dark as earth. *Le Cheval* is full of ore; you are just a secondary cargo. The food from the galley is inedible, the rice filled with sand, the fish already rotting. Once out at sea, people eye the railing but in their hearts everyone knows it is too late.

This is all you remember of the boat ride down the Vietnamese coast in the land the French call Indochine: the little white birds trailing the ship, the night sky as if salted with stars. How a man from Ninh Binh demanded drinkable water and was hit on the head only once, though the blood came down out of his scalp as if he'd been beaten again and again. On the third night a man and a woman lay writhing on their small square mat while everyone else slept, the man with his hand over the woman's mouth, and the cords in her neck either straining with pain or something you can't fathom.

On the fourth day the seabirds have doubled in number, land close enough even the weakest swimmer could make it. By the time *Le Cheval* sails into port, your mother has already finished her daily implorations to the goddess. Lady, keep us safe. Lift up our hearts in the darkness.

Once the ship docks, chaos breaks out when a foreigner boards and begins beating the air in front of him with his cane for no apparent reason. *Partez! Partez!* A woman falls clutching her head. It takes another hour to sort things out. All over the splintery wooden boards of the pier you notice rusty stains that theoretically could be anything.

The provinces are all going somewhere different. Due to war profiteering, the rubber companies are legion. Michelin. Mimot. Bigard. Cardesac. Because you and your mother hail from Nam Dinh, you will board one of the trucks heading back up north. It will take nearly two whole days to get where you are going. From time to time the truck stops so that you can climb out to relieve yourselves, then fill your arms with as many pineapples as you can carry. Some will wonder why the ship didn't just stop near Tuy Hoa and let you off, but no one dares to ask.

And then you see it slipping through the trees—Terres Noires—up in the central highlands with its fourteen villages, its million hectares. The earth is red, though the French call it black because the original rock is volcanic and dark in color. In time the dirt turns a deep red as the rock breaks down, fertility beyond anything imaginable.

In the back of the truck your mother holds your hand. Thuan, she says. Remember who you are. You don't know if she's reminding you that you're supposed to be fourteen or if she means something deeper. You jump off the truck, and a woman hands you a thin wooden badge on a tin chain. The woman's face is dark and lined, her own badge weathered and dangling around her neck like a battered soul. Your mother slips hers on first. No. 1220. Put it on, but don't become it.

Your first night in the barracks of Village Twelve you hear someone screaming from the woods. There are a hundred people sleeping in the room, but nobody rises to go to his aid. In the morning you learn that a man had gone out to meet his lover but had been mauled by a tiger. Before roll call there is a crowd gathering by the water station. The man's extremities look intact but his innards have been skillfully removed. A woman bends over the body but doesn't shed a tear. It is a crime to leave the plantation at night. There is talk of rebels proselytizing in the hills. Nobody comes forward to claim the body. Eventually two men are singled out to take it away. The men load it on a flatbed and drive it to the place where the workers are building Village Fifteen. The body will be planted where the new saplings will go.

A few days later a small shrine goes up by a storage shed, a tiny pagoda with a roof not much bigger than a rice bowl, a place to burn joss. When Eduard, the head overseer, sees it, he orders it torn down. We're not running a goddamn temple, he says. Your mother bows her head, closes her eyes. When she's done, she looks to you to do the same. You bow your head but don't know what to pray for. As the days and weeks pass, this happens repeatedly, words not readily coming to you. Like speaking into the darkness. A feeling of being all alone, though there are thousands at your side, each one stooped and suffering. Lady, keep us in Your sight.

Terres Noires stretches for miles, trees planted in straight lines as far as the eye can see. In the back of Eduard's flatbed it takes more than two hours to drive from one end to the other. Such cultivation, such care. You will be ten years old in the fall. You are too young to consider how any of this got here. How the first truckloads of men and women came down from the north in the late twenties. Men working to clear the land. Hack down the forest. Rip out the old trunks. Plant the saplings. Build the villages. The barracks and sheds and the garages and the water stations and the cooling rooms where they store the liquid rubber and the system of houses for the network of overseers, the great villa where the *propriétaire* lives with his thousand-bottle reserve in the cellar.

You will be ten years old in the fall, eyes clear as crystals. Nobody believes you are fourteen as your mother claims, though many of the women who have given birth to children are hardly bigger than you. The first few weeks you work the land around Village Twelve like everyone else. Roll call at five, then up on the trucks and out to the sectors. The day starts at six, then all day in among the trees with your pruning hook, your hand ax. The tin bucket always with you, which you use to empty the small wooden bowls that sit in hooks placed at the end of the track, the track itself a great ribbon cut diagonally around the trunk so that the latex oozes out and runs down the long slanting gouge and into the bowl. The latex white and creamy, which the workers joke about though you don't understand. You never knew there could be so much to do in the world, every hour of your life given over to something, the need to stay in constant motion. You spend the days filling your bucket, careful not to spill.

This is what you learn that first week at Terres Noires. There are no eight-hour shifts. No medical clinics worth mentioning. No thirty pounds of rice per month. On the trucks by five, all day milking the trees, then back on the trucks at six. Sundays you spend cleaning the village, sharpening the adzes and pruning hooks, cleaning the tin buckets of their residue. When it is all done, sometimes there is time for *cheo,* the traditional plays of song and dance that help the workers forget themselves. In *cheo* lovers meet in wet paddies. Lost princes wander the land before being restored. Tricksters with good hearts ultimately deliver the protagonist from his enemies. It is all a metaphor, but for what you are unsure.

In each of Terres Noires' fourteen villages there is a commissary, a small store where everything is costly and of the worst quality. Your mother is trying to stretch the money she has been paid, though the salary is only a figure in the manager's book, a number inked on a piece of paper. Last month the commissariat informed her that they were only paying you half the wages. But she's fourteen, your mother wailed. Thuan deserves a full salary. The other women in line told her to be quiet. Let them treat her as a child, one woman whispered. The women all lowered their eyes. It is the only line they respect, someone said. Your mother stopped protesting and accepted the eighteen pounds of rice without further complaint, then made her mark in the commissariat's book.

And that very afternoon as your mother is learning another of the thousand things mothers fear for their daughters, you see him for the first time—a grown man in his late thirties. Underneath the cashew tree with its white flowers the size of fists.

He sees you staring. There is something in his eyes that you have never seen before. A knowing gentleness, the palms of his hands white as clouds. It is 1940 and when he looks at you, you can feel yourself being recognized for the first time.

In each village there is a medical clinic where a Frenchman sits smoking a cigarette as the patient struggles to describe his *malade* in a foreign tongue. When the patient finishes, the Frenchman will rise and flick his cigarette out the window. Do not eat or drink for the next twenty-four hours, he will invariably counsel. Give your system a chance to purge itself. And the patient is ushered out.

When the people don't work, it means the plantation doesn't have to pay them. The company would rather you stay home and starve than go out into the woods and earn a wage.

So the workers turn to him when they fall sick, the man with palms white as liquid rubber. The people's sicknesses are predictable, the dark siftings leaking from their bodies from the poor food, the dirty water. Depending on whether or not there is blood or pus the man with the unworldly smile will brew a tea made from the bark of the philodendron. Drink this, he says. Within hours the rumblings in the worker's belly fall silent.

That first time you see him it's Sunday. He is sitting off behind the barracks in the shade of a cashew tree, legs in the lotus position, eyes shut, the white flowers of the tree big as fists. You have been working Terres Noires for months. The muscles in your thin arms are striated. The empty buckets you are carrying bang rhythmically against your knees as you walk by. You don't know the word for the thing you are feeling in the pit of your stomach, though you know it has nothing to do with dirty water. The moment like walking a long dirt road directly into the sun, the sound of the buckets like the clattering of your heart. There is something in the stillness of his body, though somehow you know there is a fire burning deep within like one you have never known. How is it possible? The man opens his eyes.

Not your mother. Not Hong Hanh, who is actually fourteen and lives in Village Eight with her whole clan from Ha Nam. Hong Hanh, whom you'll meet in the grand kitchen of the *propriétaire,* the copper pots and saucepans hanging from iron hooks. Nobody. *Personne.* Not a single soul will ever understand the unworldly rapport between you and this man. You barely understand it yourself.

It happens like this: there is a riot in Village Two. Village Two is one of the original villages. Some of the workers have been cutting the trees there for more than a decade. As Village Two is more than fifteen miles away, news of the riot doesn't reach your village for almost a full day. The night after it happens the first of the rioters begin to trickle into your sector well past midnight. When they knock on the barracks door, only he will rise and step outside, the man with the palms white as cream standing in the moonlight and patiently drawing a map in the dirt. The man tells them which river the dogs won't ford, which mountain tribes are friendly, which to avoid at all costs.

And so a new girl is needed in the kitchen. The girl from Village Two who used to work there doing whatever was needed has disappeared along with her family. The truth is maybe one of the overseers saw an opening and took it, lured her out into the field of new saplings by Village Fifteen, and did what he'd been waiting to do, ultimately burying her body there beneath the young trees where they will grow and mature and bleed for years. Who can know for sure?

Two days after the riot you are filling your bucket out among the rubber trees when one of the LeBonne brothers appears and says come with me. His skin is pitted as if with a needle. You turned ten years old in the fall, though you are starting to look fourteen. For the rest of the day your mother, who was only a half mile away when you were driven off, will be tearing her hair out.

In the grand house you see things you have never seen before. Indoor plumbing. Gas stoves. Lace so fine it hurts just to look at it. Staircases carved in teak. Ivory and china and the fabric they use to blow their noses in finer than anything you have ever touched.

This is where you will grow up, not out there under the rubber trees and the watchful eye of the other LeBonne with the battered rattan cane he is never without, your hands callused like leather, fingers peeling and raw where the white sap sticks to them and won't come off. No. This is the world the world has been hiding from you. Massenet. Lavender. Madeleines. Taupinière. A world of leisure, though the hours of sweet inactivity are not for you. You will work as hard as ever in this other world.

Time passes. The war arrives. Nobody is allowed to leave. Because Vietnam shares a border with China, the battle-thirsty Japanese invade, desperate to keep Vietnamese supplies from the Chinese. Occupied France allies herself with Japan, and now Indochine has a new ruler. On the plantation three-year contracts are extended indefinitely because where would you go, child? The Japanese have faces like yours but different somehow, eyes smaller, hard as knives, eyes as if entirely made of pupils, like insects with their compound lenses. Mostly it doesn't matter. The French are still very much in charge because business is business, and the Vichy are accommodating, though the young mademoiselle sits at the piano crying that her life has been ruined, that she will never stroll the Seventh Arrondissement with a lover on her arm. *Mon pauvre petit chou,* you say, fanning her with a banana leaf. My poor little cabbage.

You no longer sleep in the barracks but in the servant quarters with Hong Hanh and the rest of the staff. The few times you see her, your mother says she is happy for you. Your French is flawless in that way children pick up foreign languages without even trying. Once when you haven't seen her for months, you barely recognize her, the lines in her dark brown face as if gouged with an awl. The first time you call your mother *Maman,* she looks stricken, as if you've just hit her.

Though you never forget the moment by the cashew tree, as the years pass you only see the man with the beautiful palms every now and then, mostly when the French *garagiste* sneaks him into the building just off the main house where they keep the Saoutchik shipped in all the way from Marseilles so he can work on the great black car so polished it always looks wet, the thing bigger than any room you have ever shared or ever will. The way the man with the beautiful hands can intuit what is wrong, twisting the right cap, replacing the right part, with the result that the engine purrs back to life and the *garagiste* can hold his head up around the grounds. You always knew the man was magical, his hands like blank pages. This is the proof.

Today the *garagiste* yells through the back door to bring them some coffee. Though you are in the middle of boiling the napkins, there is no one else around, so you do as you're told. You make it just the way the *propriétaire* himself likes, the aroma so bitter you wince at the smell. You leave it in the press and carry the tray outside, your house dress just below the knee, your body fully blossomed, eyes clear as glass. In the night when Hong Hanh is asleep, the breath sniveling out through her nose, you are learning how to touch yourself. Sometimes you think of him, the man with the perfect hands, the light in his eyes seemingly faceted like a cat's, and when you do, it happens faster.

For a moment you stand in the light of the garage. He is under the great black hood. You can see yourself reflected in the liquid metal—a girl holding her heart out in front of her. Then he comes out from under it and everything is as you've remembered. Even under the grease his hands shine like moonlight. The *garagiste* is nowhere in sight. Thuan, the man says. It is the only time he will ever speak your name. The rooms in your heart flooding.

In the days after the European war is over, when the danger in Vietnam is at its most extreme as Indochine steadies herself to fight the French imperialists, Hong Hanh will say this is why the man with the lily-white palms befriended you. Because you have access. You can get him keys and maps and help him drug the dogs and tell him things about the cycles of the great house. You stand in the pantry with your hands folded across your chest. *Ta guele!* you shout at your best friend. And years later, after all the passion has drained from your body, you will keep the physical memory of your first afternoon of love, July 1945, the *propriétaire*'s niece to marry that very week, the tent like a great sail staked out under the flowering cashew trees, the man beaten, his back laced with welts, and how he brought out the dragon fruit nevertheless, the thing he had been hiding just for you, and the way he brought it out from the dark cave of his body where he had kept it hidden between his legs as the overseers beat him with their canes, the LeBonne brothers with

their homicidal rages blind to who he was, not knowing that
stealing the fruit was the least of it, that he was Vietminh, that
he was organizing the workers, that nights he would read to
them from *Than Chung* and *Humanité,* the French Communist
paper, tales of workers finding their voices, the collective power
of their awakening, of *sûréte* agents and managers and armies of
overseers being overthrown at last, and the memory of that first
time when the man peeled the fruit for you and watched you eat
of it, and the way he took you in his arms, and all the while you
were careful not to touch his back as he moved into you and you
felt the little death creeping up on and on until you died and he
moved in you until you died again and you said I'm yours I'm
yours I'm yours I'm yours you never stop saying it even when
someone tells the overseers about the two of you there on the
eve of the August Revolution, Ho Chi Minh with his declara-
tion prepared, the war in Europe over, the Japanese emperor
declared just a man, August 1945 and Ho Chi Minh né Nguyễn
Sinh Cung with his letter of friendship to Harry S. Truman
which will go unanswered ready to tell all the world that after a
thousand years Vietnam is Vietnam's at last but before it happens
the LeBonne brothers come and drag you out of your bed and
put you in a room where a series of Frenchmen ask you where
is he and it goes on and on until one of them puts his cigarette
out on your chest not because he thinks it will bring an answer
but because he can the burning going all the way down to your
heart a window a hole that lets the light in gives you second
sight a way of seeing in the dark which is why now at the end of
everything you see yourself lying on a highway in the middle of
fleeing millions a girl a child kissing your scar light of my blood
everything spilling into her so that you can finally rest but it isn't
the end, *n'est-ce pas?* After life there must be life.

And years later when an old medicine man with green scars in the pits of his hands moves to the same province where you live by the Song Ma, the River of Dreams, you will be vindicated. It wasn't all about access, about dogs and maps and keys. It wasn't.

This is what Rabbit sees in the instant she kisses the skin where a Frenchman burned her grandmother next to her heart. Terres Noires and everything that followed—the three or four men who came after the man with the milk-white hands, one of them the father of Tu, the subsequent fire of childbirth, the feeling of Tu's small hot mouth on Bà's breast, war and more war and war without end and the living on because you had to, the years beside the Song Ma and the years on Lak Lake and all the while the world growing dim though in the heart it was the opposite. The scar on her chest like a medallion.

She's dead, said Huyen. In among the clamoring light of the full moon, Rabbit could hear others dying farther up on the road, the closest one only a few hundred feet away.

Lady, lift us up in the darkness.

September 1945. Within two months the uprising in Indochine is over. All over Vietnam the plantations are once again under French rule. The end of the war in Europe means that France has been liberated and Indochine is still a colony. The French gendarmes and the *sûréte* agents and even a division of Allied soldiers have put an end to the revolt, rounding up as many Vietnamese Communists as they can. But what the French don't know could fill a universe.

Today the wound on your chest from the August Revolution no longer smells and is starting to heal, though it will never fully heal. Now you work the rubber trees again as you did long ago when you were a child pretending to be a woman. Each day you take up the sharp pruning hook and gouge the bark. Each tree forever scarred.

One tree over, Hong Hanh puts down her pruning hook and points. A truck is coming through the woods, but you don't stop what you're doing. It's just another truck full of prisoners headed to Con Son Island off the southern coast. Now that the revolution has failed, Terres Noires is shipping them out, anyone suspected of illegal activity, of being a Communist and organizing against the French. It isn't until your friend, who has also lost her job in the kitchen, snatches the hat off your head that you put down your bucket and look.

In the truck bed the prisoners stand shoulder to shoulder, their arms held out in front of them where, in lieu of rope, someone has speared a length of copper wire through the center of their hands, the men strung together like fish on a line, each man wired to the other. Already their hands are growing green and useless.

Calmly Rabbit kissed her grandmother's forehead. *Cô ta không chết.* She's not dead, said Rabbit, her first sensical words. She was four years old in the ancient system of reckoning. In the darkness the freckles on her face seemed to shine. Huyen put a hand over Bà's mouth, but there was nothing coming out.

And when you see him, the man you have always loved, as you invariably will, your love riding in the back of a truck with wire running through his palms under the hot September sun, don't cry out. Don't acknowledge his presence. His swollen hands sewn to his neighbors', his back riddled with fresh welts.

He doesn't see you, his mind a thousand miles away, the

anger already growing in him, a rage that will carry him through the term of his imprisonment. Standing there in the hot sun he doesn't see anything. He can't. But the Lady is watching. We are always in Her sight. And so for some reason the man lifts his heavy head and looks out at Terres Noires one last time. He turns his face toward you out there somewhere among the trees, a knife in your hand, your eyes bright and cloudless, and bows.

"And the Water Was
Made as Glass" [1979]

The Christians among us have a story about the light of the world and a voyage by water. "Now under the Semites' Barley Moon of the Strong Rain it came to pass that he went into a ship with his disciples, and he said unto them, 'Let us go over unto the other side.' But as they sailed he fell asleep, and there came down a storm of wind, and they were filled with water and were in jeopardy. And they came to him and awoke him, crying, 'Master! Master! We perish.' " This is what the Christians among us believe, and as some of us have lived it word for word, the waters serrated and thronging, our stories are not dissimilar. East and West. Night and day. The light of the world indiscriminately keeping watch over all of us.

R ABBIT AND SON WERE SITTING ON THE FRONT PORCH
with their feet in the river when the boat floated by. It was
the sixth one that month. The engine was up out of the water,
a mass of weeds threaded through the rusty blades. Two men
stood on either side of the pilothouse using bamboo poles to
push the boat downstream. The only noise was the sound of the
bamboo stabbing the water, the boat gliding down the Mekong
through the floating village of Ba Nuoc on its way toward the
sea in the darkness before moonrise.

Squatting on the porch, Son waved, but the men didn't wave
back. Nobody else came out of their rickety houses to stare as
the boat drifted by. Son knew better. It might look like nobody
was watching, but somebody always was.

Ba Nuoc was a small community of fewer than fifteen houses,
each one no more than three rooms built on empty fifty-gallon
drums along with a type of river weed that the men harvested
and the women matted together until it floated. Sheets of metal
covered the roofs, at night the rooms lit by firelight. Some of
Ba Nuoc's residents were extended families like the Dinhs, Son's
clan. Others were southern professionals like Dr. Kao who had
been pushed out of the cities with nowhere else to go but the
Mekong delta. It was thought the doctor had a wife and children
somewhere. There were rumors he had once been the personal

physician to Madame Nhu. Now his house was just a floating raft with a shack lashed to it.

The water coursed under the porch where Son and Rabbit sat waiting. There were floating villages all over the delta as well as floating markets and floating factories, in places the Mekong so wide one couldn't see the other side. In some spots the villages were built on stilts to avoid the annual flooding when the river overran its banks. Everywhere things were made to float, the whole world tying itself to something and not letting go.

The boat was almost to the bend in the river. Soon it would disappear behind the thick curtain of mangroves. There was still no sign of Son's mother, Phuong, or Huyen and Qui and the other women returning from the floating market. The moon was well above the trees. Finally the boat rounded the bend.

Let's go, said Rabbit, her voice as if inside Son's head. He jumped up before he could help himself. He was nine years old in the modern system of reckoning, two years older than her, but in every other way Rabbit was the leader, her hair cut short as a boy's, a black bowl encompassing her head. From a distance she and Son looked like brothers, their bodies lithe as saplings, Rabbit's ribs also visible when she went without a shirt. Once, out on the porch of their floating house, Son's own mother had called to Rabbit thinking the little girl was Son. Then Rabbit had turned around and Phuong had seen the map of freckles adorning the child's face. Phuong shuddered at her mistake. The freckles were unsettling, the spots so rare among the population that nobody knew what to make of them.

At the other end of the porch Rabbit began untying the sampan. Son opened the cage and took Binh out first, placing her black webbed feet on his shoulder. Binh was the first bird Rabbit and Huyen had ever trained. While other birds came and went, Huyen had allowed Rabbit to keep Binh. There was a trainer over in Sac Bao who clipped the wings of his birds, taking the strongest feathers from each appendage. That way they couldn't fly away and never come back. It also meant they couldn't dive as deep. Consequently the fish they caught were midsize and unremarkable, but the man said that was the price you paid if you never wanted to worry about losing your bird.

Son had been with Rabbit and Huyen when they'd first found the nest hidden in the mangrove roots by the water's edge. Huyen had taught them to never take more than they needed, otherwise the birds would move and never come back. Over the next three years they had returned again and again to the same nest, never taking more than one egg with each visit. It was a time-consuming process. Huyen showed them how to keep the eggs warm until they hatched, then how to feed the hatchlings tiny shrimp and bits of fish. The few times Son had gone hunting for a nest with his uncles with the intention of raising a pair of birds to sell, they had picked eggs that never became anything. By the time they realized it, they couldn't even eat them, the shells starting to grow soft. With Huyen and Rabbit it was different. Every egg they took became a bird.

Ordinarily it could take as long as six months to train a young adult, but Huyen could do it in less than three. The locals joked she was part cormorant, her betel-stained teeth the same fleshy color as her tongue. Son knew it had something to do with the silvery room inside Rabbit's head, the place where she went to listen. He imagined a cavern blasted somewhere deep inside her skull, a jagged room made of silvery rocks like the caves down by Cuu Long Bay where people hid things from one another, a place where Rabbit could hear things no one else could hear. That was the only way he could explain it. All she had to do was speak a thing and the bird would do it, Rabbit and the bird as if talking to each other. Dive. Open your mouth. Give it here. Be quiet. Sometimes Son did exactly the opposite of what she said just to make sure she didn't have any power over him, but even then he wondered.

Rabbit extended her arm. Son put the second bird, still in training, on her wrist. At two feet tall it towered over her head. We don't need the cage tonight, she said, brushing her cheeks in its ragged feathers. A few months back she had argued with Huyen. It's what people expect, Huyen had said. You can't always be there, the old woman added. A customer had come back and said his bird had flown away. After the man was gone, Huyen took the cleaver off its peg and opened one of the cages with a new bird in it. Rabbit climbed over the railing into the sampan. She put her fingers in her ears as Huyen slammed the cleaver down on the bird's wing, clipping its best feathers. Huyen breathed heavily as she worked her way through, her teeth the same color as markings on the bird's head and beak.

Unlike other fishing birds, the cormorant couldn't swallow underwater. It had to surface with its catch. Most fishermen fitted small bands made of cane around the bird's throat, the poorer fishermen simply tying a piece of string just below the gullet. When the bird resurfaced, the fisherman would pull the string tight, keeping the bird from swallowing. Time and again Huyen would tell customers the string wasn't necessary. If you respect the bird, she would say, it will respect you. Hers were the best fishers on the river.

Son stood upright paddling in the back of the sampan, Binh preening on his shoulder. The stars were out and the air was muggy. The last time he had gone out alone with Rabbit, Phuong had carried on when the two of them got back even though one of the fish they caught was the length of his arm. Rabbit was lucky that way. Qui couldn't talk. The front of her shirt was always wet, her pale face with the large eyes so filled with beauty his uncles never talked about her, as if the mere mention of her radiance were a kind of sacrilege. On the other hand Phuong was always yelling. Ever since his father had disappeared in one of the reeducation camps, Phuong was beside herself over the littlest things, wailing that if anything ever happened to him, who would take care of her? He was nine years old. There were other boys younger than him who went out fishing by them-selves, their fathers dead or off clearing land in the new eco-nomic zones. Phuong didn't care. Even when her own brothers told her to let him be, she would acquiesce during the day, let-ting him go with them to the black market in Cantho to sell any extra rice. When he came back home, it was a different story. Nights on the leaking floor she slept with her arms around him.

Rabbit didn't even turn to face him. The Dragon's Head, she said. Son kept paddling east toward the stars in the Winnowing Basket. We need the money, Rabbit said. Please. A bat swooped by his ear almost knocking him off-balance. He tried to remem-ber the last time he'd heard her say please, but nothing came to mind. She was a seven-year-old girl who spoke like an old man, addressing everyone with the pronouns meant for inferiors, her freckles cowing adults into silence. Once, unthinkingly, Rabbit had called Huyen *em,* and Huyen had slapped her. Son's older sister, Sang, liked to say that Rabbit was a tiger girl and that one day her tiger blood would get him killed.

Son sighed and swung the sampan toward the stars of the Black Tortoise. He thought of the things Huyen had told them about the river. The Mekong was a series of rivers that origi-nated in the icy mountains of Tibet and reached the South China Sea through a network of tributaries south of Saigon. It branched and forked and twisted for almost three thousand miles, the dark brown surface deceptively calm. Anywhere two or more branches met there was a dangerous current as the two rivers became one. At its widest, the Mekong stretched more than seven miles from shore to shore.

The Mekong is our mother, Huyen had said. She gives us fish and birds and a place to live. The old woman put her hand in the river and scooped up a handful. She will kill you without shedding a tear, Huyen added. In her palm the water gleamed an impenetrable brown, silt-rich. Sometimes when he wanted to hide, all Son had to do was jump in and hold his breath.

He was steering toward a spot where three fingers met a tributary called the Sap River, the waters originating from Cambodia's Tonlé Sap. By sampan it was almost an hour. He tried not to think of the way his mother would lock her arms around him when he got home. A bird that could fish the Dragon's Head was worth double, though if you fell out of the boat, it wouldn't matter to you how much the bird was worth.

Son had only been there once with his uncles in a boat with a small engine. They'd gone to look for river otters. The animal's bladder could be sold for three months' wages in the fields, the glistening sack smoked and pulverized for Chinese medicine. Otters were drawn to the Dragon's Head because of the types of fish the fast water attracted. Son had talked his uncles into bringing Rabbit along. She'll be able to hear them, he said. She's small. She knows where things like to hide. At the time his uncle Duc had intended to say no, but something about the little girl with the cluster of freckles and the boy's haircut standing there looking him right in the face as if she were his elder gave him pause. The next thing he knew she was in the front of the boat.

In their first ten minutes at the Dragon's Head, Rabbit had pointed to some dead saplings snagged in a mass of weeds. Duc managed to scoop the creature up in a net. The thing was obviously a baby, its coloring still tawny but glistening in the light. Then Hai, Son's youngest uncle, brained it, holding it by the hind legs as he smashed it twice on the side of the boat. When he was done, Son could see what looked like chunks of pink sponge coming out of its ears. Within seconds the flies began to clot.

Rabbit rode the rest of the way in silence. Something about the impassive look on her face, as if she were seeing all the way to the ends of the earth. Though they wouldn't admit it, none of the grown men could bring themselves to disturb her. They came home with just the one lying like a tattered sock in their net.

Overhead Son searched the sky for the pale green second star in the Willow, his birth sign, but the moon was too bright. He knew even his uncles would be upset. Night with just a bamboo oar and no rope and him ferrying his childhood friend to the killing heart of the river. The worst part about it, his uncles would say as they sat drinking the *ruou nep* in the light of the fire, the sweet wine distilled from sticky rice, was that there was really nothing in it for him. He had a heart like his dead father, An, they would conclude—like An, he put everyone else ahead of himself.

After a while Son changed course again, steering the sampan the final stretch toward the Great Emptiness in the western sky. How to explain? Sometimes with Rabbit you chose to do things you wouldn't ordinarily do. You became bigger than who you were. Wasn't that what the Buddha taught? He didn't think his uncles would understand. And with the government's new policies in place, in a few short months everyone had forgotten how they used to live. Son could still remember the old way of harvesting rice, everyone out in their neighbor's fields, everyone lending a hand, the whole village prospering together. And how at the end of the harvest the village would celebrate by hiring a water puppet troupe to perform, the papery creatures as if walking on the surface of the flooded paddies. Yes. The thing his uncles would chide him for was the thing he missed most about his father. When An was with you, he would do anything you needed—climb any tree, till any paddy, or just carry you on his thin shoulders even when you could have walked. Now that the

government had collectivized the countryside, declaring everything belonged to everyone, it had had the opposite effect—it
made the whole world less willing to be generous. Now nobody
gave his neighbor a hand at harvest time. Each farmer was left
to struggle on his own. Once Son had heard his uncle Hai say it
was a good thing An was dead because this new world would've
killed him.

Son steered the boat past a fisherman floating on a makeshift
raft. The man's fire had gone out. A fishing bird huddled at the
man's feet, but there was something strange about the creature.
Son wondered if the bird's wings were rotting. Unlike other
seabirds, cormorants didn't produce oil. Every day you had to
let them out of their cages to stand in the sun, or their feathers would become waterlogged. With a wingspan of over four
feet, if they stayed wet long enough, their soggy feathers could
become heavy as weights, in time their own wings drowning
them.

A match, the man said as the two children passed by, the man
gesturing as if lighting a cigarette. It was more a command than
a request. Son looked to Rabbit. Ever since the government had
begun collectivizing the farms, robbery was on an uptick. Rabbit studied the man. His conical hat obscured his face, though she
could see his long gray beard falling to his chest. He was leaning
toward them, one hand invisible under the water. She shook her
head. Son kept paddling. He could feel Binh's feet tightening on
his shoulder. He knew his father would've stopped to help.

Within minutes he could hear the shift in the current. He
kept the boat near shore. Even then he had to throw all his
weight into it, the speed of their progress cut in half. There was
no way he could row them out into the middle. If he did, it
would be like shooting a rapid, the water sending them sailing
downstream in unpredictable ways. They were still a half mile

from where the waters converged, but it was close enough. In the moonlight he could see things tornadoing past, mostly sticks and weeds but other objects as well, things bloated and shiny.

You sure about this, he said. Already she was picking the smaller bird off her wrist. Even if it comes up with all the Buddha's gold, he said, who's going to believe us? Rabbit glared. Son felt his face growing red. It was true. Nobody would question it. Adults believed every word she said.

He reached into the pocket of his shorts and pulled out a book of matches. Out here it was a formality. The light wouldn't make a difference in the fast water. He walked to the front of the boat, the sampan rocking, and raked his fingers through the basket full of twigs and leaves they kept on board. With one match he got it lit.

It was the ancient art of fishing. After dark all over the Mekong, men in boats would position baskets of fire on long poles out over the water, the innumerable flames like a flock of moons, then up out of the depths shadows massed on the surface of the river, each one attracted to the light, moths to the flame, and *splash!* The bird dives over the edge into the darkness, thrashing about momentarily, and resurfaces only to be hauled up by the fisherman. And when he whistles, the bird opens its beak, and the man reaches in and pulls one out, the bond between man and bird sealed, the fish's long silver body flashing in the firelight. At the end of the night, the horizon pinking, the fishermen load the birds back into their wicker cages, the men's movements gentle, deferential, as if they were handling gods, each man placing a dark hood over the bird's crested head and dousing the flame, putting the feathered god to sleep.

Son slid the basket of fire out over the side of the boat. Here the river was so fast the light wouldn't attract anything other than insects, but he did it all the same.

Rabbit had her face buried in the bird's feathers. She was

talking to it with her eyes closed. Son couldn't hear what she was saying. He knew her words were building a fire in the bird. He closed his eyes and tried to pretend. Someday he wanted someone to talk to him like that.

Rabbit perched the bird on the lip of the boat. The basket of fire swung over the water as the sampan rocked in the current. It was a narrow point in the river, less than a quarter mile from shore to shore, the water gray in the moonlight. The bird extended its snakelike neck as if limbering up, its dark grace mesmerizing.

Go. Rabbit's command echoed inside Son's head. He hadn't even seen her lips move. The bird opened its black wings. He could see where the pattern had been interrupted by Huyen's cleaver. Clipping could be tricky. Hit a blood feather and the animal could bleed to death.

The bird fluttered down onto the water. Already it was moving away, its powerful feet all but invisible. Son put his hand on Rabbit's shoulder. It would all be decided under the surface. The bird would slip under, then the animal would have to call on both its feet and wings to power it back up against the crushing water. Once it dove, everything would happen quickly.

Thirty feet upstream there was a series of rocks studded in the river. The one time out with his uncles they had pulled to shore at the end of the day. Something was choking the engine. While they waited for Duc to clear it, Hai had climbed out on the nearest rock and lit a cigarette. Once Duc got the engine going they were ready to leave, but Hai was still lying on a rock, his shirt off as he lay sunning himself. Hey lady, Duc had called. Get over here or we'll leave your flat ass. Now in the moonlight Son noticed the rocks strung across the river, each one silent and black.

A halo of insects was swarming around the fire. On his shoulder Binh's feet were starting to make his skin sweat. He missed the exact moment when the bird went under. One minute its long loose neck swayed like an S, the next it was gone.

They waited. Far away downriver pinpricks of light twinkled, whole universes being born and falling dead. Then Son could see it, the great neck craning. He could see the fish in its mouth. Even at a distance the whiskers on the fish's face were thick as wire. And of its own free will the bird was making straight for them with its offering, coming to lay the great fish at Rabbit's feet.

Neither of them saw it. It must have been sitting on the rocks waiting for the bird to rise, the pattern of stripes and spots helping it to melt into the darkness, the animal keeping its eye on the water, anticipating the spot where the bird would surface, its muscles tensing, its whiplike reflexes ingrained in the blood.

The cat leaped. It hit the bird square at the base of the throat. Even from where they were sitting they could hear the sound of the bird's neck snapping. It looked twice as big as a normal fishing cat, though the two black spots on the back of its ears were the usual markings. Son was still watching the animal gripping its prize in its jaws, eyes coated with night sheen, when he suddenly fell backward in the sampan as the boat shot out into the middle of the river.

At first he thought they'd been hit by a river croc. He sat back up and looked around for the two yellow eyes. Straight ahead he could see the rocks jutting up out of the water. The fishing cat had changed course. It was swimming straight for the rock farthest from shore.

Son held on to both sides of the boat. The water was swamping them. The sampan began to break apart. Rabbit was standing in the back, the bamboo oar in her hands. He knew she had set the boat in motion, that she was aiming for the fishing cat, but the sampan went sideways in the water, the boat caving in from the force. He was still sitting on what remained of the floor, Binh somehow still on his shoulder. Rabbit let the oar fall from her hands. She closed her eyes. Son imagined she was already in the silvery room inside her head. If the moment were frozen, she would have looked as if she were standing on water.

Then the boat overturned. Son went under and came back up, a flame guttering in the breeze. He took in as much air as he could. Underwater it was hard to tell which way was up. He imagined a room with no doors or windows, no up or down, the room a perfect sphere. Then he imagined a wild animal materializing in the room. That's what it felt like when he would slip under—a wild animal tearing at him in a room with no way out.

The current was stronger than he'd expected, stronger than the monsoon winds that tore roofs off houses. I am going to drown. It was as if somebody else were thinking it, a third party outside himself. He thought of the voices inside Rabbit's head and the way she would paw at her ears. He wondered if he would become one of them. He was swept downriver, a piece of flotsam. He considered just letting go. The Buddha promised a special wheel of life for children. Maybe it wouldn't be so bad.

He surfaced again, his lungs on fire. Something was poking him in the back, trying to hook his shirt. He felt it take. He was being dragged through the water. Then a hand reached down and grabbed him by the arm and swung him up out of the river. For a long time he lay retching.

It was the man he and Rabbit had left in the dark, the one who had asked for a match. The man's raft was a patchwork of logs. His long gray beard shimmered in the moonlight. You're breathing, the old man grunted, then he went back to scanning the river.

Without Rabbit, Son wished he were dead. He imagined the front of Qui's shirt, how it would never stop weeping, her long hair tangled in knots. He closed his eyes and tried to concentrate. He pictured a room on the moon. Could Rabbit hear his voice?

Rabbit, it's me, he thought, say something, but all he could hear was the sound of the river flexing beneath him.

When Son opened his eyes again, the old man's bird was standing over him. He could smell its musk. There was something different about the bird, its feathers strangely silver in the moonlight, almost colorless, its eyes as if filled with blood. The man was squatting at the edge of the raft and stroking with a crude paddle. Son struggled to sit up. One side of his face was aching where he had scratched it on a branch. Downriver he could see something, a black V floating on the water.

It was Binh. The bird had opened her wings and was marking the spot. Rabbit was drifting on her back and looking up at the stars, the bird floating beside her head. As the raft drifted closer, Son could see there was no panic in her face. Mày là con heo! Son said. *You dumb pig!* The old man laughed, his long gray beard rippling. You two married, he asked. He reached over and pulled Rabbit out of the water. She had lost her shirt in the current and was naked from the waist up, her ribs distinct as fingers.

The man placed Rabbit down on the raft. He picked up his oar again and continued paddling. He didn't seem to be in any hurry, his gray beard fluttering in the breeze. You're one of the Dinhs, he said. Son nodded.

They came around the bend that opened up into the cove where the houses of Ba Nuoc sat floating on the river. All were silent and dark except for Rabbit's. Even from a distance they could hear a chorus of voices carrying over the water. A throng of sampans was tied up out front.

It was illegal to have that many people gathered in one place, but Son figured it was all right. They were probably organizing a search party for the missing children. Son climbed onto the porch. Please come in, Uncle, he said to the mysterious stranger who'd saved them. It wasn't Son's house, but Rabbit would never think to ask. The old man just shook his head and held on as Rabbit climbed over the railing with Binh on her shoulder. For a moment the two children stood in the light of the moon. It was only after the man had shoved off that Son realized he should have run inside and found a dry book of matches for the stranger, but the old man and his silvery bird were already lost to the dark.

Inside it was crowded. On the floor lay a crude hand-drawn map of Asia. Son could see lines running through the ocean connecting Vietnam with other countries in the region. Nobody seemed concerned—Rabbit half naked, Son with a deep scratch on his cheek, the injury twisting down his face like a lightning bolt. In addition to Huyen and Qui, Son's uncles were there as well as Dr. Kao and a group of ten or so raggedy men Son had never seen before, their clothes hanging in tatters. One of them had a small red mark staining his face where his hairline had receded, the thing shaped like a jewel. Some of the ragged men spoke a language Son had never heard before, the language flat and unmusical. Then someone was coming forward, the man's shoulders thin as rungs. One eye brown, the other sky-blue. Ba, said Son, running for him.

The All-Seeing Lady is the one thing we take with us wherever we go. That's not to say it's wrong to dream or imagine ourselves differently. Some of us are still making peace with this stratum, the way we are merely rustlings in the world, crescents of light glinting on waves. Sometimes we remember what it was like to have agency, the appearance of control, which we know even at its core is only an appearance.

By month's end the streets were crowded with the Autumn Moon Festival. Red lanterns hung along Duong Le Loi, though each remained dark. Since the end of the war, nobody had candles to spare. Outside the one *pho* shop that still served white onions the four lanterns the owner lit at twilight were dark by the time the moon rose. Someone had blown out the candles as if making a wish and pocketed them.

The Autumn Moon Festival was second only to Tet in importance. Even before the war it had a reputation for being the one time of year when the whole world turned a blind eye to wrongdoing, the holiday a day of thanksgiving for a bountiful harvest, a time to be with family and celebrate good fortune. The doctor had decided they would travel in separate groups. Son and the men would walk to the rendezvous point through the city of Cantho, the women going by river. With the festival raging all night, nobody would notice a group of men slumping around the city in frayed clothes, some of them with their pants held up by rope, one man missing an entire sleeve.

All week Son's mother Phuong had been telling their neighbors that his sister was getting married. Son didn't know if Sang knew the truth or not. Dr. Kao said it would look less suspicious this way, the men and women traveling separately. Just try to relax, the doctor said, as the group of men walked through the festival. One of the sun-dark men tried to smile, but it looked more like a grimace. All the same the doctor patted him on the back.

People were gathering along the riverfront. There was talk of fireworks, but nobody believed it. The government couldn't even protect its citizens. The year before just one province west, in An Giang, the Khmer Rouge had crossed the Cambodian border, killing more than three thousand Vietnamese in a single night. The night it happened, Rabbit lay burning with fever on the floor of the floating house, her small arms cradling her head, her hands frantically rubbing her ears. In the border city of Ba Chuc there had been only two survivors.

The sky was ablaze with the Autumn Moon, the brightest moon of the year. The doctor had conceded there would be a lot of light. It's a risk, he'd said, but we don't have enough money for more than two bribes. They were counting on guards stationed around the city to leave their posts, the whole world drunk on rice wine. None of the adults had told the children what they were planning. For the past two weeks the men talked of Malaysia and Hong Kong. There was always a series of numbers in the air, the discussion dragging on into the early hours of the morning. Weight. How many days. Fuel. Water. Everything that could be planned was planned. The doctor anticipated the worst but knew, if it came, it would be like nothing they could imagine. Son could tell his uncle Hai didn't like the doctor and that the feeling was mutual, but for now they needed each other.

Tonight as they walked the streets, the doctor was dressed like everyone else. There was a hole in the knee of his pants, and for the first time his wrist was without its watch. All over the south, professionals like Dr. Kao had been replaced by northerners with little or no training. Ever since reunification, southerners were being pushed out of their jobs and forced to eke out a living on the streets. In the moonlight, Dr. Kao looked just as ragged as the rest of them.

The men who didn't speak Vietnamese were careful not to talk. Son wondered what would happen if people realized they were Cambodian. At one point one of the Cambodians bumped into a woman carrying a baby. The woman stopped and demanded an apology. The man acted as if he were drunk and stumbled on without saying anything.

Under an archway festooned with lanterns the Cambodian with only one sleeve bumped his head. He slapped himself on the cheek and laughed. There was something childish about him.

Walking the festival streets he genuinely seemed to have lost all his cares. Son kept his eye on the man. They had already lost him twice in the crowds as he'd stopped to gawk at various vendors. Mooncakes and exotic fruits. Black-market items openly displayed. American toothpaste. Potatoes. Sesame oil from Thailand. White silk gloves that ran all the way up a woman's arm.

The man with one sleeve stopped again. Son squeezed his father's hand and nodded to where the man was standing peering at a collection of jars. The seller was squatting in front of some newspaper she'd laid on the ground. When the man stopped to look, she reached deep in a sack and began rooting around in it, pulling out a live snake, in the sticky evening air its body twisting on itself like an amulet. The woman held it up by squeezing the sides of its head, the trap of its jaws sprung wide, its teeth tiny and mouse-like. She held it out for approval, and the man with one sleeve ran his finger over its cool length, its skin patterned and dark. People were starting to stop and stare. They seemed unsure of what to make of a grown man stroking the underbelly of some common snake, then clapping his hands together, delighted.

In a loud voice the woman launched into her patter. Look at you. A stiff wind would carry you away. The man didn't blink. Quickly Dr. Kao came forward and handed the woman a few bills. *Cam ơn,* she said, taking a rusty knife out of the waistband of her pants and laying the thing down in the street, all the while pinching its head, its tongue flitting like a ribbon. Even after she'd hacked through the throat, the tongue still flickered in and out, eyes glassy and black. At the first sign of blood, the man with one sleeve covered his eyes. Son could see his bottom lip quivering.

The woman kicked the head into the gutter and made an incision down the length of the body, the snake still wriggling. A small crowd had gathered to watch. With her fingers the woman dug in the stringy wet meat, then pulled out a glistening sac the size of a pea and motioned for Dr. Kao to pour himself a glass from one of the jars where dead snakes were kept preserved in a clear rice wine, the snakes bleached and curled tight, eyes pale as marbles. Then slowly, as if squeezing a boil, the woman milked something green and inky into the doctor's plastic cup, each drop falling like a tear. When she was finished, she dropped in the crushed sac.

Dr. Kao touched his elbow with his free hand in the traditional way. Một, hai, ba, DÔ! someone shouted. Một, hai, ba, DÔ! the doctor said, and downed it, his face smooth as if he were drinking water. When he lowered the cup, the gall bladder was gone.

The woman twisted her fingers inside the snake and snapped out another organ. She dropped it in a second cup, which she herself filled, the wine turning a dull pink. The moon was just beginning to rise over the cityscape. The woman offered the glass to Son's father. Một, hai, ba, DÔ! the crowd shouted. In the silver light An's blue eye looked cloudy. He seemed as if he might faint. The chanting grew louder.

Son snatched the cup out of his father's hands. On his face the deep scratch throbbed from the night out at the Dragon's Head. He closed his eyes and threw his head back. The thing hit his teeth but he didn't gag. He rolled the heart around in his mouth. It tasted like a hot coin. Son thought of the place where his father and all the other men had come from. That first night in Rabbit's house the men's stories of fields lined with skulls with the flesh still on them. He swallowed as hard as he could, the heart beating all the way down. The crowd roared.

Son lowered the cup. The bleached moon hung in the sky. The man with the bloody diamond on his face patted him on the back. Son still couldn't believe the man was Rabbit's father, that someone like Rabbit even had a *ba*. He wondered about the places his father and Tu had been, his father who they had all assumed was dead. Tu took the cup from Son and handed it back to the woman. He put an arm around him, and together they moved through the crowd.

Qui rowed the three of them up to the floating house in the last rays of the sun. Downriver a heron skulked in the tall grass by the water's edge. The second boat was full of their possessions. They would all ride together in the first and pull the second one behind. Son's sister Sang was standing on the front porch, her heavily made-up face a soft pink, skin coated as if with frosting. From her seat in the boat, Rabbit thought Sang looked as if she were posing for a portrait, her black hair piled high, lips the same blood-red as her dress.

Phuong hurried out the door carrying one last sack. It made a strange rattling sound as she walked. Her face was smudged with what looked like ashes. Child, she said to Sang. Take this. In the fading light Phuong held the sack out to her daughter. Sang stamped her bare foot. It made a damp squishy sound. Mother! she said. She hated it when Phuong used the word meant for children. Sang was fifteen years old. She was old enough to have a baby. She knew how it was done.

From the sampan Huyen spit in the river. Qui nodded to Rabbit. Even Rabbit knew they didn't have time for this. She sighed and hopped out of the boat.

Two days earlier in the floating market Huyen had traded Binh for the red *ao dai*. The silk was threadbare in places, the dress obviously used. And now Sang stood on the porch in the red *ao dai* waiting to be carried downriver. This morning she had put it on as soon as she woke up, even though they wouldn't be pushing off for hours. The night before she had laid it out at the foot of her mat. In the morning when she slipped it on, it smelled musty, as if it had been stored in a rice shed. You smell funny, Son had said at breakfast, waving his hand in front of his face. You don't know anything, Sang said. She went back to humming to herself.

The day the dress appeared Rabbit had watched Huyen load Binh in the sampan one last time. She knew Huyen wouldn't be bringing the bird back from the market. Please, Rabbit said. I can take care of her—she'll feed herself. Hush, said Huyen. It won't be happy where we're going. The old woman tucked some fresh betel leaves in her cheek. Only a fool puts his heart in things.

On the front porch Phuong handed Rabbit the sack her daughter wouldn't carry. It was heavier than it looked. Rabbit hoisted it up onto her shoulder. Her head filled with voices, some of them so old they seemed to speak another dialect. Rabbit closed her eyes and rubbed her ear with her free hand. There were so many she couldn't pick out just one, the voices unintelligible as static. She turned to climb back over the railing and down into the boat, but Sang held her back. Me first, the older girl said before climbing down.

Phuong had told all their neighbors about Sang's marriage. It's sudden, conceded Phuong, but she's ready. It explained the comings and goings of the past several days, the strange men peering out of the windows. The other families in Ba Nuoc nodded and offered their tempered congratulations. We wish you one hundred years of happiness, they droned. Mostly they were grateful for the show. When the authorities asked, they wouldn't have to act incredulous. As if they hadn't noticed their neighbors packing up all their worldly possessions right underneath their noses. They could tell the government officials we saw her standing right there on the front porch in a red *ao dai* with a full face of makeup. They could say yes, there were strange men coming and going at all hours of the day. We thought they were the groom's family.

Sang stepped down into the boat. Rabbit watched as the older girl tried to catch a glimpse of herself on the surface, but the river was turbid with silt. Then they were floating away. Qui stood in the back with the bamboo oar in her hands. Her curtain of black hair was loose and almost skimmed the water. From time to time the second boat would bump them in the back, making their possessions rattle. Sang was trailing her fingers in the water. After sunset it was a dangerous thing to do. Rabbit kept her eyes on the horizon. Downriver the heron began flapping its wings, beginning its long ascent into the air.

The man with one sleeve tapped Son on the head and pointed across the water. They had been waiting in the marsh grass twenty feet from shore for what felt like an eternity. Things had begun to fall into place when their group had left the swelling crowds at the festival. They had walked two hours east, the paths empty as the countryside celebrated in Cantho. As they waited in the marsh grass, the tide was out, but the water was beginning to rise. By the shore it was still too low for a sizable boat to clear. So far upriver the tide was just a matter of inches. There was a line of ants running up one of the tall blades of grass. Son wondered how the ants got there, how they moved over the water from stalk to stalk. Then he looked down and saw a string of ants striding on the surface, a black line snaking all the way from shore. He wondered if the moon was so bright the ants thought it was day.

The man with one sleeve tapped him again. Son looked to where he was pointing. At first he couldn't see anything, but then he saw it—in the distance the tip of someone's cigarette drifting past. Son woke his father up. They had been squatting along with the other men in the tall grasses on the edge of the Turtle Marsh for the last hour. It was well past midnight, the moon in the third quadrant. Son noticed the back of the doctor's shirt was damp with sweat, though Son himself was getting cold.

The Cambodians began whispering among themselves. The man with one sleeve cupped his hands around his mouth. He let out a series of short squawks, each one like the noise the white-eared night heron makes when disturbed. When he finished, they waited. From across the marsh a sequence of squawks echoed in the night. The doctor closed his eyes. Son could see his lips moving. With his hand, Dr. Kao touched his forehead, then several places on his chest.

They watched the drifting boat come to a stop only a hundred feet from shore. In the moonlight Son could see two sampans coming their way. The boat itself didn't seem large enough to take them all. It was a fisherman's boat built for a crew of five, ten at the most. He knew at best the motor would be a relic from before the war. There were no new engines to buy. He wondered where his uncles had found the boat, if they had actually paid money for it. If it was stolen, he wondered if that would affect their chances, the boat's karma tainted, all of them doomed before they'd even set out.

After the sampans reached them, Son and his father and the man with one sleeve were the only ones left waiting in the reeds. There wasn't enough room for everyone. Someone whispered that a sampan would be back shortly. Son could feel himself shivering, the snake's pulpy heart somewhere deep inside him. The moon lay on the water like a hole filled with fire. The man with one sleeve was playing a game with his fingers. Even as the others loaded up the sampans and moved across the water, the man kept pressing his fingertips together in different patterns—

thumb to the ear finger, the first to the ring. Son knew the man could do it all night long, could do it all the way across the sea or in the overcrowded cells his father had described where men had to take turns lying down because there was so little room.

His father had fallen asleep again. An's fatigue seemed endless. From across the water in the moonlight Son imagined An might look like something in the heron family, his delicate silhouette as if branched, bones hollow. He held a hand up in front of his father's mouth and waited until he could feel the breath on his palm before lowering it.

Son heard them before he saw them. They were rounding the headlands when they came into view. A string of shadows moved along the path like figures cut from black paper, their voices traveling over the water. A few of them carried torches, the light dancing like little souls. They were still a half mile away, but it didn't matter who they were. If they were a patrol, then they would all be arrested, the ragged men put back in cells where the whole cell had to defecate in a plastic bucket with a hairline crack running the length of it. If they were peasants, they might ask for money in exchange for their silence. Son shook his father. Ba, he said. The man with one sleeve was already wading out into the river. They couldn't wait for the sampan to come ferry them across the water. Son grabbed his father's hand and followed.

Ordinarily the swim wouldn't have been difficult, but the boat was anchored in deep water. The deeper the water, the more unpredictable the current. Son was holding his father's hand when the drop came and the current took them. He felt his father jerked downriver, their hands ripped apart. He could feel the soft earth disappear beneath his feet as the water picked him up. He knew he couldn't cry for help or all would be lost. The trick was to swim upriver. If he swam for the boat itself, the current would bring him up short. The man with one sleeve seemed to know this. Son could see him swimming for a spot thirty feet upriver of the boat. He began to head for the same spot, but he could hear the sounds of someone fighting for breath. Already ten feet away his father was floundering, his body spinning wildly in the water. There was so much light on the surface of the river, he looked as if he were being spirited away by moonlight.

An disappeared under the water. Son could still see where the tips of his fingers had scratched at the surface. Afterward Son thought this must be how the bird finds the fish through the darkness. What it feels like. No time for thought. How the body takes over. He swam to the spot where the water had closed over An and dove. When he came back up, his father was retching in his arms.

Ba, said Son. His father had taken on a new heaviness. It was all Son could do to keep An's head cradled above water. Together they drifted downstream, the boat growing smaller and smaller. He wondered if the others would raise the anchor and come after them. He knew once they raised anchor they would stop for nothing. He could feel the half-healed cut on his face starting to sting. His father coughed. Please, An sputtered. Leave me. Son held on tighter. I order you to let me go. It was as if someone else were talking in his arms.

Ten minutes passed. Son could have kicked them to shore, but he thought it best to stay in the water. For the second time in less than two weeks it was out of his hands, the Mekong charged with his destiny. If he thought about it, the one thing he'd want more than anything else these past few years had already come true. He was holding his father in his arms, the moonlight surging all around them.

Son lost track of the time. An hour, minutes, weeks passed. They were flotsam in the river, an island of two. A beating heart sailing down a dark throat until it lands where it will.

Later he would tell Rabbit that the stories were true. He could smell it before it surfaced. The animal's breath like night soil, rotten and fetid from the heaps of garbage it ingested, teeth yellow as piss, each one studded in the mouth like a series of nails. Fishermen had cut open crocodiles to find bicycle tires in their stomachs, one with an entire French tea set tarnishing in its guts. Most of the freshwater crocs weren't large enough to take a grown man, though they could take a limb and leave the victim to bleed to death. There was one said to have taken more than fifteen water buffalo in the last two years all up and down the river, though nobody had ever seen it.

The women were almost five miles downriver from Cantho when they heard the drone of a small outboard engine. It was another few miles to the spot the doctor had chosen for them to board, a wide-mouthed inlet where the water was deep enough for the boat to draft. From there it would be another mile to the spot with enough shoreline vegetation for the men to hide until they could be ferried on board. As the little motorboat approached, Phuong gripped the sampan's edges. Even in the dusky light, Rabbit could see her knuckles blanching.

They were teenagers, just boys in makeshift uniforms, jackets torn at the elbow. Everyone else was off at the festival. Huyen muttered under her breath. The younger soldiers were the worst, many of them officious and drunk on the little bit of power that came with the uniform. If someone needed to be executed, it was often boy-soldiers who did the killing. His first night in Ba Nuoc, Rabbit's father had told a story about a group of boy-soldiers on the front lines in Cambodia who had stomped a fellow soldier to death for snoring too loudly.

The older boy was working the engine. With his free hand he made a brusque motion in the air. Rabbit could see a few stray hairs sprouting on his chin. Qui stopped rowing. The boat pulled up alongside. For a spell the two boys sat staring, Qui's beauty like nothing they had ever seen. Then the boy at the engine took charge. Papers, he squeaked. None of them moved. Even though he looked older than the other boy, Rabbit thought he couldn't have been more than fourteen.

Maybe they all should have seen it coming. All day she had been working herself into a quiet rage. Sang smacked the water with her hand. The younger boy jumped. She looked him dead in the eye. Rabbit could feel the heat coming off the girl's skin. This is my wedding night, Sang said, a coldness in her voice. She was a fifteen-year-old girl on the verge of becoming a woman. Even the boys knew they had only just scratched the surface.

There were no men around, no one to save face in front of. The boys wouldn't speak of it later even between themselves. The younger boy averted his eyes. A hundred years of happiness to you, sister, he said. The older boy kept his eyes on the engine. Qui took up the oar. Rabbit looked at Huyen. She could tell the old woman was doing her best not to smile. She wondered what would happen later when Sang realized the truth.

The river croc made its first pass. It was swimming high enough out of the water that Son could see the prehistoric ridges along its back. He imagined it was looking for the spot where it might seize them in its jaws and take them under, never letting go until it had drowned them. Son tried not to look at its yellow eyes. Depending on how far apart the eyes were, you could tell how big the animal was. His uncles said if you looked a river croc in the eye, it could hypnotize you. Some river crocs were said to have been medicine men in previous lives.

The animal slipped under the surface. Son knew it would surface to attack. Once he had seen a small one take a dog in the death roll. He imagined how this one would take their heads in its mouth and begin rolling its plated body in the water, the sound of their bones breaking audible only to them.

Under the water something brushed his leg. He had never felt anything so cold. Was it the animal or a piece of debris? He began to wonder if it would hurt. Of course it would, the great mouth studded with teeth, and the added agony as the dark water burned his lungs. It was almost too much to consider. If he were all alone, he might try and do like the ancient monks and just will himself to die.

Then something was coming from out of the sky. A shadow crossed the moon. He could hear the flapping of wings. A bird landed on the water just feet away. It was a cormorant. The bird looked colorless, the long serpentine neck weaving from side to side. It seemed to be staring at Son with its bloody eyes. Son wondered if the bird sensed what was under the water. There was a possibility the crocodile might surface for the bird, pulling it under instead. From out of the reeds he could hear someone paddling toward them.

The boat was sitting in the middle of the river. It looked abandoned. The doctor's plan relied on the whole world being at the festival, all eyes on the moon. There hadn't been any attempt to hide it. It was a fishing boat with a small pilothouse, its white paint peeling from the salt and the sun. Qui quickened her pace. Rabbit could feel the sampan surge forward with each stroke. They had to board without anyone seeing. If someone saw them, there would be no lying their way out of it. There would be no shaming two teenaged boys into letting them go.

Qui rowed around to the far side away from shore. Bats were already wheeling through the air. Then Son's uncles Hai and Duc appeared. Nobody said anything as they got to work. Rabbit felt herself being lifted over the side. On deck she watched as Hai jumped down into the sampan and lifted Huyen, the old woman light as seed. Sang was standing, her feet planted like pylons. The sampan started to rock. Sit down, Hai hissed. In the fading light Sang's dress shimmered faintly. She stayed standing.

Duc and Hai worked around her, unloading and storing things below deck. Phuong herself carried the clattering sack down into the hold. On board Qui was tugging Rabbit's hand, but Rabbit wanted to watch Sang with her legs and arms akimbo in her red *ao dai,* colossal in her growing fury. Rabbit wondered if Sang had ever really believed she was on the way to her wedding. For a moment Rabbit could feel the girl's loneliness like the pale yellow aura around the moon. Finally Rabbit let herself be led below deck.

If she had stayed, she would have seen the moment when the fire burned out. Sang didn't take the hands reaching out from on deck to pull her up. Her head simply dropped. She stood a long moment in the new light of the world. Then without uttering a cry she reached over and put her hands on the splintery lip of the boat and pulled herself up.

It was a race and they were the prize. The crocodile was still somewhere under the water, its cold blood beating in the darkness. Son could feel his father growing heavier in his arms. He didn't know how much longer he could hold on, though he was prepared to hold on forever. Across the water the sound of someone paddling toward them, each stroke like the ticking of a heart.

It was almost worse this way. When the yellow eyes had been on the surface, Son had felt a terror beyond compare. But now that the eyes had submerged it was incomprehensible. There was no word for it. The idea that one moment you could be floating in the water and the next all sentience could be ripped from your body. Then Son could see a makeshift raft coming toward them out of the darkness. Ba, Son whispered, shaking his father.

When the raft arrived, a hand swung An up out of the water first. Then Son felt himself being lifted. For a long time An lay heaving, water coming out of his mouth and nose. The man who had rescued them made a whistling sound through his teeth, and the white bird lifted off the river's surface and floated up onto the raft. Lovingly the old man ran a finger down its neck, the tip of his long gray beard brushing the bird. The old man took off his *non la*. Son could see the moon reflected on his hairless head.

Twenty minutes later the raft rounded a bend. The boat was sitting in the middle of the river. It looked empty. Son wondered if the others had been caught. His father lay still. Son didn't know what to say. Everything was out of his hands. Silently the old man rowed up to the boat. Son shook his father. Ba. His father began to stir, his blue eye almost invisible in the moonlight. We're here, he said. Nobody came out to greet them. The man boosted Son up on deck. Before he even had a chance to look for his uncles, the man was already hoisting his father in the air. He turned and helped pull An on board.

Something stirred in the pilothouse. Cautiously Duc and Hai appeared like animals creeping out of the night. There were gasps of amazement. Son could hear his mother crying as one of his uncles carried him below. He could hardly breathe, it was so hot, the air like stagnant water, the whole space a crawlway, the hold no more than three feet at its highest and running the length of the boat. How did you get here, someone asked. A man picked us up in the river, Son said. What did he want, someone asked. Hai came bustling back down the steps. There's no one out there, Hai hissed. Son raced back up the steps. He looked in all directions, but it was true.

When you are called to make the passage, just open your mouth and remember the sutra. It will feel like light flowing out of the body. Even if you are just a child, do not fight the temptation to remain. All forms are impermanent. What the world is trying to teach you: the only permanence is impermanence.

ONCE THEY'D RAISED ANCHOR, THEY MADE IT TO THE OCEAN in only a few hours. Duc left the motor off and let the currents carry them along. The Harvest Moon was still in the sky by the time they arrived at the sea. Dark cliffs ringed the bay like turrets. For the most part the boat stayed in the middle of the river as far from shore as possible. From time to time the river narrowed. When it did, they passed floating villages, villages much like the one they'd left behind, houses floating on matted river weeds and fifty-gallon drums, each house soundlessly bobbing in the water, the people off celebrating in the city. Only Duc and Hai in the pilothouse could see their good fortune firsthand.

Duc was surprised by how smoothly it had gone—no patrols, no stray fishermen following in their wake demanding to be taken along. In the pilothouse he watched the bay open before them. At the back of the boat Hai began prepping the motor. The tides were right. There was no reason to hesitate. They slipped into the dark waters of the bay as if it were a lake. The setting moon wavered on the waves. Then the engine turned over, the land steadily growing smaller and more distant. Within the hour it was gone.

Hai came down into the hold. He left the door open. Rabbit could feel the heat rushing out, fresh air pouring in. We're at sea, Hai said in a quiet voice. They could come up out of the darkness. The sting of the salt felt welcoming those first few hours, their throats tingling with each breath.

For the first time since coming on board, Son could see how many people there were. Bodies on top of bodies. He didn't know how they'd all fit. In addition to his own family, there were the Cambodians plus Rabbit and her family. As people began to pour out of the hold, he noticed the doctor gathering a woman and a young girl to his side. The girl was smaller than Rabbit. One of her feet was laced up tight in a thick black shoe. Together the three of them held hands and bowed their heads.

When they were done, they touched their faces and chests in the same pattern. Son had never seen the woman or girl before, but he knew who they were by the way the doctor gripped their hands.

Son and Rabbit spent the rest of the first night on top of the pilothouse. In the sea air the deep scratch on his cheek was beginning to dry. Nobody cared that the two children had stationed themselves on the roof. It meant two fewer people on deck. The boat wasn't built to carry them all. There were four other families related to the doctor. The men of the families were lawyers and engineers, men who had been to university and were forced to work as cyclo drivers and *che* sellers after reunification. Son knew that all over the river delta, professionals like these men were now doing the same backbreaking jobs as his uncles. Southern society had been turned upside down. People were dying in hospitals because the northern doctors shipped down to replace the "capitalist sympathizers" had received their medical certificates in less than six weeks.

Just before dawn there was a commotion in the hold, the sound of someone shouting. Together Rabbit and Son peered over the edge of the roof. One of the Cambodians came scrambling up on deck, Phuong trailing behind him beating his back with her fists. Sang appeared in the doorway. She was still wearing the red *ao dai,* the dress's train flapping in the wind. Phuong was screaming about the man having his hand up Sang's dress. Nobody paid much attention. Even An was more embarrassed than concerned. Everyone knew who had started it. Sang in the blood-red dress was still furious. The doctor's wife shook her head.

The sun would be up within the hour. In the pilothouse Hai was still muttering about Hong Kong. If they were refugees in Hong Kong, it would be easier to find work while they stayed in a transit camp. Ever since the government had started harassing the three million ethnic Chinese who had lived in Saigon for generations, thousands of people had escaped the country by boat. There were refugee camps all over Southeast Asia. Hai had heard that in Hong Kong they let you out during the day. In Malaysia the people were Muslims. He had heard of the prohibitions there against pork and alcohol, even cards prohibited. Back in Ba Nuoc, Phuong had teased her younger brother. For you it will be worse than Vietnam, she said. No, Hai said, blowing a stream of cigarette smoke out through his nose. Nothing could be as bad as not having a future.

Rabbit was lying on her back and looking up at the stars. They were winking out, the sky lightening in the east. What's wrong, said Son. Rabbit glared at him, her freckled face scowling. There was so much wrong. Forty people packed on a boat built to hold a handful, the engine already starting to stutter. Rabbit turned on her stomach and peered over the edge. She located Qui among the crowd squatting on a mat, Tu sitting next to her. They weren't touching, but Rabbit could tell by the distance between them that they were aware of each other. In the wind Qui's hair tickling Tu's shoulder.

From the roof of the pilothouse Rabbit and Son watched the sun rise in the east. Each sliver poured over the horizon smooth as gold. The day passed without incident. By mid-morning it was overcast. The sky threatened rain, though none came. By noon everyone began to realize they could still sunburn even under the clouds. People took to shielding themselves with pieces of clothing. Some went back below deck. Toward evening Qui and some of the wives came around again with the rice they had cooked in advance. There was seven days' worth on board along with enough uncooked rice for another week. The doctor had decided only the men doing hard labor would get what little of the dried fish they had. Everyone else would have to make due with just the fish sauce and whatever else they'd brought with them.

By day's end the sun broke through the cloud cover. It was hanging low in the sky when Son spotted a plume of water spouting in the distance. It's good luck, said one of the doctor's relatives. People began to clamor for a glimpse of the whale. The doctor remained seated. He held his little girl in his lap, her foot laced up tight as if in a trap. The only good fortune is in Him, said the doctor.

Just then there was a loud bang, and the engine seized up. Cái thằng con heo! said Hai. The doctor scowled and pulled his daughter closer. Duc came out of the pilothouse. Together the brothers waded through the people to the back of the boat. Most of the engine was underwater. Duc tried to tilt it up, but somehow it had become locked and wouldn't budge. A few of the men began to gather. One of the engineers reached under the water and touched something. Instantly he pulled away and put his fingers in his mouth. Thing's hot as pig shit, said Hai. It's burning oil.

Duc used the bottom of his shirt to unscrew the cap. It was a modern-enough motor that there was a separate reserve just for oil. They had chosen a motor with an oil tank rather than a two stroke because they wouldn't need someone constantly feeding oil into the gas. The engineer began to explain what might be wrong. He spoke using a lot of technical jargon. Shit, said Duc. Just tell us what we need to do. It was only their first day at sea, and already it was starting. Basically you need a whole new engine, said the engineer. Fuck that, said Hai. This is Vietnam. Nothing's new.

An argument broke out, but the doctor didn't get up from where he was. One of the Cambodians slipped below deck and found the man with one sleeve. He was sitting upright under the stairs in a spot with no more space than a crate. The Cambodian began to explain the situation to him. The man with one sleeve nodded and squeezed himself out. As always, there was a small smile playing on his lips.

On deck at the back of the boat the man with one sleeve ran his hand over the engine and closed his eyes. Great, said the engineer. A magician. After a while the man with one sleeve explained that he was going to take a look. Someone translated. How are you going to do that, said the engineer. We can't even pull the engine up. Already Duc and Hai were headed for the pilothouse. The man with one sleeve was taking the remains of his shirt off and rubbing his arms as if to warm them up.

Within minutes he was ready. There was still some light left. The other Cambodians scanned the water. They hadn't seen any yet, but that didn't mean there weren't any. Tu stood holding a paddle. It was only as good as its length. The doctor and his wife bowed their heads. From his perch on the roof of the pilothouse, Son noticed the doctor's wife cradling a necklace in her hands, her fingers working the beads.

In his tattered shorts the Cambodian climbed onto the boat's edge. Somehow he managed to keep smiling. He was still smiling even as he jumped in. Ba says he can do anything, whispered Rabbit. Son had also heard the stories through the window of the floating house in Ba Nuoc. How the old southern soldiers like his father had been given a choice. Fight the Cambodians or stay in the reeducation camps. He was unclear as to the rest of it, how An and Tu had found each other, eventually escaping with the Cambodians all the way downriver to Ba Nuoc. All he knew was that their fathers had once been enemies, his father fighting the north, Rabbit's father siding with the Communists. Lying on his stomach on the roof of the pilothouse, Son had only one thing on his mind. Twenty-three. Twenty-four. The waters were dark and silent where the Cambodian had gone in.

The way Son used to jump into the Mekong to hide from his mother, the river closing over him like a door. What he knew. Twenty-eight. Twenty-nine. You can only disappear off the earth for so long.

The Cambodian came up for air three times. The sun was on the edge of the horizon. The third time he surfaced he swam for the boat and explained what had happened. They had run over an old fishing net, the thing tangled in the blades. Someone handed him a knife. He took it and put it in his teeth. As he dove under the boat, the blade cut the corners of his mouth. Instantly the blood went out in the water, a beacon calling them up from across the depths. Tu stood on deck with the paddle in his hands as if it would do any good.

The man filled his lungs to the breaking point. The light was going. Duc had turned the boat so that the engine was on the side of the setting sun. The waves were only a few feet but getting higher. The man could feel the pressure in the rib he had cracked the last and final time the guards beat him. The pain was something from his past. He put it aside and continued. How the man was able to do it. How he was able to do anything. By living in the present. The deadly fields outside Phnom Penh had taught him that. In the present there was only the pain of the present. No more. A pain you could tolerate. Endless days in the sun working the land, at night the endless rounds of meetings, of checking oneself for faults. Brother, I cut the wood in ten strokes instead of seven. Sister, I thirsted too much and didn't leave enough water for my neighbor. The Sunday speeches stretched most of the day, leaders up on the dais under a canopy and everyone else burning in the light. Even now he wasn't sure how the leaders had gotten away with it. There were so few of them and so many of the man and his family. Maybe it happened because men like him let it happen. The children dying first, then his wife falling sick with hunger. The day he came back from the forest and no one would look him in the eye. Only the oldest child left and its days of usefulness numbered. They had to save bullets. They were told the Vietnamese were always making bullets. The Vietnamese had whole cities filled with scrap metal, factories churning out bullets designed for the sole purpose of stripping the Cambodian people of their sovereignty. And so Cambodia's resources had to be allotted, rations given only to the strongest, the obedient. The herd had to be culled. Food reserved for the hardy, the weak left to perish. All for the benefit of the Kingdom of Kampuchea. Listen, brothers and sisters. We must strike the Vietnamese in their beds, crush the baby in the womb. This is our mandate. The Vietnamese are waiting to come pouring over the border, the way they have been ruling over us since the thirteenth century, effacing the great Khmer culture, which the Enlightened One brought to us through the channels of India and replacing it with their miscegenated cultural offerings dredged up from China. Using the French to annex our lands, then after the French, using our nation to stage war on themselves, the Americans bombing us without regard. Take up the hoe in your hand. The Vietnamese all look the same, the same sloping faces, the same mongoloid features. Aim for where the three plates meet at the back of the head. War a thousand years in the making. The very day after Saigon falls we will march to Phu Quoc Island when the enemy is at its weakest. We must hit them first and keep hitting them.

Presently in the water the man is floating under the engine, a cosmonaut suspended in the blue. As he disentangles the old fishing net, his blood wafts away in the currents, one part per million, ten miles away the smell of a single drop like a woman's perfume aerating a room. The man can't see what he is doing, but there is no need to see. What he has learned the hard way. Life is suffering. Desire is suffering. Attachment is suffering. He doesn't think about what is riding on his work, the broken boat left drifting at the mercy of pirates, every man, woman, and child's tongue gradually growing black and parched from lack of water, tongues hardening as if with scales. No future, no past. No sharks knifing toward him out of the darkness. No hunger, no fear, the stomach beginning to eat itself. Everything just present tense, this moment of floating in the sea, cutting the netting out of the motor's blades, the boat rocking in the water, the silence and the cold and the darkness and the heart beating in the chest.

On the roof of the pilothouse the children spot something speeding over the waves. Uncle, Son calls, his finger pointing to a spot in the future. With his knuckles Duc begins rapping on the bottom of the boat. The black knife skates toward them, the animal with its own sense of the present.

The man resurfaced with the last shreds of the net, blood dripping from his mouth. On board the people waved him on, Sang in her red *ao dai,* the long sleeves flapping like a flag. Hands were already over the side waiting to pull him up. In the present, the danger of the great dark fin doesn't register until he sees it. The man turns in the waves and spots the animal cutting straight for him. He claps his hands together in delight and shouts something. Someone translates. Arun says if we hook it in the eye, we could catch it.

A wave sweeps Arun toward the boat. Someone gets a hand on him. Later the others will explain that the thing was too large, its black eyes big as plates. Even if they speared it in the brain, the residual instinct could take over. They didn't have the space or the proper equipment. There were stories of men losing hands hours after a shark had been hung up by the gills, the massive head tolling in the air, then the sudden snapping of the jaws even after brain death. They were also afraid the shark's blood would attract more, the waters teeming with teeth. Arun will listen to his friends explain why they let the shark go. When they are done explaining, he will smile and nod the way he does with everything.

Duc climbed back up into the pilothouse as Hai stood winding the cord. There was no guarantee the fishing net hadn't damaged the engine. There was no way of knowing how long they'd been burning oil. When he was ready, Duc gave the signal. Hai pulled the cord. The first few pulls nothing happened. The doctor's wife busied herself with her prayer beads. After the third try, Arun took the cord from Hai and laced it up. All eyes were on the engine. Only Rabbit on the pilothouse could see a series of black clouds massing on the horizon. Arun's grin was almost maniacal. He pulled, the muscles standing out all over his chest. No day but this. The engine kicked on. In the distance the black clouds were already sparking, their underbellies ravenous and flashing.

When a reversal of fortune arrives while traveling on water, do not turn back but continue on. There is nothing to be done. Water is the trickster element. The way it allows you to float, how it seems to carry you along, your physical form brimming with it. Do not be fooled. Water bears the prince as well as the man in rags.

THE FOUR OF THEM WERE SITTING ON TOP OF THE PILOTHOUSE. From time to time a few fat drops fell, but it wasn't enough to make them come down. Everywhere black clouds whipped over the moon. Tu thought they had another hour before the weather hit. It was the first extended period of time either of them had spent with their children—An on the end with his arm around Son, the scratch on his face still angry and red, Rabbit on the other side of Son with her steely expression, the constellation of freckles on her nose and cheeks. It felt like only yesterday that Tu had pulled her up out of the earth like a carrot, something you harvested from the dirt, the full rabbit moon keeping watch, the scent of honey perfuming the night.

What do you want to know, said An. The clouds were beginning to win. He almost had to shout over the clamoring of the waves, each one tipped with silver. It was bearable, but soon it wouldn't be. Everything, said Son.

An sat with his memories of the past four years. As soon as he'd heard Buon Me Thuot had fallen, he had walked home through the panicking crowds from the base in Qui Nhon. He took off his uniform along the way, shedding it piece by piece like a snake molting its skin. How he'd left it lying on a low brick wall, first making sure the pockets were empty and there were no identifying marks anywhere on it. As if he could shrug it all off just like that.

The first few weeks after reunification he'd stayed hidden, never leaving home. His neighbors knew, but he'd always been the best of them, the one willing to help someone in need—An always fixing a flat, lending someone money for medicine or schooling, An giving someone the last ripe mango from the fruit bowl beside the altar. There was no fear they'd give him away.

When the posters came out blanketing the city, Phuong saw his name. An had been a captain. Before the Americans had retreated, he'd worked on an American base. The posters said things like TRANSFORMATION and FOR THE GOOD OF SOCIETY. Report with ten days' worth of food to the old army base to be evaluated. The expectation was that it would be for no more than two weeks. The government didn't have the resources for mass imprisonments. Phuong packed his bag. Ten days, she said. We are lucky the government recognizes that a boy needs his father. An nodded. There had been talk of blood running in the streets, but it hadn't happened, and it didn't look likely now.

He arrived an hour before the main gate opened. There were others already waiting. On base the lines were endless. He was surprised so many had shown up. There was a feeling of optimism in the air. Ten days and they could be done with it, the last half-century. They could finally be a country of brothers. Maybe he had been wrong to oppose the north. Inside he moved from line to line as he was moved up the chain. Each time the official on the other side of the table asked him in a friendly manner if he wanted to be a good citizen. More than you know, he said. An could feel the officers trying not to stare at his mismatched eyes. Toward late afternoon an official passed him a legal pad. Not unkindly, he was told to write out what he'd done during the war, where he'd served, what he'd been in charge of. The more detailed the better, the official said. Dates, names, places, strategies employed.

When his turn came, he was led into an empty room. He was told to sit down and wait. The guard took the legal pad with his account handwritten over seven pages. The only names he'd listed were names everyone knew, generals and such. On page five he admitted he had once shaken hands with McNamara. He was off duty, wearing tennis whites on his way to a match, when the Secretary just happened to be passing by. The American An worked with in Transport and Logistics, a Colonel Wallace, had pointed him out to the Secretary. This is Captain Nguyen. Pleased to meet you, said the Secretary, extending his hand. The Secretary's grip was beyond perfect, not too hard, not too soft. Afterward An told Phuong there was no way the U.S. wouldn't win.

The room was windowless. He knew it was one the Americans had used for debriefings. When the fighter pilots came back from their bombing runs, they would come into this room and tell what they had seen, if there had been any new bridges thrown up overnight, any supply routes made obvious by the defoliation. There had been maps and aerial photos taped to these walls. Someone had even hung a photo of Ho Chi Minh on the back of the door with the eyes X-ed out.

The official who entered the room was middle-aged. Comrade Do was clean shaven, his cheeks sunken like most of the northerners. An noticed he had cuffed his left sleeve higher than the right, presumably to show off his new wristwatch. The northern soldiers were buying everything in sight—watches and refrigerators and TVs and radios, motorbikes, even cars, things they had never been allowed to own in the north. Secretly some of them felt betrayed. All these years, decades really, they'd been told that in the south only the top echelons of the corrupt capitalistic swine owned such items and now to come all the way down here only to discover that even middle-class families had gas stoves!

Comrade Do smiled. Overhead the light began to flicker. You want to be a good citizen, don't you, he asked. Of course. An said it before the comrade had even finished the question. With his left hand Comrade Do slid the yellow legal pad with An's account on it across the table. The watch flashed on his wrist. An realized the man was left-handed and that he didn't know that one wears a watch on the opposite wrist.

The new government wanted names. It wanted secrets. It wanted even the littlest things like who took out the trash and on which day of the week. An knew he could never tell enough.

It wasn't in his nature to harm others. He closed his eyes and thought of his children. At five, Son had the face of an old man. Still, he couldn't bring himself to do it. Somewhere he could hear a door closing, hinges creaking as it blew shut.

There was nothing else to do. He threw himself on the shoals. Said he'd worked with the Americans, that he had little involvement with the Vietnamese. Comrade Do licked the face of his watch a few times and began shining it with his elbow. The Americans left in '72, he said. What did you do after that? Something about the way the comrade licked the watch, the slowness of his movements, like a cat licking its paws after a kill. An sat back in his chair. He realized everything about his case had already been decided. He didn't say another word. It was out of his hands. A river sweeping him onward toward wherever it would bear him.

After three nights crammed in a holding cell, he was taken by truck five hours into the highlands. Back in the day the holding cell had been used to keep drunk American soldiers under lock and key until they sobered up. For three nights it housed more than thirty men. Each hour they rotated positions. Three men at a time were allowed to lie down. The rest of them stayed standing, the air by the wall like being smothered alive. At the front of the cell the ventilation was the freshest, though it meant you were mashed up against the iron bars. Men stepped away from the rungs with marks running the length of their faces.

Those first days there was a Buddhist monk in the cell. His orange robe shone like a sunbeam, head smooth as a globe. Somehow he spent three days kneeling. Even when the monk's eyes were open, An could tell he wasn't there, all earthly attachments severed. He never saw the monk take any of the paltry food and water they were handed once a day in two wooden bowls for the entire cell. The monk simply knelt by the plastic bucket they relieved themselves in, the bucket with a hairline crack spidering down the side of it, which someone had tried to stop up with gum, urine and waste slowing leaking from the crack, the monk's robe soiling in the seepage. Time dripping on into more time. The monk didn't blink when men squatted to defecate right by his head.

At mealtime on the third day the guard read a list of names. An and ten others were called. They were told to prepare their things and leave without eating. None of them had anything to prepare. All their things had been confiscated the first day they came on base. By the time they got to the trucks, there were other prisoners already waiting inside along with two guards with old guns. The guards sat smoking and tossing their butts wherever, the ends still burning faintly, smoke curling off the tips. After an hour one man surreptitiously picked one up and took a drag. When the guard saw the smoke slowing forking out of the man's nose, he went over to where the man was sitting and hit him savagely in the shoulder with his gun. Then the guard lit a fresh cigarette and placed it in the center of the truck bed. They all sat watching as it burned down. Time burning on into more time. All the men with a cigarette habit squirmed in their seats, the men teased like dogs with pieces of meat. It was only the beginning. The guards didn't even laugh.

When the prisoners got off the trucks, there was nothing but jungle in every direction. They had to hike several hours. Sometimes it seemed like the guards didn't know where they were going. Under the canopy the heat felt like a blast furnace, even in the shade of the broad serrated leaves. The first few men through the path were quickly adorned with leeches on their necks, one of them as big as a plum and as dark. The very first man in line hacked at the brush with a machete, then after fifteen minutes he would hand it off to the next man and sink to the back of the line. The path was a trail animals used, scat everywhere, dried and fresh. An didn't know places like this still existed, miles and miles that had never been bombed. Places where things would still grow.

After a few hours they were told to stop. They were eighty men standing in the jungle. All around them stood a ring of men with guns, some of the guards just boys, their uniforms too big or obviously borrowed. The prisoners were told their job was to clear the land, harvest the trees, build their own shelters, grow their own food, find any mines that might still be present, prove their loyalty, redeem themselves, regain their citizenship, keep an eye out for those among them unable to be rehabilitated, realize the error of their ways.

The first few nights they slept out in the open. Each morning their mosquito bites were so bad they looked like carriers of the pox. An's unit consisted of twenty men. There was a colonel who refused to do any work, but the others covered for him at first until they didn't. Each week new trucks would arrive filled with men expecting to stay ten days. Every time the trucks pulled up, An could see the situation reflected in the new arrivals' horrified faces. How fast a man physically deteriorates. The first month he lost twenty pounds.

The very first structures they were forced to build were a series of small boxes barely big enough for a man to stand up in. The first man put in the box was a former student leader named Nam. But I protested against Diem, Nam said over and over as they dragged him in one morning. Don't listen to him, the guard said. He is a traitor who has been to the great enemy. I have been to the United States, Nam conceded, but to lecture *against* the war. He said he'd been flown to America by anti-war organizations to speak with students in a place called Berkeley, another called Madison. The guards got his arms in and closed the door. A piece of wood shot through a bolt in the front to keep it closed. All morning in the hot sun they could hear Nam's cries at first like a small child, then like a wounded animal, and then nothing. The guards made a show of taking him out that night when the others came back from clearing the jungle. When they opened the door, he fell on his face, his body shaking, mouth white with foam. Two men were ordered to carry him over to the spot where they all slept out in the open. By morning he was dead. Why, someone whispered as they walked into the jungle at the start of the day. To show us the power of the box, someone said. Why him, someone asked. Because he was weak and they didn't need him. No, someone else said. The man speaking carried a length of rope coiled around his arm, his voice a deep baritone. This is how he was meant to serve, the man said. Nobody said anything. And with that, they began to suspect one another.

In less than a week they'd built two barracks. The floors were dirt, and they were told not to hew any windows into the walls. The hardest part was cutting down the trees miles away in the jungle and dragging the logs to camp. They didn't understand why they had to use trees from so far away, but they didn't question it. The first night the men slept in the new barracks, the guards came around and bolted the door. By the end of the night the heat of fifty men created condensation on the roof, and the ceiling began to drip. There was a plastic bucket in the corner. In the long night if one of the men suffered from runny stool, it smelled as if they were all wallowing in it. Nobody said anything because they knew in time it would happen to them.

During the day there were various teams of twenty. Building was the best assignment. After a few weeks an architect arrived in one of the trucks, but the guards didn't care. Nobody is better than anyone else, they said. One of the supply sheds collapsed during a thunderstorm. For a while two of the barracks looked rickety until the men shored it up at the urgings of a newly arrived engineer. Even when someone needed medical attention, the guards didn't turn to the numerous doctors in camp, three of them surgeons trained in France. When a man accidentally had two of his fingers cut off with an adze, he died within the week from a combination of infection and blood loss.

Clearing and logging were among the worst tasks. Each group had a daily quota. If you didn't make it, your group got less of the sandy red rice they served for dinner. It was just an excuse to feed them less. Everyone knew the loggers would never make their numbers. The trees they were expected to fell were impossibly old, many as tall as city buildings, the jungle so dense you didn't know what would happen once you brought one down, how it would fall, what it would bring down with it. Their tools were inadequate—hand axes and some rope. One of the men was an old fisherman who had been denounced by one of his sons' wives because he had willed his boat to another son. The second week, the man was crushed by a falling tree. The worst part about it was that he was alive the entire time as they tried to get the tree off of him. He kept asking for water, but there was none to give him. It took all of them to move the trunk a few inches so that one of them could slide him out, the blood welling in his extremities, legs puffed up big as tires. When they got him out at last, the men cheered. Then he died.

For the first month An worked logging. It became more dangerous when one of the groups discovered that the river was the only chance they had to even possibly make their quotas. It took six men to carry a log the half mile to the river. Then they would throw it in and tie it up. When they had six logs in place, they would let them go. Each man was tied to one, logs round as fifty-gallon drums, the inner wood pale as sand. It was each man's job to guide his log the two miles downriver, making sure it didn't get snagged. It was dangerous, because you could get caught up in someone else's rope. There were also places where the trail they'd hacked became treacherous, the jungle growing so fast they had to constantly cut it, or one day there might be a vine or a root that wasn't there the day before. Sometimes if a log got swept away in a current, you could be pulled into the river before you had a chance to cut yourself free. When it happened, you were dragged who knows where, maybe all the way out to sea, your body washing up onshore a thousand miles away. The worst part was the place they had chosen to pull the logs back up on land. It was the closest spot to camp, but the waters were strong. Every week someone got pulled in somewhere along the route, his body battered among the logs. Depending on where you got pulled in, you might survive with several broken ribs, though more likely your throat would be crushed.

After three months Trinh Thi began to look like a camp. There were ten barracks, each housing fifty to one hundred men. There were houses for the guards, a proper kitchen, a small medical clinic that was used sporadically, mostly when a government official was coming to visit or when a place was needed to store someone until he died. There were two other buildings, which they used for interrogations. Every time you were interrogated you were handed a yellow legal pad and told to write out your confession. The men who couldn't write were told to draw. If they couldn't draw, then someone was assigned to write it down for them as they spoke. They all began to look forward to the interrogations. Written confessions could stretch twenty, thirty pages, a good three hours, an uninterrupted period of time when you weren't working in the jungle, a moment of privacy. After a few weeks they began to add literary flourishes. The Americans' soulless eyes pale as opals. The plane with its trail of white fire screaming through the air. The northerners brave as hornets. Ho Chi Minh with his capacious love deep as the ocean.

Once the land had been cleared, they began to plant things.

The months before their first harvest, at lunchtime they would eat whatever they could find. Wild berries. Animals the traps they'd set the night before had managed to catch. Patches of tapioca left by northern soldiers who had traveled for years along the tapioca trail running north-south along the Cambodian-Laotian border. It was how the NVA had managed to penetrate the length of the country. Each time a soldier pulled up a root, he would plant two tapioca seeds in the very same spot for the next soldier coming through, the plants both nourishment and a trail marker. A whole army had traveled south on tapioca and nothing else.

They would work from sunup to sundown. At the end of the day the men out in the farthest quadrant felling the trees had to stumble home in the dark. Then each night after their dinner of rice and fish sauce, the red sand in the rice slowly grinding their teeth down, they would attend a meeting. Often the meetings were self-directed. Each group had a leader, someone the guards randomly assigned. The team leader's job was to keep count of the tools, make sure each ax made it back into the shed. Mornings he double counted, confirming that everyone was in line by six. Nights the group leader kept them on topic. What were your errors, brother? In the future what will you do right?

For the most part they would sit around a small fire and try not to fall asleep. The mode was confessional, the favored form the self-critique. You had to talk about your daily performance, your work in the jungle, the reasons why capitalism would fail, the shadows that lingered on the surface of your heart. Often someone was assigned to give the daily reading. A citizen recognizes that a society is only as good as its citizens. A son must love his country first, his father, and then his mother. The meeting always ended with the singing of a patriotic song. An missed the old songs, the love songs about schoolgirls with flowers trailing the length of their white *ao dai*. They sang out as loud as they could. There was a constant worry about moles. You had to go through the motions, look as if you meant every word.

Ba, said Son on the roof of the pilothouse. The rain was beginning to come down harder. The moon had been utterly erased from the heavens, and the winds were picking up. Soon they would have to go below deck. Say something. An felt the water on his face. Where was he? How could this be happening? Everything he'd ever wanted for the last four years was right here on this flimsy boat in the middle of the South China Sea, which was about to turn on them. How could he have gotten this close? We never laughed, An said. I never remember laughing.

Some days, right before an official visit, they were allowed to write letters. They were each given a square of rice paper the size of a man's hand, the thing fibrous and tough, and told to share pencils. Most of the men wrote to say they were alive and somewhere in the highlands. They asked their families for letters in return, clothing, cigarettes, a better knife. They knew the guards were reading, so they kept it simple. Once a man was scolded because his love for his wife was deemed improper. He had used the word *beloved* six times on his small sheet of paper. After a while they all knew their letters didn't go anywhere. One man found his flapping in a bush beside the river with excrement smeared on it.

The dysentery. The malaria. The fevers that would never break. The lack of protein. The sun. The rain. The expected and the unexpected. The monotony. The lack of privacy. The self-critiques. The constant acting. Pretending you were ashamed of yourself when you weren't.

Time passed. Men died. Somehow An held on. He wasn't the

strongest or the bravest or the most resolved. When someone told him a year had passed, even he didn't know how he'd done it.

The first time he got put in the box it was a mistake. Even the guards knew he wasn't the one who had killed the hen out of spite. The eggs were strictly reserved for the camp chief. Comrade Ngu was a slight man with a lisp and no mercy. There was talk he had spent the war in China keeping the supplies flowing. When the hen was found with its neck snapped lying at the foot of Ngu's house, even the guards shuddered. Among the prisoners there was already a rumor circulating that one of the guards had done it because he was tired of watching Ngu eat eggs every morning while the guards had none.

They were trying to get someone to confess. The door to one of the punishment boxes was gaping open. Barrack by barrack the prisoners were lined up. The guilty one was told to step forward or there would be repercussions for all. The last time they had been threatened with group punishment they had been denied water for two days. Four of the older men had died out in the jungle. They were already late to head out. It meant none of them would make their quotas. Maybe they wouldn't get anything to eat. An looked at Mr. Lu standing to his left. Lu was in his sixties. He had once been a professor of law at Saigon University. He had helped negotiate the Paris Accords. An wasn't really thinking when he stepped out of line. He walked up to the front of the box. Behind him hundreds of men were holding their breath. Up close it wasn't even as deep as his arm, the thing an upright coffin. He closed his eyes and stepped inside. The guards stood staring at one another. Well shut it, someone said. The door creaked shut behind him, hinges groaning as if with pain. He could hear the sound of the bolt being rammed home. Inside there wasn't even room to turn around or raise his arms.

Later he tried to tell the others it hadn't necessarily been unpleasant. That when the discomfort came you had to settle into it. You had to make peace with the ants crawling up your leg, the smell of urine and feces as if you were steaming in them because essentially you were, the sweat trickling into your eyes and the sting that became a blurring. He tried to remember the orange-robed monk from those first days in the holding cell in Qui Nhon. The monk whole worlds away, his robe caked with shit. He began to see colors. He could hear the sounds of the sea. Each time his blood coursed through his body, he felt the tiny kick as his heart whooshed it through. There wasn't even space to fall down. Before he blacked out, he knew if he came out of the box alive, he would make it through absolutely everything. It was out of his hands. The world would decide if he should live or die. He was starting to merge into an even greater darkness, heart shuddering like a drum, somewhere the ocean swelling like a graveyard. He knew somewhere someone was crying for him.

Today all over Cholon in Ho Chi Minh City there are small plaster statues of the Lady of a Thousand Eyes, an eye nestled in the palm of each of Her thousand hands. When you can't hear yourself screaming over the rancor of the waves, She will hear you. And even if She doesn't hold out Her various arms to you like the branches of a tree, be comforted in the fact that She hears and sees everything.

Tu WAS RIGHT. AN HOUR PASSED BEFORE THE WEATHER HIT. The ship groaned through its joints. All but a few of them were crammed in the hold. Body on top of body on top of body on top of the calamitous waves, the water a foot deep and rising. Rabbit was lying on top of Qui. Even amid the turmoil, she could smell the sweet milk sloshing back and forth in Qui's chest. With each thirty-foot wave, the cold waters rushed straight down the stairs. Water like dark hands looking to drown them.

Just before the four of them had scrambled down off the pilothouse, Rabbit had seen something off in the distance twinkling like a star on the ocean. Ba, she said, pointing. Tu had been looking at the sky and remembering the sounds of men being lined up and shot. He wondered if the karma was now bearing down on them. Then across the thronging waters he could see something in the troughs of the waves, a tiny light cutting through the darkness. It was another boat. He realized the boat he was on must look like that, a mote in the vastness. He hoped for the distant ship's sake it wasn't a boat just like theirs, a vessel stuffed to the rafters with refugees. On the other hand if it were anything else and if they escaped the jaws of the storm, there would be it to deal with.

On their way off the roof, Tu and Rabbit stepped into the pilothouse to point out the distant boat to Duc. Duc was standing at the wheel. Beside him Hai was shouting directions—when to speed up the side of a wave, when to ride it back down. In the chaos of the small room Rabbit's head suddenly filled with a silvery light. Her ears began to itch. She felt dizzy as the voice grew stronger. Someone had died right there in the pilothouse. It had happened recently. And now someone was trying to talk to her, a spirit desperate to be heard. She closed her eyes. Please, the voice said. Take whatever you want, then the sound of a fishing knife punching two holes in the side of the throat, the air hissing out red. Rabbit could hear a body slump to the floor, blood pooling around it like a halo. I hear you, she said. Already Tu was ushering her out the door and down into the darkness.

In the hold the smell of urine and vomit was overwhelming. They had to crawl over the others to find Huyen and Qui nestled up against a wall. Qui pulled Rabbit to her chest, and Rabbit let herself be held there among the sweetness. Just this time the day before they had been gliding down the Mekong, the Harvest Moon like a lantern. Now they found themselves counting the seconds it took to crest a wave.

They were still counting their way up one. In the hold there was utter silence as the boat ascended. Even the smaller children kept still. The way up seemed interminable, the time lengthening, then longer. Huyen thought of the night she had wriggled the abraded cone of the cypress tree up inside her granddaughter. How she had told Qui it was a trick to ensure the birth of a boy, the cone oblong like a penis. All night Qui had stayed curled up by the fire with what Huyen told her was the pain of creation, Mother Dragon in the same pain when she had thrashed over the formless waters and created the earth, Mother Dragon's drops of sweat diamonding the sky and turning into stars, that inner space burning until Qui wanted to claw it out with her own fingers. In the morning Huyen had tugged on the fishing line she had tied to the cone. The wet thing slipped out sending the dark blood gushing. In Huyen's mind it was the only course of action. Wartime was no place for a child to have a baby. Parts of the cone came out in gelatinous pieces, though Huyen didn't see the thing itself.

They were nearing the top of a wave, the monster close to fifty feet. At the top there was a cusp between states as the boat shifted momentum. They found themselves waiting for it, that split second of balance, the neither coming nor going, the worst over, the worst yet to come, the blood darker and more plentiful than anything Huyen had ever seen. When would it stop? Qui lay hot as a tick in the light of the fire. They hit the top of the wave. At one point Huyen looked down at her hands, her palms as if someone had dipped them in blood.

Like a waterfall, the great wave crashed on deck. Boards splintered. The front window in the pilothouse blew out. Duc slammed into the wheel, pulled the rope tighter that lashed him to it. Their one compass and all their maps were washed out to sea. The door to the hold caved in. Water cascaded down the stairs. Phuong grabbed the sack, the last thing she'd removed from her floating house, the one that clattered when she walked, and cradled it in her arms. The engineer slogged his way to the opening, taking his family up above. He yelled they would drown down there, but no one could hear him. People sat dazed in the cold. The other families followed the engineer up into the outer dark, the children in their parents' arms. Qui started to move, but Arun reached out and shook his smiling head. The doctor also sat back down. Later when they left the hold, everyone who had gone up on deck was gone.

Then Arun was holding a piece of wood. He was hammering at a spot in the wall. After a while he managed to make a small hole. No light came pouring in. He crawled on his belly to another spot and made another. He made four in all, each high up in a corner. When they were riding a crest, a man would stand at each hole furiously scooping out water with a pot or bucket. When they were coming down, he would flip whatever he was holding in his hands, using the bottom of it as a shield and with all his might try to keep the water out.

There was nothing left to throw up. They felt themselves being lifted. Huyen threw more dirt over the bloody spot growing between her granddaughter's legs. Somehow they all knew if they could just make it to the other side of the wave. The blood so thick it gleamed black. It wasn't like anything Huyen had ever seen. Qui whimpered. Rabbit latched on to her body looking for the peace of the world. Huyen assumed it had been flushed out in the first blood, but now it was just coming. She could tell by the way Qui lay panting. Riding the wave all the way to the top, Rabbit sucking on her chest. Then the deep root snapped. A body lay floating in a river. A family was swept overboard out into the open sea. A door blew shut behind them. Huyen peered in the dirt. Something stirring like the silky threads that cling to a yolk, the thing the size of her ear finger, all of it there in miniature. Their ears began to ring. They felt themselves lifting off the floor as the momentum shifted. In the dark, hair floating like a star around each and every head. A tiny golden fish glittered in the blood. Huyen scooped it up in a bowl and swept it into the fire.

The fundamental difference between lights is forgiveness. Among the Christians forgiveness is everything. Ask for it as you lay dying on the jungle floor, the bloody work of your hands lying all around you, and the Christian god will grant it. In the Eastern cosmology the Lady will come to you and bathe your wounds and listen to your suffering, but She will absolve you of nothing. Absolution comes in the next life if you live within the path.

QUI SKIMMED THE FAT OFF THE BOILING WATER. MOST OF THE foodstuffs had been ruined. They had enough gas left for three days, maybe enough oil for one. Nobody wanted to say it, but with the other families gone their chances of surviving had increased somewhat. What little rice there was would go further. With less weight the boat rode higher in the water. From the pilothouse Duc and Hai had nothing left to steer by but the sun and the stars. Hai said they could do it, but Duc knew a few cloudy nights and they could get turned around, plus after the storm they couldn't be sure of where they were. The doctor's wife said she hoped the good lord had taken the missing families all together. Rabbit was thankful they were far enough away she couldn't hear them. She didn't want to know if the children had gone first, the parents left searching their empty arms, or if it had been the other way around, the children standing all alone on deck looking up into a wall of water.

The engineer had brought a small wire cage on board with him. In it was a rooster and a hen. On deck there had been a heated argument between Hai and the doctor as to whether or not they should cook the birds now or wait and see if they got an egg. Then Arun had explained that they could use the fat to make oil. Mixed with gasoline it might buy them a day or two. With that, Hai swung the chicken in the air by its neck. The way he swung it, he just missed hitting the doctor. He didn't apologize. He just swung it a few more times before handing it to Qui and storming back to the pilothouse.

Son and Rabbit weren't allowed up on the roof anymore. The structure was too shaky. Inside Hai swept the glass up and threw it overboard. More and more the doctor let his daughter sit with Rabbit and Son in the front of the boat, Minh's foot baking in its black boot. Everyone slowed down as they ate less. The children tried to stay out of the way. From time to time they pretended they were the captains of the ship. They would send

Minh on make-believe errands, telling her to go wash the deck. She would hobble away, eager to please. Below deck the sound of her walking like someone knocking erratically on a door.

Once when they sent her to mend a net, Rabbit said to Son do you think your uncles could kill somebody? In the silvery room inside her head she could still hear the voice in the pilothouse— the voice all breathy and scared, the air hissing out like a hole in a tire. You mean in a war, Son asked. Okay, she said. Yes, said Son. They sat for a while thinking about it. Rabbit could feel the skin of her shoulders starting to burn. The freckles on her face were growing darker in the strong light. You know our fathers killed people in Cambodia, said Son. An didn't, said Rabbit. Of course he did, said Son. She looked down at her arms. My father did too kill people, Son repeated. Rabbit considered her burning skin. The tingling felt strangely good.

Rabbit considered telling Son the story, but she didn't know what exactly she had seen. Her family had all been asleep one night as they lay on the leaky floor of their floating house in Ba Nuoc, Huyen softly snoring on her mat, the moon growing fuller in the window. Tu had only been back a few days. Qui? His voice sounded childish as he whispered. Then Qui rolled over and lifted her head. Rabbit could hear her father exhale. Most nights he tossed and turned, eyes glassy, his words few. Tu began to tell Qui about a place called the Parrot's Beak. How the Vietnamese, with all their years of fighting western forces, had easily crushed the tactically inept Pol Pot, defeating his nineteen divisions in just days before settling in Phnom Penh for the occupation. That's where I met An, he said. The government had let the southern prisoners out of the reeducation camps, telling them they could earn their freedom by fighting the Cambodians. One day after the battle of the Parrot's Beak, An was sitting up against a tree with his eyes closed, said Tu. There was blood and dirt on his face. I thought he was dead. Then he opened his eyes.

The left one blue like a flower. I did what he'd asked me to do a long time ago on the night Rabbit was born when a kindly soldier drove me to the banks of the Song Ma. I remembered him.

Tu talked for hours. He told Qui how he and An had stayed together digging graves. Even during the American war he had never seen so many bodies, the flies thick as thunderheads. He said often the only way you could tell the Vietnamese dead from the Cambodian dead was by their weapons. Most of the Cambodians were armed with just axes or hoes.

Not everyone was dead, Tu said. The man in charge of our unit pointed to a ridge and told us what to do. I don't know why he picked us. He should have picked some of the teenagers, the ones drunk every night who would cut off fingers from corpses the way they'd heard the Americans used to. We were each given a pistol, said Tu. An didn't know how to load his. The man pointed to where a ring of them were sitting on the hillside. Said take the ones who have hoes. Tu laughed at the memory. You could say they came prepared, he said.

We took a dozen of them up over the ridge. I picked a spot, but An said no, there was more shade just a few hundred feet over. Like he was trying to make their last moments on earth more comfortable. I didn't argue. I thought the shadows might be good. Keep their faces in the dark. I could feel my knees trembling. Twelve human hearts beating in my hands. I thought I was going to be sick. Somehow I was on the front lines and I had never killed anyone that I knew of. But I kept going because we all kept going—An, me, the constant flies, even the men marching onward, one of them smiling like he was just out for a walk.

I thought they knew. It made me mad. Every one of us playing his part. When the war with the Americans ended, I thought I'd never have to look at another dead body. Bodies clogging the rivers. Bodies sitting upright in their houses like they were waiting for a visit. We stopped walking and told them to start digging. One of them started to talk to the others in their language. I thought they were trying to figure out if they could overpower us. Twelve of them and two of us and one of us An, green as a leaf. I put the gun up to one of their faces. The man looked tired. Too tired to even flinch.

It took them three hours to dig a trench. They had no reason to work hard. I thought they just wanted it to be over. We didn't know then what had been happening in Cambodia, everyone starving and a quarter of the population dead. The smiling man crawled out of the trench and surveyed their work. He looked pleased with what they'd accomplished. He went around patting the other men on the back. They didn't just shrug him off, so I knew they somehow valued him.

An and I decided how we wanted to do it. Then An was miming what we wanted, but none of them would turn around. It was then I realized they didn't know we were going to shoot them. In Cambodia, they killed people with clubs and hoes, smashing them in the back of the head. It never occurred to them we might actually shoot them, that they were worth spending a bullet on.

One of the men started walking back down the hill. I imagined him making it all the way back to camp. The way everyone would laugh at us, saying An was the reason the south lost the war. Then someone would come right back up there and kill all of them. If it was the teenagers, maybe they'd cut up their faces, pull out their teeth even before they were dead.

I could hear a red-vested parakeet singing in the trees, Tu said, its song like a man's whistling. You don't hear them much anymore. Birds just go where they want. Nothing to keep them from flying away. Listening to its song I knew what we had to do. Everything was a mess. Vietnam was a mess. Cambodia was a horror. Ever since reunification, rumors of people just sailing away across the sea for the chance to be free and start all over again. We could do it. Me and An and these men who had seen the worst. We could do it if we all stayed together. We could be our own army, build ourselves a new home, but the one Cambodian was walking away back to camp as if the day's work were over. He was walking away from what we could become. Stop, I said, but he kept walking.

For the second time I raised my gun. I don't remember what I was aiming for. Suddenly it felt like I'd been punched in the shoulder, my arm jerking back from the recoil. The parakeet went fluttering up out of the tree. I could smell the smoke weaving itself into the fabric of my clothes. The man who was always smiling looked puzzled. He ran to where the man I'd just shot in the back had fallen, but when he turned him over, there was blood on the man's lips. With every lungful there was more of it, the blood coming out with every breath. At the sight of the blood the smiling man's face crumbled.

It took them days to trust us. Even after An helped one of them remove a small burr stuck in his eyelashes. Even after I burned an infected leech off someone's leg. You could still see it floating in their eyes. Like a dog that's been beaten its whole life, the constant suspicion. A few of them could speak Vietnamese but were pretending that they couldn't. I realized it one day as I was talking to An. We were talking about how our families lived in the same spot on the river, how it was fated. I looked over and noticed two of them straining to hear what I'd been saying. You understand me, I said. They just looked at me, but from that point on I talked to them in a normal voice. By the time we reached the river, one of them had started openly translating. We began making better time.

After I shot the man, An and I dragged him into the trench and buried him so that his hand was barely visible. That way it would look like he was one of many. Then we pointed the guns at the others and told them to run. An in the front, me in the back. It took us sixteen days to reach Ba Nuoc. All we had were our two guns and their hoes. They were used to living off the land. Once we shot a bear. The smiling man, Arun, roasted the kidneys. That night Arun said each of us was infused with the strength of the bear. The only thing that could stop us was steel.

Rabbit heard noises. She realized her father was crying. I still see him sometimes, Tu said. Only in my dreams I shoot him in the face and not in the back. His head comes straight up off his neck, the blood pumping like a fountain. An says we killed one to save them all, but An didn't kill him. He didn't see the blood lacing the man's breath. The feeling as if my arms were bathed in it all the way up to the shoulders.

After a while Qui rolled off her mat and onto Tu's. Rabbit had never seen anything like it. There had never been a man in any of their houses. The way Qui's back arched in the moonlight, hips locked, the muscles tensing in her thighs, her body riding over him, cresting, the long black hair rippling down her back like water, the bloody diamond on the side of Tu's face flushed a darker shade of red, and the way Qui, who never said a word, said many, though Tu put his hand on her mouth to keep them from spilling out.

My father killed a lot of men, repeated Son. Rabbit knew they should move below deck. The tops of her ears were beginning to burn. When the little girl came limping back, they would move downstairs. She wondered why Son needed to believe his father was a killer. Anytime she went near the pilothouse the voice called to her, her ears as if on fire. The voice saying please. Take whatever you want.

A thief finds a golden ax deep in the forest. Even before he picks it up he knows it will be light as water, strong as diamonds. With such an ax the thief could cut his way into anything, penetrate any wall, dominion at last over the hills and vales of the world. In his excitement to master the ax, the thief rips his own thigh open all the way to the groin. Eventually in his search for relief the thief begins climbing a mountain up to the home of the gods, the blood spoor soaking the earth. As the thief rifles through the gods' domain, he stumbles upon a thing of infinite value locked away in a wooden chest. He cannot believe his good luck. Without hesitating the thief begins to pack his wound with it, the pain lessening as the injury fills, and in time he smuggles the thing back down the mountain following the trail of his own blood. In a wet place between two rivers the thief lays his body down to sleep, and in his sleep his body breaks into blossom. When we eat, we eat of him. How rice enters the world.

THE ROOSTER AND HEN HAD PRODUCED MORE FAT THAN EX-
pected. Arun said the makeshift oil would last three more days.
Since Hai had poured it in the motor, the smell of cooked chicken
wafted over the boat. The smell made their mouths water. They
were only allowed a spoonful of rice twice a day and two pulls
of water from the jug. They had been out at sea for five days.
Sometimes Duc would cut the engine and let them drift to save
fuel. Now he kept the boat running. Since morning, the mystery boat Rabbit and Tu had spotted before the storm had been
trailing them in the distance. Among the waves the strange craft
glinted like a tooth.

From her spot by the wall, Huyen knew what Qui was considering. Don't, she growled, baring her ruined red teeth. Then
everyone will beg for it. The hunger was just starting to kick in.
Already Huyen had seen Hai eyeing Qui the few times he came
below deck.

Down below deck two of the Cambodians were dying. Their
health had been ruined from years in the fields, worms in their
major organs. Still, the doctor brought them their two spoon-
fuls of rice a day. Arun insisted on it. He wouldn't take his until
they'd had theirs.

Huyen knew that even if they made it to a refugee camp, she
herself would never get up from the spot where she lay by the
wall. She was just glad not to go the way Bà had—people having
to cart her crooked form from place to place, strangers lighting
her roadside pyre. When the time came, there would be no cer-
emonies. They would launch her off the back of the boat, Qui's
breasts silently crying, or maybe not. The humbler the send-off
the better her chances in the next life.

It was clouding up again and looked like rain. The doctor's wife
plied her beads. They were all hoping for water. With the clouds

coming on, everyone who could went up out of the hold. The deck filled. The salt air stung their lungs. Sang was still in her red *ao dai,* her makeup long since faded. Only Arun, Qui, and Huyen remained below deck with the two sick Cambodians. Silently Qui inched forward. The night of the terrible storm was the first time Rabbit had taken any in years.

Qui lifted her shirt and cradled the first man's head to her chest. Arun never looked away. Then for Qui the old feeling again, light streaming out of the darkness. She thought of the night she and Tu had locked themselves together, a different kind of light forming out of the dark. She hadn't known it could give such pleasure. The one other time all those years ago it had been an ARVN soldier on the riverbank of the Song Ma, the river weeds poking her in the back. The soldier had simply popped up out of a thicket. Hello, he said, before looking around and untying his pants.

Qui took up the second sick Cambodian. The man was missing teeth, the remaining ones tainted with rot. His pull was so weak Arun had to help hold the man's head as she milked herself into him, the milk silver in the darkness as it spilled from the sick man's mouth onto the floor.

When the southern soldier cast his arms wide on the banks of the Song Ma, Qui didn't run. The thing was already out and pointing at her. She had seen them before. Men urinating by the roadside. The great sacs that hung on the undersides of the male water buffalo. The occasional bright pink tongue that slipped out of a dog. She knew it was what made men men. She didn't know that when it tunneled its way into you, it burned whatever it touched like salt inflaming a wound. She was barely thirteen. Over the soldier's shoulder she could see the sun struggling through a cloud. She closed her eyes and waited to die.

When Qui was done, Arun laid the Cambodian back down next to the other. Only then did she realize why it had been so difficult. The second man was dead, his face reposed with the peace of the world, the milk of her breasts dribbling down his chin. Arun didn't cry. He leaned down and pressed his forehead to the dead man's. Then he looked up at Qui and smiled.

The doctor's wife didn't let the children watch the makeshift funeral, but Sang stood in the shadow of the pilothouse in her red dress. For the first time in days she looked calm. The Cambodians had wrapped the dead man's head in his shirt. One of them spoke. Then four of them each took a limb and hoisted him up. For a moment it looked like a prank among sailors. The other man Qui had fed was already up on deck, his eyes vibrant though his frame was still emaciated. Later below deck Rabbit didn't understand why she couldn't hear the dead man's voice. She sat in the very spot where the Cambodian had died. She searched the floorboard looking for a sign of him, listening, but all she could hear were the sounds of footfalls up above.

The sack Phuong had carried on board was lying in a corner. Voices emanated from it in a thick chorus. Then Rabbit understood why she couldn't hear the dead man's voice. The man had transcended. The Cambodian had broken the endless cycle of life and death and was at peace, the sweetness of Qui's milk in his mouth. He didn't need Rabbit. He wasn't ever coming back. He was free.

By mid-afternoon it was foggy. The strange boat that had been following them was lost in the haze. The fog hung thick and mysterious, the world revealing itself in pieces. The children were playing near the back—Son, Rabbit, and the doctor's daughter. Their tongues were starting to itch, though they didn't talk about it. When she wasn't looking, Son would sometimes poke the little girl's boot just to see what it felt like. She pretended not to notice. They were performing a funeral for an

imaginary corpse, the little girl playing the part of the grieving widow. In their lethargy the adults were indifferent to the
children's fun. Without warning the little girl wilted, falling to
her knees. For a moment Son and Rabbit thought it was part of
the game. The doctor and his wife were down in the hold. Hey,
Duc called from the pilothouse. Bring her here. He nodded the
children in. Son picked up the little girl and carried her over.

Hai stood smoking behind the wheel. He had pilfered all his
used cigarettes for their last shreds of tobacco and stood smoking what he'd been able to roll together. Duc pulled a flask out
of one of the cupboards. He sloshed it around before unscrewing
the cap. What is it, said Son. Duc held the flask up to the little
girl's lips. Buddha water. Some of it spilled down her chin. Rabbit could tell it was regular water. The voice she'd heard before
in the pilothouse started up again inside her head. She winced.
Take whatever you want. Just don't hurt me, the voice wailed.
What is it, said Duc, but she didn't say anything.

With one last swallow of water the little girl perked up. All
better, asked Duc. How did you get this boat, Rabbit said. He
stared at her, her eyes blacker than any he'd ever seen. He remembered her looking him right in the face the day they'd gone to
hunt otters at the Dragon's Head, her freckled face so stony it
made him afraid. The doctor bought it, Duc said. Rabbit looked
confused. She closed her eyes as if calculating an equation. Yes,
there was something almost surgical in the way the knife punc-
tured the throat, the efficiency of the thrusts, the aim exacting.
The voice apologizing over and over as the air hissed out. Saying
I'm sorry. I won't say anything. I promise.

What do you know about this boat, said Duc. Rabbit opened
her eyes. It was a long time before either of them spoke. Then
Duc said in a small voice what they say about you is true, isn't
it? Rabbit thought of Phuong's sack down in the hold, the thing
constantly babbling. She wondered how many people's bones

were in it. The entire Dinh family tree uprooted and being carried across the sea. She looked out over the water. Fog and more fog, the sun a blur in the west. Well fuck all, said Hai from behind the wheel. I told you he didn't buy it. Someone was calling from the back by the engine. The children raced out, the little girl limping along. Already they could see them needling in and out of the fog.

A whole school was swimming off the portside. The water plumed up out of the tops of their heads. The pod came right up by the boat. Dolphins. They're saying hello, said the little girl. For the first time any of them could remember Arun stopped smiling, the urgency apparent in his voice. What, said Son. Even the Cambodians seemed confused. What is it, repeated Son. One of the men translated. He says they're warning us.

Just then the other boat came racing out of the fog. One minute there was nothing and then it was right behind them. Hai and Duc were busy yelling at the doctor in the pilothouse, An and Tu standing between them. You lied to us, the brothers said. We were each supposed to put in a third. The doctor was wailing that he had to get out of Vietnam. My brothers and sisters got out, he said. There is nothing left here for me.

The other boat was less than a hundred feet away. Clouds of fog passed in front of it as if it were flying through the sky. Rabbit could see someone standing on deck holding a gun. One minute the man was there, and the next he was gone, lost in the fog, then he was back again with another man at his side. I was going to pay, but he wanted more or he said he'd tell the police, sobbed the doctor. Arun was tugging An's arm and pointing. Hai took a swing at the doctor. He hit him in the face. The doctor fell on his knees. They all looked to where Arun was pointing. Beyond the little girl in the strange black shoe a boat was racing toward them. The man at the wheel of the other boat stood with a knife in his teeth.

Most likely the pirates were Thai, but they could have been from anywhere. The occasional Vietnamese word floated across the water. Stop. You can't escape. The other boat wasn't as good, but it had fewer people on board and probably more fuel. Arun ran down below and got the last of the chicken fat. Duc opened up the throttle. They could keep the pirates off for now, maybe a whole day, but eventually they'd run out of gas. The best they could hope for was another storm or dense fog or a commercial ship passing by or land, but even land wasn't a guarantee of anything.

When the doctor got his senses back, he stood up and limped down into the hold. What is it, said his wife. What's happened? From a worn black medical bag he pulled out an old handgun and some bullets. Lord God, she said, crossing herself. Then he pulled out a bundle of raggedy towels. Husband, what's going on? Slowly he worked his way to the center like a surgeon removing someone's bandages. His wife crossed herself. It was a foot-tall ceramic crucifix, the thing cream colored, though the drops of blood adorning His head and hands were painted a deep red, the scarlet tears running down His ribs like falling petals. The doctor kissed it before screwing it onto a metal pole. He handed it to his wife. There was blood trickling out of his nose. Together they crawled through the filth in the hold and came back upstairs hand in hand. Hai eyed them as they made their way to the back of the boat.

Duc wanted the doctor to shoot, but An said the pirates might shoot back and the doctor only had four bullets. He told Sang to round up the children and keep them below deck along with the other women. Son didn't want to go, but his sister had him by the neck, her grip like iron. Down in the hold he could smell joss burning. Phuong had set up a small altar with a bowl of hardened rice ruined by seawater and a few small portraits. It was too dark to make out any of the details in the faces. Son could just see the poses. Men and women looking head-on into the camera, their faces frozen and unsmiling.

The sack was lying on the floor at Phuong's feet. Make an offering to the spirits, she said. Son knelt beside his mother. Though he wanted to be on deck with his father and the other men, he knew now wasn't the time. Phuong handed him a joss stick. He clapped it in his hands. Smoke clouded the air. The scratch on his face started to itch. Rabbit could hear one of the voices in the sack wailing that the mandarin was just a man. Who will look out for us, the earth's meek, the voice said. Above deck the doctor and his wife stood waving the dead figure of their god at the enemy. Below Phuong called on Quan Am, the many-armed Goddess of Compassion, to hear them.

Nobody heard the shot over the incessant roar of the waves. In the fog, the gun's flash was barely perceptible. From below deck they could hear the doctor's wife screaming and feet pounding the boards as someone ran toward her. In her red wedding dress Sang gathered the little girl Minh in her arms. It's all right, Sang said. Just hold on to me.

The doctor and his wife had been standing on the starboard side, the wife waving the crucifix in the air. The other boat was close enough they could see two men leering at the front. One of them was holding a whip. The second man held the gun, steadying it with both hands. His shoulder jerked back as he pulled the trigger. Then the doctor crumpled. The wife dropped the crucifix. It shattered on the deck. Her screams brought some of the Cambodians. When Arun saw the blood pooling under the doctor, he put his hands over his eyes.

They all knew what would happen if the pirates boarded them. The pirates would ransack their possessions, taking all of their valuables. The marauders would beat and kill some of the men. Sang in her red *ao dai* would be passed around. Qui would be kept alive as a slave. The pirates would take everything and leave the survivors adrift to die at sea. Even Huyen might be raped.

The pirates pulled up alongside. They stood on board holding ropes with grappling hooks. There were less than twenty feet between the boats. One of them was swinging his rope. He threw it, the hook glinting in the light, but when it landed, An threw it overboard. All the while the doctor's wife was screaming, her body prostrate over her husband's. Nobody could tell if he was alive or dead. Pieces of the shattered crucifix lay in his blood.

Then it happened. They heard it down in the hold, though they didn't know what it was. One minute the other boat was chasing them down, and the next it was engulfed in flames. A man ran on deck on fire, arms flapping like a bird. The explosion sent pieces of flaming debris onto their own deck. Even before they could sort out what had happened, the Cambodians were running around throwing the burning pieces into the sea.

The doctor was still alive. Across the water the man on fire screamed as he leaped into the ocean. The sound like the end of the world, skin crackling like a burning log. Thy will be done, the doctor said weakly. His wife helped him make the sign of the cross. Then he died.

It took a long time to realize what had happened. The pirates had hit a mine. There were minefields all over the South China Sea. Governments ringing their waters with them, some governments to keep refugees out, others to keep their own people in.

On deck they stood watching the pirates' boat sink in the distance. For the moment they forgot their own hunger and thirst. Black smoke raged up into the air. After a while only a faint glow was left illuminating the haze. Duc only told Hai. Hai had already been thinking the same thing. Where there's one, there's many, Duc said.

Less than fifteen minutes later they threw the doctor over the side. The shards of the crucifix were tied around his neck. With the little girl standing in her black boot beside her mother, there was no attempt to keep the other children away. Rabbit could hear the doctor searching through the darkness. *Ora pro nobis peccatoribus.* For the briefest instant the body was sailing into the fog. Pray for us sinners, now and in the hour of our death. She didn't even see it hit the water. As if he were flying off a stage. All around them the waters were eerily smooth. For the first time since they'd entered it, the South China Sea was calm as if made of glass. What were you arguing about, said his widow in a quiet voice. Her face like the face of her god, long and impassive, all attachment severed. Duc and Hai looked at each other. Nothing, said Hai. At the front of the boat Tu asked Qui to watch the widow. He was afraid she might throw herself and the little girl overboard. Briefly he touched Qui's cheek with his hand. Her sorrow is deep, he said. All around them the fog was starting to lift. Just as he said it, he felt himself flying through the air. Please, he thought, only I deserve this, and then everything went black.

Renovation [1986]

The poets say the rabbit on the moon pounds the medicine in vain. Some say it is the elixir of life she is grinding in her stone mortar, others that the rabbit mills rice for mooncakes. Along the Silk Road there are triadic images of three hares with only two ears between them. Among the Reindeer People there is a tale of the rabbit who had nothing to give the wanderer-god but the flesh of her own body and so threw herself into the fire and was immortalized on the face of the moon.

It was a full month before the Russian stopped to ask for a lemon. Rabbit saw him standing by the iron gate. Farther up the boulevard the sun rose over the distant yellow hills. The other Russians were headed for the trucks that would take them out to the Nam Yum, the river often iridescent with runoff, pearly. She wondered what they did out there at the old battleground. With each trip they trucked the equipment back and forth to prevent the locals from scavenging and selling off the metal. Some of the more daring locals remained undeterred. They would come out at night after the Russians had left and begin tapping the ground with sticks, at times digging with nothing but their own bare hands.

Even among the Russians who drove out to the Nam Yum each morning he was like nothing Rabbit had ever seen. A long scar braided the side of his neck, twisting down his throat in three sections as if someone had taken an iron to the skin and kissed it here, here, and here. She remembered the first time she'd ever seen him. She had been boiling water for the Vietnamese laborers building the school across the street. From out of the crowd a pair of icy eyes trained on her. She thought of Bà on the rubber plantation and the man with the milky-white palms sitting cross-legged under the cashew tree, Bà's heart flooding. Rabbit could feel the heat gathering in her own blood. The heart flooding maybe once in a lifetime.

Through the days and weeks she had come to notice a silver ring on one of the Russian's fingers. The ring face was flat but embossed with a flowery creature shaped like a dragon. Mornings he would wander up the dusty boulevard toward the trucks, the sound of the ring clanking on the metal as he ran his hand along the iron fence. For a long time afterward she could hear a soft ringing hanging in the air.

At the end of the government's third five-year plan the Russians were everywhere. Rabbit couldn't remember when they began appearing. One day the streets were simply filled with men pale as milk, bodies like mountains, even the women big as trees, and the men with hair blanketing their faces, not the sparse wiry hairs of the Vietnamese men, boys her own age searching their chins for just one, the mark of wisdom, these men with their entire throats furred like wild animals. There was talk that their whole bodies were like that, their torsos like pelts, the dark hair growing coarser as it moved down their forms.

It's cold in their country, said Giang, who walked out through the unlatched gate of the foreign workers' dormitory every morning before the sun came up, her scarlet lipstick long faded. In the dark Giang would hand Rabbit five hundred *dong* and watch the honey run into the cup. It's so cold, sometimes the sky freezes and falls to earth, Giang knowingly said.

Then the trucks were pulling away. Their black exhaust stained the air. Each one could hold as many as fifty men. The Russians would be back long after sundown, their instruments caked with clay. The men would be tired and dirty but glad to be alive after toiling in the minefields of the old French battleground. Rabbit had heard that the Russians preferred the sea.

Down south between Danang and the clear waters of Nha Trang, there were accommodations built just for them, small furnished rooms that would cost the average Vietnamese six months' wages for a single night. Everywhere they went in Hoa Thien the locals would sidle up on the muddy streets to buy whatever the Russians had on them—clothes, sunglasses, tennis rackets, sneakers—anything that could be sold on the black market. The policemen who escorted them through town would often listen as the illicit buyers named a price, the police sometimes translating, telling the Russians yes, comrade, it is fair, then taking a cut for themselves and leaving them to trudge back to their hotels in their socks.

Ever since China's month-long invasion of the northern border at the end of the decade, ties between Russia and Vietnam had strengthened. Workers came from all over the union, the republics and satellites as well. The government in Hanoi needed them and their scientific know-how, their rubles that kept the economy afloat. The country was still in the first year of *Doi Moi*. Renovation. The end of collectivization, the government starting to reform. Some of the Russian soldiers who looked for mines out at the Nam Yum had been reassigned out of the Hindu Kush in Afghanistan. The soldiers came and let their beards grow wild. They did what they were told to do, which was easy compared to what they'd done.

In the east the sky was growing light. The brighter the morning, the harder the rain to come. Rabbit looked at the sun. Qui was late again coming back from the early market. It meant they would have to wait for the midday break to make back the money they'd spent on supplies. Overhead, Son was sitting on the highest limb of the only tree left on Duong Khiem. It was a cinnamon tree. The branch was gray and leafless, but he looked so much like his old self, sitting in the cinnamon tree staring out over Duong Khiem, that Rabbit didn't say anything.

Across the street the Vietnamese laborers were already at work building the school for foreign children. A group of men stood in a clay pit mixing concrete with their feet to keep it from setting. The men moved as if dancing, the sweat beginning to bead on their foreheads. Van was among them, the muscles in his legs striated from hours in the pit, his mangled hand hidden at his side. At lunch the laborers would shuffle across the street with their rumpled bills. Most of them couldn't afford the hundred *dong,* but they still came just to gaze at Qui, her unearthly beauty still intact.

Under her conical hat Rabbit herself was far from beautiful, but she had a presence that made men look twice. The fearless little tomboy was gone. In her place was a demure young woman on the cusp of adulthood, her straight black hair falling to her shoulders. In adolescence the handful of freckles sprinkled along the bridge of her nose and cheeks had taken on an exotic air. People often stared. Freckles were a rarity among them. Sometimes Rabbit could hear people whispering, the locals speculating that she had foreign blood in her. She was fifteen years old in the ancient system of reckoning, older than Qui had been when Qui started nursing her. She was almost the same age as her grandmother when Bà took the dragon fruit from the untainted hands of the medicine man on the fecund grounds of Terres Noires.

By the dormitory gate Rabbit sat watching the laborers mix the concrete. She could see their bodies glistening in the sun, hips twisting in the sludge. Within minutes she spotted Qui pedaling up Duong Khiem, the basket perched on her handlebars. Qui's hair spilled down her back. It was so long it could have easily gotten tangled in the spokes, but it never did. Sometimes Rabbit didn't recognize her. There were moments when from a distance Rabbit found herself thinking who is this old woman coming toward me? Then the moment would pass and Qui would emerge from the crowd with her stained black shirt and big western eyes, her exquisitely structured face. It still startled Rabbit. Qui's hair no longer night-black, each strand white as pearl and as luminous.

Except for the color of her hair Qui hadn't aged since the night they pulled Rabbit newly born out of the ground. If anything her face looked even younger. Her complexion that never burned was still bright and soft as the skin of a baby, only now her long silvery hair gave her an unearthly glow. On occasion Rabbit had trouble remembering how Qui used to look.

Qui propped the bicycle against the wrought-iron fence. The front of her blouse was dry in the early hours. She swung the basket off the seat and put it down next to the metal drum where the two of them kept a small fire burning as they worked. Their tabletop was a piece of cardboard covered in plastic, which they balanced on bricks they'd scavenged from a work site. Rabbit could still hear the sound of the Russian's ring singing in the air from when he had brushed the metal earlier with his hand.

Suddenly Son popped up from behind the fence. He glowered at her. The scratch on his face flared as if fresh. Rabbit put her fingers in her ears. More and more he wasn't the boy she remembered, the quiet boy who'd slept in his mother's arms, the boy on the roof of the pilothouse searching the stars. As she herself moved into young adulthood, he'd become her second conscience, a being who knew things about her that no one else knew, the secret thoughts racing in her blood.

As swiftly as he appeared, Son disappeared without a word behind the gate. Rabbit took her fingers out of her ears. The reverberating sound of the Russian's ring on the metal fence had gone dead.

The morning passed slowly, the July heat like moving through water. Across the street some of the men in the concrete pit had taken off their shirts, the sweat raining down their bodies as they lifted their legs in the thick mud. Rabbit tried not to stare. A delivery man carrying some packages stopped on his way out of the dorm and bought a tea. What's in there, she said. The man wiped his brow and held his cup out for more hot water. For a moment he stared at Rabbit, the strange freckles spotting her face. Mostly just beds, he said. Rabbit couldn't tell if she felt disappointed or not.

A few minutes before noon Rabbit stoked the fire with an old broom handle. The sparks flew loose, the air rippling over the barrel. Each day she and Qui set up under the cinnamon tree, the fragrant trunk twisted and crumbling. The men who had paved the road had orders to cut down everything, but they left it standing. It was then that the tree stopped producing seeds, the shallow roots damaged by the heavy road equipment and the run-off. There were still patches of green sprinkled through the canopy, but mostly the tree was dead. Over time the wood of the trunk was growing less and less fragrant, though the woman who sold pancakes across the street still pounded a few wood chips into a fine powder at the start of the business day.

When the lunch hour came, a group of Vietnamese workers walked over from across the road. Then Rabbit was taking money and pouring hot water, Qui squeezing the lemon in and adding just the right amount of honey. As always there wasn't much talk, just the quick exchange of bills. Qui and Rabbit had been selling tea for the past year. Under *Doi Moi,* individuals were allowed to start their own businesses, and private enterprise was flourishing. Today the line seemed longer than usual. Rabbit could see Van standing among the workers, holding the rag in his hands. As always Van waited until the other laborers had been served before hobbling forward. Some days they ran out of lemons before his turn came. Rabbit wondered if Qui's silence made her seem all the more approachable to him. Van with one hand missing all but its two primary fingers, his hand like a fractured smile.

Ever since the first week they'd set up on Duong Khiem, Van appeared every noon with a red chrysanthemum that he presented to Qui. In the midday sun he would stand and carefully unwrap it from an old rag he kept damp to keep the flower from wilting. When he learned Qui didn't speak, he stopped saying anything. He would simply touch his forehead with his two remaining fingers before holding out the great whorled bowl of the flower. Qui always took the chrysanthemum with a small smile and tucked it behind her ear. In her silvery hair the flower gleamed like blood on snow. Each night in their one room near the bus depot Qui would carefully remove the flower. Rabbit never saw where she put it. In the morning it was never on top of the trash heap by the door or in the small chest where Qui kept the few things she treasured—the chipped blue rice bowl from the grave where Rabbit was born, the burlap sack filled with bones that Phuong had carried out of her floating house once long ago. By morning, each blossom was gone.

The line inched forward. Van held the flower out and touched his forehead. Where he got red chrysanthemums in Hoa Thien in the northwest corner of the country nobody knew. The other men stood in the shade of the cinnamon tree. Through the leaves the sun dappled the ground. Then the twenty minutes were over. The workers filed back across the street. Qui began to tidy up. There would be one more rush when the workers went home before sunset. Van would be back with just his sad little smile, his mangled hand. As she did each day, Qui would hold out a second cup to him, but he never accepted it. They both knew he didn't have the money. He would simply touch his forehead and smile. Qui would nod, her silvery hair tinted indigo in the twilight.

Rabbit took a deep breath. For a moment she thought of her

father, the strange red diamond marking Tu's face, and the night Qui had touched the birthmark with her fingers, her long black hair cascading over both of them like a blanket as their bodies rocked back and forth. Abruptly Son popped up behind a crate. You're too young, he whispered, then disappeared again.

They were still tidying up from lunch when the first truck turned up Duong Khiem. Something was wrong. The Russians never came back early. The pancake seller across the street boldly stood up to watch. Two men in the concrete pit stopped moving altogether. Only Rabbit averted her eyes. She could hear the tired sound of feet scraping the pavement as the men filed past in silence on their way through the gate and up the steps into the dorm. Most of them gripped their cigarettes with all of their fingers.

Within minutes a second truck turned the corner. The men off-loaded with their frozen stares. Rabbit let herself look, but she didn't see him among them. She watched as a pack of dogs jumped out. Something in her stomach began to tighten.

Fifteen minutes later the last truck roared up the boulevard. This time only a few men got off. They seemed more distant than the others, their faces hardened as if they had come from the very ends of the earth. A handful of them were spattered from head to toe, some with bits of matter dried in their hair. One of them was so spattered it was as if he had bathed in it. His cold wolf eyes were the only part of him that wasn't bloodstained. A silver ring encrusted with blood gleamed on his finger. Briefly the knot in Rabbit's stomach loosened.

Son was sitting on the curb holding a piece of tree bark in his hands. He watched Rabbit as the men walked into the dorm. The blood-soaked specter with the icy eyes was the last one up the steps. You should have been there, Son said. He held the bark up to his nose and inhaled deeply. It wasn't a criticism, just the truth. Rabbit felt her eyes burning.

The day dragged along. Across the street the school rose a few feet. Some stray customers bought tea. The honey started to harden. The sky grew dark and menacing, but for the time being the rain held off. Qui began to pack up. At the bottom of the basket there was a single lemon left, the thing hard and misshapen. Rabbit tucked it in her sleeve. Maybe she would use the rind for something, add twists of the peel to a soup. With the broom handle she raked through the fire, spreading the ashes around until it went out with a small hiss. A strand of smoke curled up into the air. Rabbit helped Qui load their things onto the bicycle. Van nodded to them before heading the other way down Duong Khiem.

Rabbit and Qui were almost to the first intersection when the pancake seller who was still packing her things whistled. They turned around and saw the fire burning strong in the metal drum they left each night under the cinnamon tree. Quickly Rabbit ran back with the broom handle. She didn't understand. There was hardly anything left to burn. After she put it out, swirling the broomstick around in the flames, she touched the side of the drum with her fingers. It was cool to the touch. She put her whole hand on it just to be sure.

Rabbit walked away, peering at the skin of her palm. The pancake seller whistled again. The flames leaped up like the branches of a tree. This time after she put it out, she peered deep into the drum. There was nothing in it, not even ash.

The final time she and Qui stood together watching from a distance up Duong Khiem. The pancake seller was at their side.

The sun was going down on the other end of the boulevard. Bats were beginning to knife through the evening air. The women stood for whole minutes, universes born and falling dead. A bat dropped out of the sky. The pancake seller nudged the creature with her foot. They all looked up at the exact moment when the fire ignited. The thing lighting as if the drum were full of gasoline, and someone had tossed in a lit match.

For a long time none of them moved. Then the pancake seller turned the bat over and righted it. The thing spread its wings and shot straight up into the air. Down the street the fire was still burning. Go on, Rabbit said to Qui. Go home. I'll see to this. Qui fingered the flower in her hair and nodded. The pancake seller clucked her teeth and went her own way.

There was no rush as Rabbit walked back. Maybe this time she would let it burn. Even from down the street she could smell the cinnamon tree on the wind. She breathed the scent in, filling her lungs. Overhead black clouds raced through the sky. She thought of the ocean at night, clouds like an invading army. Peering up into the tree's boughs, she could see a cluster of long yellow flowers studded with the little round fruit black like pepper. It hadn't been there in the morning. She stood studying it. She had never seen the tree flower.

When she looked back down, he was standing by the fire. His hair was wet, eyes blue as stars, the skin of his face pink where he had scrubbed it raw. He was wearing a pair of blue jeans and a white T-shirt. She didn't know how to tell him. Chúng tôi đóng cửa, she said. We're closed. He shook his head. Я хочу избавиться от этого вкуса во рту. *I have to get the taste out of my mouth.* The first flashes of lightning appearing in the heavens. Already she could feel a dark wave cresting in her body, though where it would lead she didn't know. The scar on his neck glowed in the light of the fire. And so it began. The two of them speaking in their own languages, though it didn't matter. Each one talking as if to comfort himself.

Rabbit reached up her sleeve and took out the small misshapen lemon. The Russian had to look at it a moment before realizing what it was. Прекрасно, he said. He took it and tore off the rind with his bare hands. Then he shoved it in his mouth and bit down. Slowly his face changed, the skin trembling around his eyes. Finally the taste of something besides blood in his mouth.

The fire turned a steely blue, then abuptly died out, the color like stars twinkling on a mountain. The Russian banged the barrel with the side of his fist. The metal rang on and on. Rabbit flashed on the image of a dead sow, its stomach rowed with big rubbery teats, things buzzing in the charred barrel of its torso. She wondered where she had ever seen such a thing. Already the Russian was walking away down the street. He spit the lemon out into his palm and turned around. Ты идешь, he called. *You coming?* Overhead the sky at once darkening and growing lighter as the thunderheads flashed. Rabbit took a deep breath and ran to catch up.

They walked side by side without touching. The Russian's strides were long, but Rabbit managed to stay with him. They passed a group of Black Hmong scurrying along the road. The Red and Black Hmong lived up in the terraced hills stretching all the way to Sapa. Gradually their culture was being erased. Ethnic Vietnamese were flooding into Hoa Thien, the government anxious to build up the towns along the border with China, Vietnam's ancient enemy. The Hmong women wore deep indigo scarves in their hair. The matriarch of the group walked at the front chewing something, the muscles tightening in her jaw. One of the younger women eyed the Russian, her curiosity evident.

Xin chao, said Rabbit. *Xin chao,* said the matriarch. When the old woman smiled, Rabbit could see she was missing several teeth, but the ones she had left were a familiar dark red in color.

Rabbit knew the Russian was taking her to the quarter where the Russians went to drink *kvass* and listen to music. There was a café run by a mixed breed who was said to be the granddaughter of Lenin. Rabbit didn't know what happened in that part of town, but once Giang had told her she didn't need to know, Giang's lips stained and swollen. The Russian was striding up ahead. Rabbit could hear music playing like the kind she sometimes heard coming from the dorm. Мы оживаем в ночи, he shouted over his shoulder. *We Russians come alive at night.*

They passed a café. Men sat out front smoking water pipes and waiting for the rain to arrive before moving inside. There was a Vietnamese policeman in his uniform sitting at one of the outdoor tables playing chess with a Russian. The policeman had his hand on his queen as he sat studying the board. He looked up at them as they passed. Спокойной ночи, the policeman said. The other man sitting at the table laughed.

The Russian led her straight to the house. From the outside it was western looking. He pulled a key out of his pocket and opened the door. There were newspapers and ashtrays piled on a card table. A small Japanese refrigerator buzzed in a corner. She watched him walk up a flight of stairs. When he didn't come back down, she put her hand on her chest to slow her heart and followed.

Son was sitting at the top of the steps, the scratch on his face inflamed the same as it was the night he'd injured it fishing the Mekong long ago. Looking at him, Rabbit marveled that she had ever been that young, that the two of them had ever been mistaken for brothers. Son looked her full in the face. He was crying. I hear you, Rabbit said, stepping over him and on up the stairs. But he just cried harder.

When she entered the room, her heart fell silent. There was nothing but a western-style bed and a table with a chair, in the open closet a few suits and a pair of shoes. She felt something stirring in her body. Every morning for the last month she and the Russian had stared at each other as he walked by on his way out to the Nam Yum to search for the dead among old mines. She took a deep breath. She could smell cinnamon coming from her hair.

Outside, the sky opened up with a tidal roar. The rain fell like nails on the tin roof. She knew it would only last ten, fifteen minutes at the most, the monsoon rains always torrential but brief. When it stopped, it would stop on a dime. In fifteen minutes the moon would be out, sailing through the heavens, the world left dripping, cleansed.

On the table a candle was burning. Shadows quivered on the walls. The Russian was curled up in the bed, his clothes heaped on the floor. The rain hammered the window. Rabbit looked at his body, the dark tan and the dramatic lines where the skin went white. She could see a spot he'd missed. She twisted a corner of her shirt and wet it with her mouth. The bed sank slightly with her weight. A spot just behind his ear. The blood came away easily.

When he rolled over, his eyes gleamed, the blue flecked with gold. Then he was slipping off her pants, the ring on his finger cold on her skin. She could hardly hear the sound of her own breathing through the thunder. He ran his face over the inside of her thighs, the pale blond hair of his young beard like a stiff brush, his hair light with sun, skin dark with it. The rain was erasing the outside world, leaving only this room and the bodies in it.

He put his mouth on her. She stopped breathing. She felt herself riding a wave. The long interval as it crested. She could feel her body crying, every door opening in her skin. When he pulled his head away, he was laughing. You taste like honey, he said. He reached up and kissed her on the mouth as if trying to explain.

That first time the two of them seated and facing each other. Legs tangled together. Both of them with their hands on each other's back. Rhythmically pulling themselves closer and closer. The room abruptly illumed with lightning, their bodies incandescent in the flash. Periodically she would look him in the face. His cold blue eyes on her until the feeling swelled and she had to look away.

When she kissed his scar, the silvery light dawned in her head, her ears itching as if an insect had wormed its way down the aural canal. Then it was all there, the disembodied voices of the dead—Afghanistan, a small boy in a long shirt running away, then the sudden explosion in the Russian's neck as the grenade went off, the concussive bang, the air like a hammer, his best friend Mikhail running toward him with the blacksmith's iron that had been heating in the fire right when the grenade exploded, the smell of his own burning flesh filling his nose and lungs.

The moon sat squarely in the window. Already the rain was down to a light patter, outside the sounds of things dripping from a great height. The Russian put her fingers in his mouth. She could see where he had smeared her blood on his chest. Nothing about it had hurt. Lastochka, my little swallow, he said, drifting off to sleep. She had to fight to keep all the voices rising off his skin out of her head. There were so many dead by his hand in that foreign place. I hear you, she whispered. His name was Levka Zaytsev, the lion and the hare. He was nineteen years old. He had seen literally everything.

Two hours before dawn Rabbit opened the door to the room she shared with Qui in the row of flimsy rooms next to the bus depot. The moon was still in the sky. Qui was sitting in the corner milking herself into a jar, her silver hair flowing down her back like a mirror. With one hand she was squeezing the swollen orb of her right breast, with the other plucking bits from the red chrysanthemum and quietly slipping the tufts in her mouth.

THE THIRD TIME LEVKA TOOK HER TO THE HOUSE, SHE TOLD him everything. They were lying in bed. Outside, the water was rising in the streets. The daily rains had been harder than usual. Together they had waded through it to the house. At one point Levka had carried her on his back. Now in the sparsely furnished room on the second floor he was telling her about the fields of Dien Bien Phu, the little orange flags dotting the valley. He walked his fingers down her belly. The ring winked on his finger. You have to be careful where you step, Levka said. She smiled as he got closer. He made a noise with his mouth. The way he shook his fingers, as if he'd burned them, she knew it was supposed to be an explosion. One wrong move, he said. He pulled his hand away and rolled over.

Moonlight tangled in the sheets. Rabbit knew he was lying in his own world far away, that he was thinking of Mikhail running to help with the red-hot iron glowing in his fist, the smell of Levka's flesh burning as Mikhail cauterized the wound. Mikhail who was always running to help. Running through the shadow of the Urals where they had grown up together as boys. Running out into the sector of Dien Bien Phu the French had called Huguette, near the old airfield, to help with the excavator, the machine's left track jammed up with rocks, the little orange flags flapping in the wind as far as the eye could see, then an old wound opening up in the earth, the air transformed into a hammer, the hammer striking Mikhail.

Rabbit could feel a tension in the mattress. She knew Levka was still awake. She didn't expect him to understand. He was the perfect audience. She reached over and kissed his scar, saw the little boy in the long shirt running away, the grenade sailing through the air. There was a man on fire, she said. I could hear him screaming. We were below deck, but I could hear him. For me, to hear something is to see it. The flames raging off him like the sun.

It has always been like this, Rabbit said. Even the three days I lay in my mother's arms in the ground, her fingers slick with honey. Maybe it started because I had no sight. I could only hear the sound of my own heart filling the dirt, the sound like water dripping from a great height.

Those first years I listened. The world was full of them. Everywhere we went. In the paddies. In the ditch beside the road. In the temples. In the rivers. A nation of people who have been dying from war for over a thousand years. Everywhere their faces buried in the road.

Levka was still lying with his back to her, in the window the moon cocked like an ear. She closed her eyes. I don't understand it myself, she said. I hear them stretching their voices out to me. They call to me and they tell me things and I say, I hear you. The simple act of someone hearing them, an acknowledgment, and then they can go wherever it is they go.

That dark week I almost became one. All those families swept overboard. The Cambodian who left the earth for good. The doctor lying with his broken god in his arms. The pirates' boat exploding. Then the hold was filled with the brightest light I have ever seen and I felt a thousand arms lifting me up. All around me the waters becoming as glass.

When I woke, there was a lump on my forehead and it was night. The moon was out. It looked full, the rabbit with its long bright ears as if stamped on a coin, but I knew it couldn't be full. We had just celebrated the Harvest Moon the night we escaped. Then I saw Son and Qui drifting on a piece of wood. Son was staring at me. There wasn't a single wave in the ocean. The moonlight shone on the water like a white robe stretching to the horizon. It does look full, said Son, but yes, it can't be.

We drifted for three days, each night the moon as if whole, the three of us adrift, Qui almost naked where the explosion had ripped her clothes off, her milky-white skin without a single bruise. When the sun rose that first morning, Qui climbed onto my piece of wood, shielding me with her body that never burns, the sun hammering down on us all day without pause, Qui's body always the same ghostly hue. I imagined from a distance her body flashing like a mirror in the sunlight.

On the second day Qui lifted her head and pointed. A boat, Son shouted. I looked up. It was so close I could see the people on board. The boat was riding low in the water. I couldn't see the boat itself for all the people spilling out on every surface, a ship made entirely of people. I know they saw us. I could see the desperation in their faces. They didn't stop.

How did we keep going? When I was thirsty, I would take Qui's breast in my mouth. It tasted like mountain air passed to a man floating hundreds of feet below water. Sometimes I would pass the milk from my mouth into hers.

The second night I heard something chittering in the waves. Then I saw them—a family dancing in the watery light of the always-full moon. Dolphins, their skins like silver. All night they stayed with us, keeping watch.

The morning of the third day the dolphins disappeared. One minute they were singing their high-pitched songs, then I closed my eyes, and when I opened them, the waters were empty. I could see seabirds circling in the distance. I watched them get closer. Among them there was one dark bird, the others white as salt. Then the dark bird left the group and flew toward us. None of us said anything even after the bird landed by my shoulder. I put my hand on the elegant S of her neck, her feathers fully formed. Binh, I said. The bird that had been traded for a red wedding dress. Rabbit looked out the window. She died just last year, Rabbit said.

Toward afternoon we heard the boat. None of us had to look. It took more than forty minutes before they reached us. The waters were so calm we could see it a hundred waveless miles away. The sailors pulled me up first. When they pulled Qui on board, I gasped. I hadn't noticed while we were drifting on the ocean. Standing on deck, her skin was still as pale as the underbelly of a fish, but over the course of three days lost at sea, her long black hair had turned white from root to tip.

Someone brought us a blanket. I can't say they were unkind. On top of the boat the red flag waved with the yellow star, a single lidless eye.

Where's Son, I said. I became frantic. One of the sailors put his arms around me to keep me from jumping back into the sea. Where is he, I shouted. A sailor came and handed us a burlap sack and a pale blue rice bowl. This is all that was out there, he said. The sack rattled as Qui took it. I could hear voices chattering softly. I knew it was full of the bones of generations.

Levka rolled over and ran his fingers through her hair. A few pieces got stuck in his ring. Gently he freed them with his other hand. With his finger he traced a pattern in her freckles, connecting them one by one. She could see tears glistening in the corners of his eyes. Почему ты всегда молчишь? She lifted her head as he inched himself into her. She was fifteen years old in the ancient system of reckoning. The way they moved together she thought of the ocean. Why are you always so quiet, he cried. You never say a word. She felt the wave cresting in her body, and even then she stayed silent, every muscle in her body screaming. The gibbous moon hung in the window, the long bright ears of the rabbit just starting to show.

TOWARD THE END OF THE SUMMER RAINS VAN DISAPPEARED. Each day Qui searched for him across the street in the concrete pit, but he was never there, a figure with muddy feet coming toward her bearing a red chrysanthemum. A light seemed to dim in Qui's face, the flowery perfume on her breath receding. The few nights Rabbit slept in their one room by the bus depot she could hear Qui shivering, her bones rattling in their sockets. Rabbit thought of the year the two of them had spent in the reeducation camp after the government sailors pulled them out of the sea. How one night Rabbit watched a new arrival, an old Chinese woman deprived of her nightly tar, the woman shaking uncontrollably, spit running down her chin.

The final night when Qui's sickness was at its worst, Rabbit got up off her mat. Qui, she said, placing her hand on Qui's forehead. Let it pass. Qui put her hand on Rabbit's neck. After a while, Rabbit let herself be pulled down to Qui's chest. It was the first time since the long days floating off the tip of Vietnam in the Gulf of Thailand almost seven years before. Air where there shouldn't be air. Light spilling out of the darkness of the body. Rabbit had forgotten how sweet it tasted.

In the morning Qui was bright as a star, the pain of withdrawal long behind her, her skin and hair the same unearthly white. In the days that followed, Rabbit began to find small gifts left in front of their door or under the cinnamon tree on Duong Khiem. At first Rabbit thought they were from Van. Then early one morning as she returned from the Russian quarter, she saw one of their neighbors leaving a bowl of rice. The woman bowed her head and clapped her hands together in front of her face the way people did in the temples. It was obvious she was praying, but for what, Rabbit wondered. Then the woman scurried off.

Two weeks after Qui pulled Rabbit to her breast, Van appeared on Duong Khiem just as they were packing up their supplies for the night. His mangled hand was heavily bandaged. Just by looking, Rabbit could tell he had only one finger left.

Van kept himself in the shadow of the cinnamon tree. Qui put down the basket of leftover lemons she'd been packing. I have to leave Hoa Thien tonight, he whispered. Qui took his hand in her hands and held it to her chest. The blood seeped through his bandages. She let go and disappeared behind the iron fence. A few minutes later she came back with a jar filled with milk. Tell him to bathe his wound with it, said Son from his perch in the tree. Bathe your wound with it, Rabbit said. Qui handed Van the jar. He touched his forehead with his one remaining finger and disappeared down the street.

Years later they would see him again in Hanoi's Old Quarter on the shore of Hoan Kiem Lake, Rabbit's fame having spread all over the north. At first she didn't recognize him, his shy smile, his finger fully restored, the finger warm to the touch but heavily scarred at the knuckle. He had come to ask Rabbit of his wife and son. After all these years, had they made it to safety? Were they alive? Van would tell her of his fears, the smugglers always searching for him, constantly ratcheting up the price of his family's escape. In her grand house on the Street of Shoes, Rabbit will wrap both her hands around the two fingers Van has left and look him in the eye. Your son lives, she will say. Your wife and your enemies are dead.

They were sitting under the cinnamon tree. Rabbit, Qui, Son. It was two hours past noon. A bird was singing in the branches, the sound like a man whistling. The three of them were drowsing peacefully by the fragrant trunk, each with their own thoughts, the smell of the cinnamon perfuming their blood. How do you think it will end, Son said suddenly. The question floated up into the air.

Rabbit thought of the planets spinning wordlessly in space. She knew nothing was permanent, Levka's body arcing over her as he cried in his helplessness, the skin trembling by the corners of his eyes. She repeated Son's question. End? She looked and saw the wetness growing on the front of Qui's shirt, the stain expanding like a map. Maybe Qui knew. Maybe they all knew. End? That instant, forty miles away in the scrubby brush of Anne-Marie, it was ending.

The French named everything after their mistresses. Anne-Marie. Beatrice. Claudine. Dominique. Eliane. Flavie. Gabrielle. Huguette. The whole of Dien Bien Phu feminized and quartered. 1954 and we saw men we had never seen before—the Senegalese with their skins like night, the Moroccans and Algerians with their centuries of mixed blood, their bowing down to a fixed spot on the horizon in the middle of battle five times a day. After us, the Africans would also take up the gun against their oppressors, but we did it first though in our war many of our colonized brothers put down their weapons and lay back in the trenches, even the Black Tai who had allied themselves with the French slinking off into the hills. And at the end of two months, we won. Then the Americans, the Cambodians, the Chinese as it has been between us for a thousand years. But those months in '54 on the plains and in the valleys of Dien Bien Phu, our bodies mixed unintelligibly. Black, white, yellow. We whisper together. There is so much we know that we cannot say. So many of us are still here sleeping in the earth until someone decides it is time to sort us out and take us home.

IT HADN'T RAINED FOR DAYS. NOW IT LOOKED LIKE IT wouldn't. The season was still some months from the deepest cold of a temperate winter. At the foot of the cinnamon tree Rabbit sat studying the cloudless sky. The red-breasted parrot from earlier in the day had flown away. Overhead the stars were beginning to appear. She always missed the rains when they stopped. There was something comforting about the sound of water hammering the roofs, the sound as if you were being given a second chance, the world washed clean.

The trucks began to return at the usual hour. Qui had already left for home, her body floating down the street as if the moon were walking the earth. Son was sitting in the highest bough of the cinnamon tree. The bats were beginning to appear, overhead Venus turning on in the twilight. Rabbit was sitting with her back against the tree, the scent of cinnamon filling her head. The first truck was off-loading. She didn't pay it any notice. Levka was always in the last truck. Any minute now the last truck would come barreling up the street, loose grit swirling through the air. He would leap off and sneak up on her, running his finger over her freckles. She was thinking of the way she had taken him in her mouth for the first time the night before, the intimacy of his cries as she hummed. She played the moment over and over in her head, the secret moments between two people. Just the moon in the window and all over the walls.

There was a deafening crash. Rabbit sat up. A tree branch was lying at her feet, a cloud of dust kicked up in the air. Son was standing by the dead limb. The trucks were gone, Duong Khiem utterly still. Rabbit rubbed her eyes. The stars were out in their entirety, Venus already starting to set.

Son stood toeing the branch with his foot. Rabbit didn't understand. She had simply fallen asleep, the cinnamon like a soporific. Maybe Levka was tired too, maybe he had seen her sleeping there peacefully under the tree and decided not tonight.

No, she said out loud. The moon was already halfway up the sky. She jumped up and ran through the gate.

At the top of the stairs she pushed open the door and entered the dormitory where the Russians slept. The corridor was dark. She could see a blue glow flickering from a room at the end of the hallway. Then she was running for it. Crying please, anyone, the corridor growing longer as if extending. She felt as if she would never reach it, the glow flickering like moonlight on the ocean.

In the room at the end of the hall an old samurai movie from Japan was playing on the TV—the men's topknots blue-black and gleaming. There were a few sofas and chairs scattered around, a refrigerator humming in the corner, the room some kind of lounge area. The smell of cigarettes was etched in the upholstery, even in the dark the walls tobacco-stained. Giang was propped up on a small counter by a sink with her shirt still on as a man stood pumping between her legs, his body with the same sun lines as Levka's, the same patches of light and dark.

The man didn't stop even when Rabbit came running in. Giang kept panting, her eyes closed, grimacing as the man moved faster. The secret moments between people. The man moaning and Giang answering, his movements faster and faster, a sheen forming on his skin. Then the man shuddered. Rabbit could see the muscles go slack, the urgency melting away. Giang opened her empty eyes. She seemed to know she and the man weren't alone, but she didn't hurry. The man disengaged and turned around, lit a cigarette before pulling up his shorts. Just then another man walked into the room. He looked at Rabbit and then at Giang and then at Rabbit again and smiled.

They picked Rabbit up off the floor and carried her to a sofa. When she opened her eyes, there was a small group in the room. She didn't remember collapsing. Giang was sitting on the arm of the couch squeezing her hand. There was a spot in Giang's eyebrows. Rabbit realized it was lipstick. Someone must have kissed her lips and then smashed his stained mouth all over her face. Rabbit could hear two voices rising off Giang's skin, the voices faint like a campfire in a vast canyon. Rabbit's ears began to tickle, but then Giang pulled her hand away.

Most of the Russians didn't even know anything was wrong. They were only hearing about it for the first time. The last truck had only just come back. The men in the earlier trucks were already sleeping. One man from the last truck sat smoking by the TV. On-screen a woman was singing in a white dress, in her wide sleeves her arms floating up and down like a moth's. The man said they had sat waiting and waiting for Levka and the two others to come back from the trenches of Anne-Marie, but they never did. What do you think happened, someone asked. The man lifted his eyebrows and opened his face the way Rabbit noticed their people did when something was of little concern to them.

The man perceived Rabbit staring. His name was Anatole— daybreak—though the others called him Grischa. His hands flew as he spoke. The others understood the theatrics, the heavy sighs. It wasn't that he didn't care. It was that many of them were soldiers. They had seen things, which they'd lived through and then put from their minds. In their time they had all known men who had cared too much. It was hard to explain, but when you cared too much about one thing, it made you careless elsewhere. Vietnam was a respite, the Hindu Kush still looming in their dreams. Vietnam with its white-sand beaches, the girls with waists you could put your hands all the way around until your fingers touched, who would lie with you for only a few rubles. Why come here to help these people extract the long dead from the earth and then die yourself? Maybe they had seen this coming. There were always men like Levka, Levka running into the arms of this child when his friend Mikhail was killed. As if he could find what he needed lying between her legs.

They didn't come back from Anne-Marie, Grischa said. Levka and Andrei and Little Vadim. Anne-Marie was just north of Huguette at the end of the airstrip. We went out looking for them, but then the sun went down and it was too dangerous. Grischa lit another cigarette and closed his face. I remember Levka saying something or other about a deep pocket, he said. Proof of atrocities. Grischa raised his eyebrows again. I tell him why bother. Yes, there are probably bodies there. So what? There are fucking bodies everywhere. The other Russians nodded.

Возьми ее туда, Giang said. Some of the men jumped at the sound of her voice. *You must take her there.* Giang pointed at Rabbit. The men looked at the two women sitting on the sofa. On the TV a group of children were singing a patriotic song. Giang knew what the local people said about Rabbit and Qui, the people bringing them gifts and offerings in the hopes that the two of them might console the newly dead and ease their passing. If you want to know what happened, Giang repeated, take her.

Grischa lifted his eyebrows. What's it to me, he said.

How do you prepare yourself when death is moving down the line? The man standing next to you and the man standing next to him and the man next to him all the way to the horizon. How you can see it coming but there's nowhere to run. Trees falling in a ghastly forest. Blood mingling in the dirt.

THEY LEFT JUST AFTER SUNRISE. RABBIT GAVE QUI A SMALL wave. Qui was standing by the metal drum stoking the fire as the trucks started up. Her skin burned brighter than the flames themselves, her hair like snow. From a million miles away she probably looked like a star, Rabbit thought. A planet rising in the east of some long-distant world.

Son was sitting in the cinnamon tree watching the convoy drive away up Duong Khiem. The scratch on his face looked as if a drop of acid had rolled down his cheek and burned the skin. Rabbit felt something tighten in her chest. She thought of Levka somewhere sitting in the branches of a tree scanning the earth for her.

The trucks turned at the first intersection and rolled out of sight. Within minutes most of the men fell asleep. The air was dry, the first hint that summer was over. At the front of the truck up by the cab lay a pile of shovels and buckets. In one of the buckets something bloomed like a bouquet of flowers. The color was right, but the effect was wrong. Rabbit stared harder. They were orange flags with little black skulls and crossbones printed on both sides. The words were written in French. FAITES ATTENTION.

Overhead the metal ribs of the truck's canvas roof shuddered with each turn. Rabbit tried to imagine Levka sitting in the very same spot where she herself was sitting, each morning the coldness of the metal floor seeping into his skin. Maybe each day on the drive out to the Nam Yum River he thought of her, their secret room in the moonlight, the taste of honey still in his mouth.

Giang had fallen asleep. She was still wearing her tiny yellow skirt and cheap plastic heels. Even in sleep there was something guarded in her face, as if somewhere in her dreams she were clutching her purse and closing herself off. Giang, Rabbit whispered. She wanted to know why her friend spoke Russian, but Giang didn't stir. Somehow in her sleep she was moving herself even farther away.

On the other side of the truck Grischa was awake. He looked at Rabbit and nodded. She could feel his eyes on her as if he were trying to connect the freckles on her face and find a pattern. She wondered if he were worried about how they would sneak her out into the fields. Before they had even boarded the trucks, he had explained the situation to Giang. The Commandant has a house in the Russian quarter in Hoa Thien, Grischa said. He raised his eyebrows and held his hands up palms to the sky as if testing the air for rain. None of us have seen him in weeks. Giang looked at him, but Grischa simply nodded. I know I know, he said. Why go out there every day if no one is watching us? He lowered his hands and shrugged. We Russians and our suffering, he said.

Then Rabbit could feel them rising, the sound of the trucks switching gears. Out of the back she could see people walking downhill into town. She closed her eyes and imagined a young woman riding a bicycle, her long black hair streaming in the wind, the woman's conical hat blowing off as she raced past a group of water buffalo. A young man standing in a ditch by the side of the road, watching the woman, the small red diamond staining his face, his heart flooding.

When Rabbit opened her eyes again, they were there. Two men helped her and Giang out of the truck. The sun was just over the hills, but overhead there was a three-quarters moon in the pale blue sky. In the daytime it was just a ghost of itself.

The Russians from the other trucks were already organizing themselves for the day. One man stood with headphones draped around his neck and a large metal machine by his side. She saw four other men with headsets, each one connected to the same kind of machine, each instrument long and cylindrical like the vacuum cleaners she'd seen once in a window in Hanoi.

The dogs looked anxious. Their handlers stood a few feet away poring over a map. The dogs kept their eyes on the men. One of the smaller dogs passed too closely to another. The bigger dog let out a deep growl and bared its teeth. The smaller dog quickly moved out of the way, its tail between its legs. Rabbit could see a scar on the smaller dog's muzzle, a spot where the fur no longer grew. Something about it reminded her of Son. She looked around but didn't see him anywhere.

For all the climbing the trucks had done out on Highway 19, the land was surprisingly flat, as if they were standing in the bottom of a bowl. In the distance the mountains and rolling hills looked like turrets. She wondered why anyone had ever chosen to fight there. Whoever had the highlands would hold the advantage. If you were down in the bottomlands, it would only be a matter of time. Even she could tell that.

After a while the various groups began to move off. Each man had his task. There were close to a hundred of them in all. Some carried shovels and buckets, some with metal detectors, which they carried on their shoulders, some straining to hold the dogs back. At the front of each group a man walked holding only a map, the responsibility evident in the slowness of his movements.

Grischa came over and spoke with Giang. He had one of the dogs with him. Rabbit offered it her hand, but the dog growled and flattened its ears. Laika, barked Grischa, tugging the leash. Giang looked at Rabbit. You ready, she said. Rabbit nodded. With her hands Giang twisted her loose hair up into a knot. Rabbit could see a small mark on Giang's neck, the mark as if someone had bitten her. Grischa says stay single file, Giang said. No matter what, stay in line. Rabbit pushed her hat back out of her eyes and took a deep breath.

It was a thirty-minute walk to the trenches of Anne-Marie. They walked on the airstrip, the asphalt long decayed and over-grown by shoulder-tall plants with small green berries gleaming in clusters. Grischa yelled something over his shoulder. Coffee beans, Giang said. To the east the land was dotted with orange flags. The Russians had been working different areas for the last year, looking for the French dead. The Vietnamese government was eager to normalize relations with their former colonizer, bodies offered up as a sign of goodwill. Repatriation was one step in a long process.

Their group was small, just six of them plus the dog. One man carried the metal detector. Two other soldiers were tot-ing shovels. They looked like boys, barely teenagers, their skin ruddy and somewhat blemished. A few orange flags poked out of their pockets. Grischa was still holding the leash, Laika trot-ting by his side. Rabbit could see something rolled up tight and tucked under Grischa's other arm, the thing shiny and black. In her mind a memory floated up of a black bag lying on the ground under a sugar-apple tree, beside it a hole growing in the earth. There was a body zipped up in the bag. She knew there was a body inside the body.

As they walked Grischa explained procedures to Giang, who translated intermittently. In each sector they would first sweep the land for unexploded ordnance. Afterward they would deto-nate the larger bombs, only defusing things when it was abso-lutely necessary. There was so much left in the ground that they would mark the smaller incidents with flags and leave them be. Once an area had been marked, they would come through with the dogs. If the dogs scented something, then they would begin digging.

The two women walked along, everywhere cicadas buzzing

like invisible engines in the grass. At one point Giang stopped to tip a pebble out of one of her shoes. Rabbit stood waiting for her to begin moving again. Why do you speak Russian, she said.

For a moment Giang stood studying her heel. I grew up in Russia, she said. I was born in Stalingrad. Rabbit waited for her to say more, but she put her shoe back on and started walking again.

Soon they were beyond the airstrip. The grass was a dull brown from years of chemicals leaching into the soil. My father was a party leader, Giang suddenly said. When I was twelve, my parents were killed in a car accident. Rabbit remembered the faint voices rising off Giang's skin when she had held her hand back in the dorm. So I came back to Vietnam, she said. After my grandmother died, I was on my own. She turned and smiled at Rabbit. At least I'm keeping up my Russian. She laughed, but Rabbit could see the effort it cost her.

Now that she knew the circumstances Rabbit could put it all together. The voices she had heard as she held Giang's hand had been crying out for acknowledgment. Giang's father closing his eyes as he pushed down on the gas, steering the car into a guardrail. His wife sleeping beside him, only rousing herself at the last moment, her eyes shocked open. In the husband's mind the desperation and the feeling that there was nothing left to do. The wife didn't think he knew, but he knew. He had always known about all of them. The low-ranking Russian colonel just the latest in her endless string of lovers.

They were only a few hundred feet from the spot where Levka was last seen when Rabbit stepped on one. She felt the air rush out of her lungs. Someone's here, she said, rubbing her ears. Giang let out a sharp whistle. The Russians turned around and came back. Giang tapped the ground with her foot. Здесь кто-то есть. The men huddled and talked among themselves. Impossible, Grischa said. He pointed to a spot up the trail. They were up by that grove when we last saw them. Giang kept tapping the ground. Grischa sighed and said something to the dog. Laika sniffed around, then squatted and urinated. The other men laughed. Please, said Rabbit, but nobody moved.

Giang reached over and grabbed a shovel from one of the boys. Without another word she began digging. Grischa pulled out a pack of cigarettes. He struck a match along the bottom of his work boot. The flame burst forth with a loud hiss. The men sat down on the ground. The man carrying the metal detector said something to one of the other soldiers and sniggered.

Less than two feet down Giang hit something. It was as if a leather glove had disintegrated, the desiccated skin hanging in shreds on the bone. Grischa ordered one of the boys to help. After another twenty minutes they could see that the body had fallen backward with both hands shielding its face, a small clean hole through the front of the skull. A large ragged hole gaped at the back.

They spent all morning going from spot to spot, Rabbit walking between the orange flags. After the first one, the noise was deafening, the whole field groaning. I hear you, she said. Be patient. At one point the Russians marked the earth with their shovels for later, the places they would come back to and dig up. It was as if they'd hit a vein of ore, a river of bodies snaking north-south. Each one with the same trauma to the face, the same holes in the skull.

They're Black Tai, aren't they, said Giang. In hole after hole the fabric was in tatters but still evident, tibia and femurs draped in indigo rags. Rabbit nodded. The Black Tai were one of the ethnic minorities who lived along the Black River and had sided with the French. Rabbit could hear the terror in their voices. As the battle raged, the men deciding one by one and then collectively to stay in the trenches and lay down their guns. To abandon the French. It wasn't our fight, said one of the voices. Overhead the daytime moon hung in the sky like a whisper.

They shot them, said Rabbit. Who, said Giang. Rabbit closed her eyes. The French. Then she could see it. As night fell the killers came back, the Foreign Legion and the *tirailleurs*. It was a small group, ten at the most. The French soldiers were acting on their own without orders, thinking they could persuade the Black Tai to come out and fight for them if the ethnics woke in the morning and found some of their comrades dead, presumably at the hands of the Vietnamese. The French soldiers assumed the Black Tai, hungry for revenge, would pick up their guns again and rejoin the battle. Instead when the fog lifted, the French looked out over the bodies of the fifteen or so Black Tai they had killed in the trenches of Anne-Marie and saw that the remaining Black Tai had fled.

The Russians were marking up their map. Rabbit was sitting stroking the dog when Laika's ears twitched. Rabbit had heard it too. She got up and began walking toward the voice. The dog trotted by her side. Giang was back with the men marveling over the number of bodies they had uncovered.

Fifty feet up the trail Rabbit and the dog came to an open pit. Laika lay down flat on her belly and began to whine. My lion, Rabbit said. On the ground something winked in the sunlight. She imagined bending down into an open grave and kissing a bright yellow bead on the tip of a dead woman's finger, the sudden taste of honey. Then she could see Levka and the other two men reaching down into the earth, a belt of old hand grenades lying underneath the corpse which the soldier had been wearing when he was killed. As the three men gingerly lifted the body out, the belt exploding. Tenfold. Twentyfold. Infinity. Lastochka, my little swallow, Levka said, his mouth on her as the wave crested in her body. I hear you, she said. Something glinted in the grass beside the pit. She stooped and picked it up. It was his ring. She kissed it, but it didn't taste like anything.

VIETNAM

⊙ HANOI

CHINA

Wandering Ghosts
[1996]

L
A
O
S

17th Parallel
Ben Hai River

Hue

THAILAND

South China Sea

CAMBODIA

HO CHI MINH
⊙ CITY

Someone has locked the door. Or imagine yourself at the bottom of a mile-long well, the wooden cover on tight so that you are forced to rely on your memory to conjure up images of what is on the other side. Then for the briefest instant the wooden cover that keeps the world out is lifted, the opening like an oculus but from a mile away the opening no bigger than a distant star. This is your chance to be heard. Say only what needs to be said. Someone is lying. Someone doesn't want you to be found because you'll ruin the whole effect.

WHEN THE WOMAN ENTERED THE COURTYARD, CHILD-sized shoes in hand, the female parakeet sitting in the lemon tree began to cry. For the past few years mourners had been coming to Hang Giay straight from the funeral procession. Most times the hearse would park out front with the six-foot-tall portrait of the deceased still draped with flowers. Then the widow would float through the grand wooden doors and on into the garden, one son at each shoulder, everyone in white like a battery of moths. Invariably joss sticks burned between the widow's fingers, her hands as if on fire.

But today was different. That night the moon would be full, the moon like a white hole on the waters of Hoan Kiem Lake. It was the full moon of the fifth month, the day the Buddha died, the unluckiest day of the year. The streets were empty. People stayed indoors, waiting for the day to be over.

All afternoon the three of them had been sitting in the court-yard shielding themselves from the June sun. The lemon trees were adorned with fruit. Linh was just coming out of the house with a pitcher of drinks made from fresh mango and milk. Despite her angelic face something about Linh reminded Rabbit of herself at that age. There was a steeliness to the child, the way the girl would slip in and out of rooms without anyone notic-ing. The way she too could stare down a grown man. Rabbit and

Qui had taken Linh in just after they'd moved onto Hang Giay. She had been one of a group of street children sent out each day to beg for money from the western tourists. Once the girl was inside the great wooden doors of the house on Hang Giay, Qui had cut Linh's hair into the same shapeless bowl Rabbit had worn at that age, but on Linh the haircut looked feminine, her delicate features emphasized, cheeks dimpled and pink, her mouth pursed like a cat's. Sometimes when she lay sleeping Rabbit had to reach out and touch the child's warm cheek; Linh looked so much like a doll, her perfectly upturned nose like something an artist would sculpt in wood.

Rabbit and Qui couldn't be sure how old Linh was. Between malnourishment and the slightness of most Vietnamese girls, she could be anywhere from eight to twelve. For all the years she'd been with them it was as if she hadn't grown an inch. She seemed frozen in time, like Son, the scratch forking down his face as permanent a feature as his nose or mouth. The two women had decided that when Linh began bleeding, they would officially declare her thirteen in the modern system of reckoning. Each day both women eyed her for the first signs of change, but each day there were none.

Qui sat by the fountain nursing another baby from the foreign orphanage that had recently returned to Vietnam after more than twenty years. Each morning Linh went out to bring back a baby for Qui. Today Linh had left the wooden doors unlocked after returning from the orphanage. At the sound of the great doors opening, Rabbit sat upright, the hinges creaking like swollen joints. In the air something hummed imperceptibly. Like a needle drawing blood from a skull.

The woman didn't even knock. She simply pushed open the doors and stepped over the threshold, her sandals in her hands, the sound of the hinges like a body in pain. There was usually a policeman at the door to keep the curious away. People were eager to contact their loved ones or even just to catch a glimpse of Rabbit. But on the unluckiest day of the year the chief of police had decided it wasn't necessary to station a guard at the door.

As the woman entered, Rabbit felt something tighten in her stomach. The woman clapped her hands together in front of her face, a cigarette burning between her fingers. I have no money, the stranger said. The baby at Qui's breast let out a small sigh. Overhead the male parakeet turned to his weeping mate and softly clucked *remember this, remember*. Linh came back outside with a clean glass and poured some of the mango and milk into it before handing the glass to their guest. Rabbit hadn't even noticed Linh get up.

Why would you travel on this day of all days, said Linh, offering the woman a chair. The woman didn't put out her cigarette. She took a long drink, finishing the whole glass at once. Nothing fazes me anymore, she said, setting the glass back down and taking a deep drag, the cigarette suddenly half as long. Not even the death of our lord, asked Linh. Not even, said the woman.

Overhead Son was sitting on the railing of the third-floor balcony, his legs dangling over the edge. It was one of the grandest houses on the street. There were others like it, houses with air-conditioning and western appliances, running water, tile floors, teak furniture. Foreign money flowed in from the overseas Vietnamese who had left years ago. Families who just decades before were peasants now built pastel-colored confections all through the thirty-six streets of Hanoi's Old Quarter, each house tiered like a wedding cake.

Across the table the baby began to coo. Qui ran her finger along the fontanel at the top of the baby's head where the bony plates had yet to close. In the lemon tree the female parakeet was still weeping. A single tear rolled off the end of her beak and fell on top of the baby's head. All her life the baby in Qui's arms will insist that she can hear voices coming from the trees, though no one will believe her. I do too understand the language of birds, the grown-up baby will tell herself when friends scoff at her assertion. The landscape will be empty except for the pied kestrel sitting in the nearby eucalyptus, the kestrel sympathetically vocalizing *klee klee klee, pay them no mind.*

In the courtyard the strange woman sat smoking, her shoes lying in her lap. After each inhalation, a thin gray cloud hung on the edge of her upper lip before she fully exhaled. If I tell you what you want to know, said Rabbit, it will cost me everything. Overhead in the lemon tree the female parakeet continued to cry. The woman made no sign that she'd heard what Rabbit had said. And if I don't help you, Rabbit continued, it will cost me even more. Lightly the woman ran a finger around the rim of her empty glass. She bent over and stubbed her cigarette out on the ground but managed to keep the smoke cycling a few breaths longer, blowing a stream of it out of her mouth and inhaling it back in through her nose.

In the lemon tree the male parakeet fluffed his wings. When Gautama Buddha cut His long princely hair and left the palace of His father, said the male bird to his mate, legend has it Kanthaka, His milk-white horse, openly wept.

Street of Wooden Bowls, Street of Instruments with Strings. Street of Sandals, Rafts, Cotton, Sails. Street of Hemp and Paper. Sweet Potato Street, Street of Tin and Oils. Street of Pickled Fish, Pipes, Sugar, Silversmiths, Street of Baskets and Brushes. Scales. Street of Hats, Fans, Aluminum, Combs. Street of Pipes and Bottles. Street of Thread, of Onions, Mats, Incense, Bricks. Street of Worms, of Shoes, of Silk. Street of Bamboo Screens. Street of Coffins, Medicine, Jars. Street Strewn with Salt.

ON THE STREET OF FANS THE VAN CAME TO A HALT. TWO TOUR-
ists went running by with their cameras jostling around their
necks. Rabbit sank back in her seat. Outside the window the
storefronts were cluttered with icons. Since the government had
begun modernizing the economy, Hang Quat was rife with religious images, row after row of plaster figurines. There was Quan
Am with Her multiple hands, statues of Mary and the Christ
child, the baby Jesus with the face of a grown man, Mary's eyes
almond-shaped and heavy-lidded, eastern. The sidewalk in front
of one store brimmed with images of the seated Buddha, His
earlobes elongated. But who hears the hearer, Rabbit thought.

Then the funeral procession came around the corner. She
was surprised to see a band with instruments. Usually a woman's
recorded voice warbled like a bird over a sound system as someone plucked the long strings of the *dan bau*. Today the musicians
walked dressed in matching uniforms. One man was playing
a long flute pocked with the markings of an actual bone. The
musicians were all white-haired. Young people weren't inter-
ested in learning how to play traditional instruments, though
in Vietnam there is a saying: the living need light and the dead
need music.

In the van Rabbit could feel Linh's eyes on her, the child hungry for an answer. Rabbit remembered the day last year when
they had woken up to find the parakeets nesting in the tallest
of the lemon trees. Linh had stood underneath the bough and
pointed. Lady, said the male bird. We have come to serve you.
Did you hear that, Rabbit said to Linh. The bird opened its wings
and flapped them a few times, the sound grand and majestic as if
coming from a much larger creature. Hear what, said Linh.

Rabbit ran her hand down the leather seat. The air-
conditioning was on, but Linh had opened a window. Up ahead
Rabbit could see a large flatbed truck crawling along behind
the musicians. She knew the family would be up at the front.

There might be as many as a thousand mourners wailing behind them. On auspicious days the Old Quarter could host up to four funerals before noon. How each one would stop on Hang Giay before the great wooden doors, the closest living relative entering the courtyard and bowing before Rabbit with a pained look in the eye.

All right, Rabbit said. There was a weariness in her voice. Linh slid open the door and scurried out into the crowd.

From the backseat Qui put a hand on Rabbit's shoulder. I'm okay, said Rabbit. For the past few years she knew what the local people had been saying about her, the rumors that flew about the city, that she herself no longer took earthly food. She was afraid Qui might lift her shirt and pull Rabbit to her pale breast right there in front of the driver and this strange woman who was the sole reason for this trip. In the backseat next to Qui the woman was staring out the window, her jaw working a piece of gum. Yesterday when she had walked into the courtyard, they had learned her name was Tao. *Apple.* It was difficult to determine the woman's age, but Rabbit figured she was in her late thirties. And now, less than twenty-four hours after meeting her, they were all in a van headed south to the small hamlet just outside Hue where the woman said it had happened.

When she had held Tao's hands under the lemon trees, the taste of dirt had welled up in Rabbit's mouth, her ears stinging. Quickly she pulled her hands away. I have to see where it happened, she'd said. There are so many voices. During the past year her encounters had become more draining. Every time she listened, she became less herself, the dead filling her with their own stories—tales of betrayal, murder, loneliness, and pain. In September it would be ten years since Anne-Marie, the Black Tai lying patiently in the ground waiting for someone to acknowledge them. And the one thing she had never considered as she walked the scrubby earth of Dien Bien Phu that first time long ago was the politics. Which stories the world is eager to bring into the light. Which stories it doesn't want told.

When Linh came back to the van from the funeral procession, Qui and Tao and the driver climbed out. Linh held the door open and nodded. It was a widower, a young man, his suit white as salt. When his mother tried to climb in after him, Linh shook her head. Rabbit slid the door shut.

The space was so small she didn't even need to take his hand. His suit and jacket and vest were all the same blinding white. She noticed his tie clip was a small jade figure of the goddess, Her arms posed around Her head like a spider. The clip looked overly smooth from wear. Maybe he thumbed it when he felt nervous. No, it was something else, the ridges of his thumbprint whirling over the goddess's face, yes, the man thumbing the clip whenever he thought of the one who had given it, his thumb working the small jade figure like a tongue worrying a sore in the mouth.

She was your cousin, said Rabbit. The man nodded, blinking back tears. Rabbit began to open herself, the silvery room in her head coming onto her, the room as if descending, the moon plunging toward her and swallowing her whole, the orb all around her with its silvery light and Rabbit like a candle burning brightly in the center of a lantern. Yes, she was there in the silvery room where no one else could enter, and she was waiting for the other to arrive.

She was my cousin, the man repeated. She was the daughter of my second aunt. For a moment his face seemed to brighten. We had never even met until a few years ago, he said. There was so much pressure on Xuan, the man whispered. We are both the last of our bloodline. I am afraid for her in the next life. The man was thumbing his tie clip. Rabbit couldn't be sure if Linh had told him what would happen. Some people were eager to tell their loved ones something or to ask one final question. Some people tried to slip *dong* into her hand as if it were only a matter of persuasion. Okay, Rabbit said. She closed her eyes and waited.

Sometimes they came to her instantly and sometimes they were shy as deer. The experience like kneeling by a river and slowing her heartbeat to the rhythm of the landscape. The sounds of water lapping on the shore, waiting for the creature to come and drink, then raise its head.

Before I met Nhat I knew it would be difficult, said a voice. In the silvery room Rabbit opened her eyes, her ears tingling. I've known it my whole life, the voice continued. There was neither happiness nor sorrow in its intonation. Everything about my monthly blood was haphazard, it said. When it would come, how long it would last, the color and thickness. Everything. The words hung in the silvery air. All those years Nhat coming home from the company every day at noon. On auspicious days the two of us lying down on the floor in the old way because the doctor said western beds were too soft. My tailbone bruising.

It had been a long time since Rabbit had spoken with one so young. At the end of the first year I made a pilgrimage to the Perfume Pagoda, said the woman. All the way down the Swallow Bird River I tried to imagine my body as a nest. I imagined lining it with bits of paper, clumps of hair. I spent a full week on Huong Tich Mountain walking from temple to temple and touching every lucky thing I could touch.

Then Rabbit began to see her. She had shaven her head and was wearing a plain white robe, her sleeves long and breezy. Rabbit knew that under the robe every one of her ribs would be articulated, her rib cage jutting out like the prow of a ship. On the front of the robe there was the spot where she had aimed for the heart. The stain was not unbeautiful, like a red chrysanthemum pinned on a sheet.

Rabbit stood in the silvery light and listened to the voice of the woman once named Xuan explain herself. Each time she found herself listening to yet another soul, Rabbit wondered at the marvel of it all. In ten years' time she had become a national treasure. The government trotted her out when they needed to know where their soldiers were buried, where to erect another monument for the northern martyrs. In the American war alone there were more than three million dead, and the end of the war was more than twenty years behind them. But as long as there were unnamed dead left in the ground, it would never be over. What the dead know. What you remember shapes who you are. The government was trying to create one memory, one country, one official version of what happened. Everything else was allowed to disintegrate and fall off the bone. All over the countryside southern remains were going unacknowledged. One side had been victorious. The other was turning into earth.

When almost two years had passed, I went to the grave of Grandmother Phan, said the woman once named Xuan. Grandmother Phan's burial mound in Lake Bien was accessible only by elephant. The woman patted the red flower on her chest as if checking to make sure it was still there. A boy brought a ladder and helped me up, she said. I remember he wasn't wearing a shirt, his young back already dark and leathery. I climbed up to the spot just behind the head where there was a dirty blanket and a place to sit. Rabbit began to feel herself melting into the voice until she too could see it, the boy momentarily walking away with the ladder across his shoulders, the elephant's mammothness between her legs, the bristles of the great animal's hair scratching her skin.

When the boy came back, he hit the elephant with a stick with a metal hook on the end. Together we waded into the water, said Xuan. It took us forty minutes to get there. Sometimes the boy would swim. Mostly we tramped through the tall grass, but when the boy swam, the elephant swam, too. In the silvery light

Xuan began to play with her long white sleeves. Then we came to the island where my ancestors are buried in mounds, the grass green and thick, and at the head of each mound there's a small hole boring straight down. Grandmother Phan's resting place was under a camphor tree. I poured a bottle of rice wine down the hole. I left a cassette player made of paper along with a paper tape of Grandmother's favorite music. Xuan was sitting on the ground running her hands over her scalp. Within three weeks of my visit to Grandmother Phan's grave, my blood stopped.

I don't know which is worse, Xuan said. I only know what happened to me. For six months my body was home to someone, the nest I'd visualized for so long finally full. Which do you think is worse, she asked. Rabbit knew the question before Xuan even posed it. To lose it before the blood has had a chance to form or to lose the form itself?

I tried to keep going, Xuan whispered. Everyone said there would be others, but I knew. I've always known my body wasn't meant for it. We never should have married, she said. Rabbit was beginning to lose her in the glow of the silvery light, the light growing brighter and brighter until Rabbit would find herself back in the van. I didn't do it out of grief, said the voice. We were cousins. He was the son of my only uncle, our blood from the same line. Through the children he will someday have, I will live on.

I hear you, Rabbit said. She opened her eyes. He was sitting next to her in the van. His thumb rested on the green tie clasp carved with the goddess. She turned to him. The dead live in us, she said. From outside Linh opened the door. A wave of air rushed in. The man let out a deep breath. So many of them expected a conversation. Time and again people sought her out for their own sense of closure. But it wasn't about the living. The man jumped out of the van and disappeared into the crowd. It was perfect. He didn't even thank her.

The old songs seem so foreign to us now. Like Soldiers of Vietnam, forward! / The flag's gold star fluttering in the wind / Leading our people, our native land, out of misery and suffering / Our efforts unified in the fight for the building of a new life / Let us stand up and spiritedly break our chains / For too long we've swallowed our hatred / Keep ready for all sacrifices and our life will be radiant / Ceaselessly for the people's cause we struggle / Hastening to the battlefield / Forward! All together advancing / Vietnam is eternal.

Just before sunset three motorcycles passed them on the highway heading south. On each a Vietnamese man sat up front driving, a foreign woman in a tank top and shorts on the back. Ever since the country had opened its doors to western tourists earlier in the decade, there was money in places where there'd never been money before. From the passenger's seat Linh waved, her dimpled cheeks shining. One of the women raised her hand. All the way down the highway the woman remained with her hand in the air until she was gone. Her long blond hair streaming from her helmet.

Just this morning they had closed up the house on Hang Giay. When the policeman arrived for the first shift, Linh told him they needed a van and a driver. Tong looked confused. There were no official events scheduled. It wasn't the day just after Tet when every year they threw the doors open and allowed anyone to come and sit under the lemon trees, though the visitors were screened ahead of time and asked whom they wanted to contact. Every year Tong knew what happened at the end of that day, though out of politeness he never said anything. How Qui would close the doors of the house and pull the weary Rabbit to her chest, the official hearer of the dead limp like a rag doll. Then Qui would fill Rabbit back up with her own silvery light.

The parakeets were preening themselves in the lemon tree. Tong was still mulling over Linh's request. A van and a driver, he repeated. She is too important to just disappear. Linh began to pick something out of her teeth. Child, Linh said, the top of her head just reaching his navel, her chubby cheeks pink as if painted. She looked him square in the face. Do as you're asked. The year before Rabbit had helped Tong's cousin find her son. The child had been trapped in a fire as he was playing in an abandoned factory. In the courtyard Rabbit told them the boy died instantly. His soul was so bright, said Rabbit. He will come back to the world as whatever he wishes. Linh stood by the wooden doors still picking her teeth. Tong got back on his moped. In less than an hour a van pulled up out front.

And so there they were heading south to the city of Hue. The sun was in the west. The highway stretched before them. The driver called over his shoulder. We should eat, he said. They had brought food with them but had eaten it all for lunch. The driver's name was Viet. On the left side of his face a piece of his nostril was missing. All that was left was a clot of white scar tissue, all day long the sound of his breathing whistling in and out of his nose. Linh didn't even confer with the others. Okay, she said.

They pulled off the highway. Within a few miles they came to a village. The sun had gone down, but there were still people out on bicycles and mopeds. Along the main street the shops were still selling. They passed what looked like a school, then a community center with a great thatched roof and a series of loudspeakers ringing the grounds. Viet pulled up at a small restaurant. In front there was a sign with the number 7 painted on it.

Inside a teenaged girl sauntered over to take their order. The girl's hair was bleached a brassy orange color and boldly cut in what looked like a western style often worn by tourists. Rabbit realized how long she'd been living in the north. The girl's accent sounded strange to her ears. Technically they hadn't crossed the Ben Hai yet, but the girl pronounced several letters in the southern style. It reminded Rabbit of the years she'd spent living on the Mekong, the way the people spoke as if they were singing.

It's a delicacy, said Viet. He sat systematically rubbing his knees. This town is known for it, he added. Even outside the confines of the van Rabbit could still hear the air whistling in and out of his nose. They were sitting at a corner table in an array of small plastic chairs suited for children. There were a few other families crowded around tables, a group of workers up front. A day's worth of trash lay strewn all over the concrete floor—scraps of food, dirty squares of coarse gray paper that the restaurant kept piled on the tables as napkins. Shall we order it? Viet lit up a cigarette. Tao reached over and took a cigarette out of his pack without asking. Linh didn't know what Viet was talking about. Yes, she said eagerly.

Their food came quickly. Bowls of rice. A plate of morning glories for Qui. A steaming bowl of *pho ga*. Viet slurped the soup down loudly in the way Vietnamese men did, the noise like a drowning man struggling for air. The teenaged girl came over with the tray. There were a few greasy vegetables arranged around the meat. Viet spit on the floor, then picked up his chopsticks and began portioning it out. Qui shook her head. Tao accepted a plate but kept smoking, blowing the smoke out through her pursed lips before inhaling it in through her nose as if to make it last twice as long.

Rabbit ate just enough to be polite. Do you like it, Viet asked. She nodded. It's salty, she said. Viet nodded. But tender, he said. Yes, said Linh, lightly pulling a piece of meat off the bone. This little one eats like a man, laughed Viet. He reached across the table and put more meat on Linh's plate. When she finished it, he spooned out some more.

Linh wiped her lips on a slip of paper and threw it on the floor. The teenaged girl pointed her through a doorway at the back. When Linh didn't return after ten minutes, Rabbit went to look for her. Rabbit had been sitting with her back to the other diners. As she got up she noticed them staring. Some of the men were eyeing Qui. Others sat watching the smoke scroll endlessly through Tao's face. One young boy sat studying Rabbit and her map of freckles. Chào buổi tối ông cụ, Rabbit said. Evening, child, an old man replied. Rabbit could see he didn't have any teeth.

The bathroom was in a stone building out back. When she entered, a cord hit her in the forehead. She pulled it and a bare bulb flickered on, the light scarcely stronger than a candle. The room was mostly empty with a concrete floor and a trough running the length of the wall. In a corner there was a water spigot and a plastic bucket with a small pail. Quickly Rabbit approached the trough and pulled down her pants. When she was finished, she filled the bucket and poured water on the spot where she'd squatted.

Back outside the moon was beginning to rise over the trees. Linh, she called. She could see the light from a fire dancing in the distance behind a wooden shack. She went toward it, almost stepping in something along the way. Rabbit bent down for a closer look. Scattered on the ground were several shallow tubs filled with water, the plastic tubs like something one might wash dishes in. In each, two or three big black fish were swimming in circles. One of the fish was too big to swim, its back sticking up into the air, the fish lying in just a few inches of water, the sound of its gasping strangely human. I hear you, Rabbit said.

Linh was standing by the fire, her eyes as if stuck open, the dimples erased from her cheeks. There was a black cauldron in the center of the flames. A young boy poked the fire with a stick. It was happening off to the side. Again and again a shirtless man lifted what looked like a tire iron wrapped in a towel over his head. At first Rabbit thought he was beating an old blanket, the dust rising in the air from the pale and dingy thing heaped at his feet. A few small children squatted around the fire without pants. One child seemed in charge of the others. In the firelight the muscles of the man's chest glistened with effort.

Rabbit put her arm around Linh and tried to pull her away, but Linh was rooted to the spot. The sound of the tire iron whizzed through the air as the thing lay whimpering in the dirt. Surprisingly there was no blood pooling around the body. The man was careful to avoid the head and set the hot blood loose. Mostly he worked the haunches, the ribs, the sound of each dull thud strangely wet. Rabbit couldn't believe it was still alive. Its back was obviously broken though its hind legs kept twitching.

Then the teenaged girl who had waited on their table was standing beside them, her hair a shade of gold in the firelight. It's a local secret, she said. It's what makes the meat so tender. The man beat it until it stopped whimpering. He put the iron down and wiped his brow. The dead dog lay in the moonlight on the edge of the fire. Rabbit imagined the dog was nothing more than a skin filled with dark soup. It was the ancient method of tenderizing meat. If you beat something to death, the softened meat separated from the bone even before you cooked it.

Linh reached for Rabbit's hand. On their way back to the table they passed the tubs with the fish circling in the dark, the sound of the one gasping fish still tinged with the human. You don't hear the suffering of animals, do you, said Linh. Overhead the moon hung like a mouth. Anyone can hear that, said Rabbit.

When they got back, the others were waiting by the van. Linh pointed to something across the street. What's that, she said. Viet took a small flashlight out of the glove compartment. Okay, captain, he said, handing it to her as they all crossed the road, Tao with a fresh cigarette clamped between her lips.

The object was perched on a wooden post. Linh turned the light on it. A bat went sailing over their heads. It was a temple the size of a dollhouse, the structure perfect in every detail. Linh ran the light over it. Rabbit could see it was painted with red lacquer and topped with a black tile roof adorned with a stone dragon running along the peak. There were tiny Chinese characters painted over the doors and windows in gold like the temples in Cholon or even like the Temple of Literature in Hanoi. Rabbit looked closer. Inside there was a bowl full of rice and a small trough filled with sand and the charred remnants of joss sticks. Dried husks of a few dead water beetles lay scattered on the polished floor.

Qui clapped her hands together three times and bowed her head. When she finished, she began picking the joss sticks out of the sand and sweeping up the insect husks with her pale fingers. Did someone die here, asked Linh. Rabbit could barely hear the question through the tumult in her head, her ears throbbing. Voice upon voice upon voice. It's a refuge for wandering ghosts, Viet said. Anyone who dies away from home out in the open. They can come here at night and rest, he added. Qui put a hand out to steady Rabbit. The voices were so loud Rabbit thought her eardrums might burst. She leaned on Qui as they walked back to the van.

Within an hour they came to the Ben Hai. The moon was up, the light shining on the river. A monument stood next to the riverbank, an obelisk recessed in a circle. At the front of the statue a worker stood in a Soviet-style uniform. Let's keep going, said Linh. Viet looked in the rearview at Rabbit. She nodded. Okay, said Viet. They continued south. The 17th parallel, once everything and nothing, grew distant and farther behind them.

They were coming up on the first stone gate into Hue, the ancient capital. Linh was sleeping in the front seat, in the darkness her face smooth as porcelain. Gently Viet put a hand on her shoulder. The moon gleamed on the Perfume River like a layer of silver. Let her sleep, said Rabbit. The sound of Linh's breath sawed in and out of her mouth. She should be seeing this, said Viet. All Vietnamese should see the great works of the emperors. There will be plenty to see when we get there, said Rabbit. There will be nothing worth seeing when we get there, Viet mumbled. What, Rabbit said, but he didn't repeat himself.

They crossed over a narrow bridge and turned left. On the corner a few cyclo drivers were stretched out asleep on their passenger seats. Within minutes the van floated past Flag Tower.

The whole structure appeared surprisingly flat like a grounded barge. Even in the night the flag of Vietnam was lit up bright as day. They say that's the biggest Vietnamese flag in the world, said Viet loudly. There was hardly any breeze. The flag hung limp, but its size was still evident. The one yellow star in the field of red, the sun and the blood of the people.

The ancient Imperial City closed at sundown. Even from the street Rabbit could catch glimpses through openings in the wall that ran the length of it. Most of the buildings had been constructed during the Nguyen Dynasty a few hundred years before. During the war the Vietcong had occupied Hue for four bloody weeks. The American bombings that retook the city destroyed much of it, the Forbidden Purple City completely razed. Recently Hue had been designated a World Heritage Site even though there were places where there was nothing left to see, not even rubble.

They passed another of the grand stone gates leading into the Citadel. It's magnificent, said Viet. The streets were empty, the stonework adorned with intricate carved designs, mythical animals covered in scales with the haunches of lions and the faces of unicorns. Beyond that is the Forbidden Purple City, said Viet. I hear it was even more beautiful than the one in China. He slowed the van down. It must be more beautiful, he said, because the foreigners call it by its rightful name. Purple after the North Star, which was the Emperor's celestial home in the sky. Viet's voice went soft and dreamy. The Forbidden Purple City, his home on earth.

There were women born in the Forbidden Purple City who were never allowed to leave, said Tao. Her intonation was flat, but Rabbit knew rage when she heard it. Through the darkness her words filled the van. Rabbit didn't turn around to look. She knew if she did, she would see Tao's face still as an icon, only her lips moving, a lump of gum tucked in her cheek. My great-

great-grandmother was one of them, Tao said. A woman with feet small as fists. They say she had to be carried everywhere. Viet stepped on the gas, gunning the engine as if trying to outrun something.

From the backseat Tao kept talking. When the emperor died, his concubines were killed and buried with him, she said. Everything he would need in the afterlife heaped with him in the earth. Trusted advisers. Favorite horses. Even illegitimate children. For a moment Linh shifted in her sleep.

My family comes from the stars, Tao said. I am the last of us on earth. Ridiculous, said Viet. In the rearview Rabbit could see the anger brewing in his eyes. Tao continued untroubled. My great-great-grandfather was a eunuch, she said. As a child, his father didn't have the money for a surgeon, so he took up the knife himself. In the firelight the boy's face was stoic even as the sweat dripped down his chin. Afterward his mother rose in the middle of the night and slipped out to the trash heap by the animal pens to find them. She wrapped them up in a soft cloth and placed them in a box, which she gave Great-Great-Grandfather, who kept them through the years as he passed his examinations and was accepted into the imperial household, his body not a threat to the emperor. His mother told him when he died, he would be buried with them. He would be whole.

Rabbit found herself growing sleepy. In the seat next to her Qui had closed her eyes. The van floated along like a boat gliding downstream. They say he loved her from the very moment he saw her, said Tao. The girl with the feet small as fists. They say her feet smelled like roses and that she was the favorite of the man destined to become the sixth emperor of Vietnam. The other girls kept their feet bound and spritzed with cologne to hide the unnatural smell of bloodless flesh, their feet discolored. But Great-Great-Grandmother's feet were pink as health, her long black hair sweeping the ground when she sat, her tiny feet resplendent as flowers. She never wrapped them a day in her life.

You are ignorant, said Viet. All the old families in Vietnam make outrageous ancestral claims. You lost everything in the war because it was never yours to begin with, he said. Tao continued as if he'd never spoken. He was her attendant, she said. He gave her baths, braided her hair, wrung out her menstrual cloths. One night she caught him staring at her in the mirror as he oiled her shoulders, his eyes burning. I think you are not what you appear to be, said Great-Great-Grandmother. He made his face into a blank slate. If you are honest and hardworking and you believe in something strongly enough, she said, it will come to you. Then she covered her shoulders.

Great-Great-Grandfather gave himself a year. Each night he opened the box his mother had handed him and unwrapped the soft cloth, kissing the shriveled skin and holding them up to the starlight in his palms. In the purple light of the North Star, the skin looked fleshy again, warm to the touch.

It happened one year to the day after Great-Great-Grandmother had first noticed his look in the mirror. At the same hour of the same day they lay together for the first and only time. It was she who beckoned him into her chambers, she who lay down on her back on the red and black silk duvet and pulled him into her, whispering have you wanted it enough? The room filled with a soft purple light. In the window the stars salted the sky. For both of them the pleasure was as it should be, Great-Great-Grandfather gasping at the simplicity of it. That you could want something badly enough and your disfigured body could respond.

When Great-Great-Grandmother began to show, she cloaked herself in rich tunics, the fabric enough to clothe ten women. The one who would become emperor never noticed, his mind full of other things, the empress dowager and the regents plotting for power. He never noticed the changes in his concubine's weight even in the brief moments when he was with the girl with the redolent feet, her body swelling and then unswelling months later, her breasts loose with milk. Her lover never noticed even through August of 1883 when he became the sixth emperor of Vietnam, the Son of Heaven, his emperorship lasting only four months.

In the end the French navy was too much. At the signing ceremony, he could feel his ancestors crowding the room. What choice did he have? The French had made it clear they would keep blockading the Perfume River, bombarding the coast. His signature felt like ashes in his mouth. Sign and become a French protectorate or be destroyed.

What an emperor will do for his people, keeping them from the worst possible harm. Even when his imperial court turns on him. Even when his own regents demand it. In the end you do what you have to do and you do it with honor. The Son of Heaven lifted the cup and drank. Opium and vinegar. Like so many emperors before him, he felt the poison burn all the way down.

But the story doesn't stop with the suicide of the emperor. In the days that follow the entire household is killed, all those loyal to the Son of Heaven. They say my great-great-grandparents drank from the same cup, Great-Great-Grandmother tottering to the spot on her own two feet when their turn came, Great-Great-Grandfather standing beside her with his treasure tucked away in a small velvet bag hung around his neck. The sudden realization as the poison aerated his blood that he'd always been whole.

With her finger Tao lightly traced the outline of the moon on the window. But their daughter, my great-grandmother, had been smuggled out of the palace months before, she said. My great-grandmother, a little girl with a stony face and the sweetest-smelling feet. She was raised in an orphanage. Rabbit could see a vein beginning to bulge in the side of Viet's temple. Then how do you know any of it is true, he hissed. Even in the dark Rabbit could see his face twisting in strange ways, the dark blood lumping under the skin. She watched as it grew bigger and bigger, the vein knuckling on the side of his face to the size of two, three, four fingers, five, and counting. How do you know, Viet screamed, the lump bright purple and half the size of his head.

Rabbit bolted upright in her seat. Outside a series of paddies floated by, the rice gently waving as if underwater. Inside the van was silent. Up front Viet peered off up the road. Tao was slumped asleep in the back, mouth closed, the moon in the sky following them south.

Hours later, just before dawn, after they had walked the muddy fields they had come all that way to stand in, Rabbit will see for herself. It will happen on her way back to the van that will carry them back to the thirty-six streets of Hanoi's Old Quarter, the portraits of the dead rolling through the district. As Rabbit, more tired than she has ever been, is about to climb in the van, she will look over at Tao standing in a nearby stream, Tao humming to herself, face calm as a cloud as she balances on one foot while washing the other, each of Tao's feet perfectly formed but small as fists. Even from where Rabbit is standing she will catch the scent on the wind. Tao rubbing the dirt from her soles, her feet fragrant as roses.

From the Latin for "terrible," "cruel." Atrox, atrocis. When did the word come to take on such scale? Endless pits gouged in the earth. The Americans in the hamlet of My Lai, some of them shooting themselves in the feet to get out of it. The South Vietnamese with their tiger cages, their filing a man's teeth down to the gums. And what happens if we don't remember? What happens if we never knew? Too many of us are here in the dark because in the rush and clamor of blood the third reptilian brain takes over, the one that says I do not recognize anything of myself in you, and so you are less than nothing.

On the way back to Hanoi, Rabbit was surprised by how many wandering ghost temples they passed. In the daylight each one was clearly visible. A few of them looked weather-beaten but still intact. The intricate scrollwork flared off their roofs in the Chinese style. In the night she hadn't realized there were so many, each one a sanctuary for the dead. How long do they stay, said Linh, turning around in her seat. Rabbit was tired. She could barely bring herself to answer. It had taken them thirteen hours to get to My Kan. It would take them another thirteen hours to get home. As long as they need to. Qui looked at Linh and nodded. In the front seat Linh turned to Viet. Uncle, she said quietly, please pull over. He glanced in the rearview. I will find us a spot, he said. Eventually they came to a banyan tree growing by the side of the road, the one tree sprouting several trunks as if it were a whole grove. Viet pulled over and parked the van in its shade. After the others climbed out, Qui pulled the curtains shut and unbuttoned her shirt. Rabbit was so weak from the few hours spent in My Kan she could barely lift her head.

Listen. There are things we know that we cannot say. For example, if you were to ask him, Viet will say he has never been married, that he has never had a child, but in the last room of the museum down in Saigon there are shelves lined with jars, pale bleached things held in suspension. The room is overwhelmed with them, in places the jars two deep, each different in its own way. Some contain two-headed cows, others dogs and cats with massive deformities—prehensile tails, the stumps of extra heads growing out of odd places, one a fetal pig, but the moony thing has flippers. Work your way toward the case that contains human fetuses, somebody's baby preserved in formaldehyde. The children are grotesque and seem to shine, their skin luminous and unfinished. Many are conjoined, some at the head, others in the body, their shapes alphabetic and strange. Because of the long years of defoliants, unnatural clouds sprayed without mercy, ours is a land with the highest rates of deformity. How these creatures must have killed their mothers, torn them open in the long hot night of their births. Rest assured that there is no one in there, each one just a vessel, nothing more. Pick a jar off the shelf and clasp it in your arms. Sing to it. Rock it to sleep, the liquid softly sloshing like blood through the heart. Despite their monstrousness, they are unmistakably human; one with his intestines on the outside of his body floats sucking his thumb.

THERE WERE STILL TOURISTS WANDERING THROUGH THE OLD
quarter when the van arrived back in the city a little after ten at
night. The humidity hung in the air, the mugginess like being
trapped in a net. Viet turned onto Hang Giay. Linh waved at the
old woman on the corner selling postcards and potato chips. A
small fire burned in a basket at her feet.

None of them noticed the shiny black car parked across the
alley, its windows tinted, the great wooden doors leading into
the courtyard reflected in the car's glossy paint, the strange car
the color of night. None of them gave it any thought as they
arrived home, the car simply melting into the landscape.

Viet pulled up out front. The wooden doors looked darker
than usual. Sometimes the doors still seemed like they were part
of a living tree. On occasion the wood sprouted burls, grew
new knots, an occasional twig forking out of the grain, the twig
often topped with a small green leaf. Each morning the guard on
duty checked the doors for growths, taking out a pocketknife to
prune any.

Qui slid the van door open and climbed out, her white hair
briefly scraping the ground. She fished the iron key out of her
pocket and unlocked the gate. Linh finished putting her shoes
on and jumped out of the front seat. Qui gave her a look. Linh
sighed and turned to bow to Viet, placing one hand in the palm
of the other. Uncle, she said. Thank you for expanding my
knowledge of the world. He nodded. Yes, thank you, said Rabbit. Before climbing out of the van, she reached forward and
patted his shoulder. For an instant she flashed on a woman in
horrible pain, a body stuck inside another body, the pelvis starting to crack, Viet with both hands up in the darkness all the way
past the wrist. Quickly Rabbit pulled her hand away. Thank
you, she said again, then climbed out.

In the courtyard the parakeets began to caw the few words
they spoke to everyone. *Xin chao,* said the female. Hello, said

Linh. She reached her hand out, and the bird landed on her finger. Where is the other lady, said the male, the one named Apple? Rabbit looked around. Already she could hear the van motoring back down the street. She ran out through the wooden doors and looked in all directions. There was just the old woman on the corner with her small fire going. Rabbit rubbed her eyes. Tao was nowhere to be seen, though the faint smell of cigarette smoke hung in the air.

Rabbit closed the doors behind her, the sound like joints filled with water. Isn't that how you prefer it, said the male bird, no word of thanks, no gratitude? Rabbit nodded. No, you're right, she said, as if trying to convince herself.

Linh pointed to something in the sky. Is that the North Star? Rabbit and Qui both looked. They were surprised to see anything at all, the thing faintly purple and twinkling. No, it's a satellite, Rabbit said. There's too much light here for stars. Qui clapped her hands. It's bedtime, said Rabbit. The three of them walked into the house. I never see anything, said Linh petulantly, her fatigue obvious. The three of them climbed the stairs. Be thankful for that, said Rabbit.

Even before she entered her own room, Rabbit could see a long shadow quivering on the floor. Not tonight, she thought, but there he was, the scratch rivering down his cheek. He was sitting on her bed, his legs knotted in the lotus position. His hands were in the fear-not position, both palms facing her, his right pointed to the sky, his left straight down. In the moonlight everything took on the same silvery hue as the room inside her head. You may never see me again, Son said flatly. Rabbit's heart went cold. He never lied.

Quietly she closed the door. Tell me what to do, she said. He got up off the bed. Life will decide, he said. He turned to her and smiled. She was twenty-four years old. He was still a child. She went to him and got down on her knees. He put his arms around her. Outside the moon had slipped behind a bank of clouds, but the room was still strangely bright. It took her a moment to realize. The light was coming from him.

Rabbit closed her eyes. Gently Son kissed her on the forehead, on each cheek, then on the mouth. With his fingers he traced a path through her freckles. For the second time in a lifetime, Rabbit's heart flooding.

What she will always remember long after the moment is over: the image of his hands in the fear-not mudra as he sat on her bed. The hand position derived from the story of the Buddha's stroking the head of an elephant sent to kill Him, the elephant maddened by alcohol, but the great beast falling to its knees at the feet of the Buddha because of the Enlightened One's radiance, His right palm open toward the sky signaling there is nothing to fear, His left lowered to pet the fallen head of His killer.

When she opened her eyes, Son was gone. The sliding door leading out to the balcony was open. There was just the taste of honey on her lips.

Qui knocked on the door and poked her head in. The female parakeet was sitting on her shoulder. The bird's color looked startling in contrast to the white of Qui's hair. Lady, said the parakeet. Are you all right? Yes, said Rabbit. She was still down on her knees. Tell the truth, said the bird. When Rabbit didn't answer, Qui entered the room. She closed the sliding door, untied the mosquito net hanging from the ceiling, and draped it around the bed, then helped Rabbit up off the floor, undressing her before tucking her in and pulling the sheet up to her knees. Close your eyes, said the bird softly. Qui began stroking her hair. After a few minutes Rabbit reached for her. Light from the darkness. Comfort beyond anything imaginable, the sweetness erasing any bitterness she'd felt. The bird began to sing:

Beloved, stay with me. Do not go home!
Your leaving makes me weep inside
And the collar of my dress is wet with tears as if it has rained.
Oh my beloved, stay. Do not go home!

When Rabbit gets out of the van, she can hear bells ringing. In the distance the night sky is lit up with fireworks, the sky softly purple like a bruise. They are ten miles south of the City of Peace in the hamlet of My Kan. As they move about there is the feeling of walking through water, everything slow and deliberate, the earth spongy under one's feet. Look at me, says Linh. She holds her arms out like a tightrope walker and tiptoes around as if she weighs nothing at all.

So, says Tao. Her voice is casual as if they have come all this way on a whim. In the sky a full moon sits at twelve o'clock with a halo around it, the halo so sharp and clear one could mistake it for a second moon. What happens next? The smoke billows in and out of her face without end, though she doesn't appear to be holding a cigarette. Shhh, says Rabbit. She is already turning and walking out into the middle of the field. Overhead the dual moons shine like a double-yolked egg.

Rabbit stops and twirls around three-hundred and sixty degrees. Flatness in every direction. A small creek gurgles by the roadside. Nothing. No landmarks. No houses. No animals. Something is wrong with the earth and everything smells scorched. She twirls around again only faster. This time as she moves she catches glimpses of figures slipping over the horizon. The sound of fireworks intensifies. The burning smell gets closer. She twirls faster. The field fills with voices. Anger and fear. She is spinning so fast the world is a blur. Something swoops down out of the sky. Rabbit stops. Through the dizziness she can see the ruins of a building in the purple light. When she regains her equilibrium, she begins to walk toward it.

It's a Catholic church. She can tell by the broken steeple lying on its side, the roof mostly missing, exposed ceiling beams running crosswise. Bowls of dried grass lie in piles where things have nested. Other pieces of the building are scattered in the tall weeds. An iron bell sleeps hidden in the brush. When she raps it with her knuckles, the metal rings as expected. Tap it twice, the metal doesn't sound at all.

Rabbit picks her way inside. The wooden floor is cracked and furred with plant growth and animal droppings. By the door is a marble font filled with debris and a single plastic shoe. Nothing is left inside. The windows are all missing, just one shard of blue glass hanging in an alcove over the altar. Probably the remnant of someone's holy robe or maybe the ocean somebody walked on.

Then Rabbit sees her. A small girl is standing in the doorway where the sacristy should be to the right of the altar. The door itself is missing and the opening leads directly outside. The girl is no taller than Linh and completely naked, her impassive face smeared with dirt and maybe worse. The child's ribs run up and down the sides of her chest like a ladder. There were more than four hundred of us in here, says the girl. She runs a finger through the filth on the altar. Though Catholic, we still celebrated Tet, she says. We were going to begin our feast after mass when the first knock sounded on the door. The last thing I ever ate was *banh chung*. Do you like *banh chung*? Rabbit pictures the small green squares of rice and bean curd wrapped in banana leaves. Very much, Rabbit says. The girl smiles.

Moonlight pours through the empty windows. The dirt and grime blaze silver, a magical dust coating everything. There were fewer than a hundred of us when it started, the girl says. We were giving each other the sign of peace. Even when the others began to arrive and beg us to let them in, people were still greeting the new arrivals with the traditional salutations. Security. Health. Happiness. May you live a hundred years. Gracious wishes for the new spring. Peace be with you. Behind them the night lit up with fires.

The first ones who came were a mother and her three children. The woman was what my father called shell-shocked. It was the little boy who told us they were killing the monks in

Hue, lining them up and marching them outside the city. I still remember something he said. "I saw the monks in their orange robes floating peacefully along like suns." My mother pulled me to her. One of the elders said out of the mouths of babes.

We took refuge in this church for nineteen days. After ten days there was nothing left to eat. The *banh chung* all gone. The fish and the chickens and the two pigs. More and more people coming. Telling us they were rounding up the civil service workers, doctors, lawyers, teachers, the intellectuals. After the monks they went after the families of the southern soldiers, then anyone they suspected of having ties to the Americans. The girl puts her palms facedown in the grime on the altar. It was the Year of the Monkey, she says. Monkey is a trickster. Firmly the girl presses her filthy hands on her chest. When she pulls them away there are handprints on her skin, fingers splayed like the twinkling of stars. She smiles. Nothing was as it seemed, she says.

The northern soldiers finally found us. They told us to come out. They said they wouldn't hurt us. They said they'd just send the bad ones among us to reeducation camps and then we would all be brothers and sisters. For nine days we had been praying to the Lady, someone among us always reciting a Hail Mary. When one person would tire, someone else would take up the thread, the words like a constant river. The girl stands drawing on her body with the dirt from the altar. She traces a circle around her belly button, and through the open roof the halo around the moon intensifies.

The soldiers threw a grenade through one of the stained-glass windows, she says. Three people died. She looks at Rabbit. Would you rather die instantly or piece by piece? In the sky the two moons are beginning to merge. Instantly, says Rabbit. The girl considers this.

When they took us outside, my father still had some old C4

on him. We had been using it to cook inside the church. Months before my brother had found a brick of it along a trail. We used it the way the Americans did. We'd shape small balls and light it on fire. The Americans were always heating their rations and leaving the metal tins lying around. We'd use the C4 when we didn't have any firewood. The flames aren't the color of regular fire, you know. The girl stops to think. I don't know how to describe it, she says. Almost a gray-blue.

The girl claps her hands together, sending the dust on her fingers up into a small sparkling cloud. As she breathes her ribs expand and contract like bellows. They shot Ba right away, she says. Afterward they said he was an American stooge. The C4 proved it. Why would an innocent man have the trappings of the capitalist pig on his person? The soldier shot Ba through the neck, but I know he meant to shoot him in the head. His aim was bad because he was weak and hungry. I remember he didn't look much older than my brother. When he shot Ba, none of us screamed. I don't know why. Maybe we were too hungry. I just stood watching the life leak out of him.

The girl stops talking. She turns her head as if listening for something. The moon is a solid mass in the sky. The girl looks at Rabbit and backs out the open door of the sacristy, the dust glowing on her body. For a moment all Rabbit can see are handprints and a circle glittering in the doorway. By the time Rabbit gets there, the girl is gone.

In the field behind the church Rabbit can hear the sound of running water. In the distance a creek cuts along the edge of the land. Rabbit begins to walk toward it. She takes her shoes off and walks barefoot. The earth feels spongy beneath her feet. Her soles are stained a dark red, but with what she doesn't know.

By the creek, Rabbit lets the history wash over her. The occupation of Hue and the surrounding countryside lasts a month. At first the Communists are almost reasonable, thinking they can hold the city. When it becomes evident they can't, they begin gouging bottomless pits in the earth.

Then Rabbit hears it, the vein throbbing under her feet. What she has come here to find. She thinks back to the Black Tai in Anne-Marie. She can feel the nausea rising in her throat. It's like nothing she has ever experienced. One could walk right over the spot and think nothing of it. In this tiny hamlet of My Kan, the number of people killed is three times the number of people who lived there, four hundred and twenty-eight dead, and they're all right here where Rabbit is standing, though the government in Hanoi would deny it.

Rabbit can feel the earth being shoveled over them. Many of them are still alive when it happens, everywhere people drowning in earth. A handful will survive this moment, carrying the taste of dirt in their mouths with them forever. Toward the end two little girls are thrown in hand in hand, one shadowing the other, both their faces still as stone, one with a bullet through the stomach, the other intact, their feet small as the rose before it blossoms. The girls are obviously sisters, perhaps even twins, their eyes starry as the night sky from which they come. The young soldier in charge misbelieves what he sees, maddened by the blood and gore. I've already shot that one, he thinks. Look. Her own ghost already walks at her side.

From here it all grows stranger. Everywhere the dolorous ringing of bells. A roomful of jars filled with two-headed babies. Women in red *ao dai* flying through the air. A man playing a bone flute, the instrument as long as the man is tall, the music like the crying of seabirds, their voices calling Lamb of God, you take away the sins of the world. Then Rabbit sees Her. It is the only time She has ever appeared to Rabbit in any form. The Lady robed in what appears to be a burlap sack, Her thousand arms wilted like the petals of a dead flower. In the sky the moon has separated again, the two moons distinct and some distance apart, the whole sky between them, each one shining in a different direction, light falling on opposing paths. Then the Lady arranges each of Her hands in the fear-not position, five hundred palms blossoming skyward, the others pointing to the earth, Her hands radiating from Her body like the brilliance of a star. Rabbit can feel her mouth filling with dirt. Everything grows dark. The last thing she sees is a small green bird sitting on each of the Lady's many splendid shoulders.

In your travails on earth, do not forget the wisdom of the animals. Even the Conquering Buddha lived numerous animal lives as the Monkey King, the Deer King, the Goose King, the King of the Elephants, the King of the Rats.

RABBIT OPENED HER EYES. THE DISTANT RINGING OF BELLS
lingered in the air. The heat in the room was unbearable. She
could hear the wood swelling in the door jambs, tears raining
down the mirror. Moonlight poured through the window hot
as sunbeams. She threw back the sheets and got out of bed. For
the moment nothing else mattered. After the darkness she'd witnessed in My Kan, she needed to see it, needed it to rise to the
surface of the water with its ageless face and wrinkled carapace
and bestow its good fortune on her. She pulled on some clothes
and slipped downstairs and out into the courtyard.

From the color of the night she guessed it was well after
two. In the courtyard there was the smell of lemons. Something
stirred in one of the trees. Lady, said the male parakeet, hopping
out on a branch. May I serve you? Yes, said Rabbit. Swiftly the
bird flew down off the bough and landed on her shoulder.

The strange black car with the tinted windows was still
parked outside the gate, but she paid it no notice. For once the
great wooden doors swung open silently as if oiled. On the
right-hand door a small twig shot straight out of the wood, a
furled green bud just at the tip where a leaf would open with
first light.

Rabbit turned left on Hang Buom, the Street of Sails, and
headed east to Hang Ngang. Everywhere people slept out on
the sidewalk. On hot summer nights families dragged their mats
down out of the upper floors of apartment buildings to sleep out
in the open. At the end of the Street of Beautiful Women, Rabbit could see the water shining through the trees. The city was
preternaturally quiet. Nothing moved, not a leaf or a blade of
grass. Even the few fires they'd passed along the way burned as if
frozen, their flames scarcely grabbing at the air. Rabbit began to
wonder if something else were at play, if the world had stopped
and she and the bird were walking outside of time. What if it

doesn't come to you, said the parakeet. Then that will be my answer, said Rabbit.

A couple was sitting on one of the stone benches beside the lake. The woman was straddling the man's lap, her dress hiked up over her thighs. Rabbit breathed a little easier. Time had not stopped for these two lovers on the stone bench, each of them rubbing their arms up and down the other's back. Rabbit thought of the palest shade of blue, a memory of a man's ring on her skin. On the bench the woman threw her head back and moaned.

On the other side of the Bridge of the Rising Sun she could see Jade Island where Ngoc Son Pagoda rose just behind the trees. A little farther down the path she chose a bench and sat down, the smell of lemon just at her ear. I will never leave you, said the parakeet. Hush, she said. I know. Rabbit began to scan the lake. Even when you should, you won't.

They could see things floating on the surface of the water. Plastic bags, empty soda cans, candy wrappers, all manner of trash blowing down out of the Old Quarter and into Hoan Kiem Lake. In the moonlight everything looked like something else. They sat watching the surface for any changes. After a while Rabbit said do you know the legend of the lake? No, lied the bird. Please teach me.

There isn't much to it, Rabbit said. The Golden Turtle God gave young Prince Le Loi a magical sword called Heaven's Will. The prince used it to defeat the Chinese. When the battle was over, the Turtle God reappeared and snatched the sword out of the prince's hand and carried it back to the watery kingdom of the gods. And that's why they call it Lake of the Restored Sword, said the parakeet, but just then in the water the animal lifted its great head, neck ridged where the thick skin folded up on itself, its aged face somehow full of both benediction and indifference.

The turtle moved as if bearing a great weight. In the moonlight the animal was as long as a man. As it came forward, it wagged its ponderous head from side to side, swimming right up to the edge of the lake and stopping as if to speak. The animal floated in the dark water, its eyes glistening. Lady, is this all you wanted, said the parakeet. I don't know, said Rabbit.

It was a soft-shelled turtle, its carapace without scales, its back leathery rather than infused with the intricate series of plates like its hard-shelled cousins. All throughout Asia the soft-shelled turtle was preferred for eating, its shell smooth, almost pliable at the edges where the upper shell met the lower shell. In Chinese medicine the turtle was associated with the liver and kidneys. Nobody knew how old the turtle of the Lake of the Restored Sword was. Some of the local people said a hundred years. Some said it swam these very waters two thousand years ago when the Buddha walked the earth.

Uncle, said Rabbit. She remembered how as a child she addressed everybody as *em*, even her elders. The turtle extended its head, its wrinkles disappearing as the skin grew taut, its head and neck almost annelid in nature, not the bulbous head of a tortoise but something more like an eel, smooth and gelid. In the moonlight she could see the open sores on its back, each one the size of a dinner plate, the inflamed skin pink and suppurating. It's dying, whispered the parakeet. No, said Rabbit. It's just manifesting the world it lives in.

Rabbit sat for a long time simply looking at the animal, the moon casting everything in a silvery light. The local people believed a sighting of the turtle would bring you good luck. At New Year's the shores of Hoan Kiem Lake were crowded with people straining for a glimpse. And if I never see you again, thought Rabbit, would I still be me? Nearby a fish jumped in the water.

Suddenly a moonbeam came pouring through the trees. For an instant the turtle appeared healed of every sore, the skin of its back smooth and healthy looking. Then the animal retracted its head and turned to swim back toward the center of the lake. As it began to submerge down into the dark waters, Rabbit could see the sores still oozing on its back.

Lady, said the parakeet. Rabbit opened her eyes. Had she fallen asleep? The moon was shining in the heavens, another moon on the water. It was almost like the dream she'd just had—two moons at opposite ends of the sky.

Someone was sitting on the other end of the bench. Neither she nor the parakeet had seen him sit down. He turned to her and smiled. Even in the shadow of the trees she could see it. I have been waiting for you, the man said. If we are to have any chance at all, we must leave tonight.

Rabbit rubbed her eyes. After all this time. More than half her life. It was true. Life is a wheel. A small red diamond shining on the edge of the man's scalp.

*Life is a wheel. The way we end up where we begin. From here every-
thing rises—the worn path, the moon with its long bright ears. Imagine
water traveling back up into the sky, the sound of it climbing like a question. Who would we be if we had stayed?*

LINH WAS STARTING TO STIR IN THE BACKSEAT. THERE WERE goose bumps on her arms, the AC on the highest setting even though the sun was still rising. Rabbit didn't know what to tell her when she woke up. In the rush to leave they had left almost all of their possessions behind. Rabbit herself wasn't sure where they were going or how they would get there. For the past few hours the moon followed their every move, but it was starting to fade. Outside, the terraces were scattered with dry rice, the hills stubbled with stalks. Dry rice grew easily. The local people prepared the land by burning it and then threw the seed out on the bare ground. The yield was only a quarter of the harvest from a traditional paddy, but it was the way people had grown rice for thousands of years when traditional paddies weren't possible.

They were almost to Nam Xoi. Tu said there was a small gatehouse on each side of the Laotian border with a soldier in it, and they wouldn't need any paperwork. The soldier would simply check to make sure they weren't smuggling any illegal timber from the old forests, that there were no small logs tied to the car's undercarriage.

In the east the sky was a soft pink. In the backseat Qui sat bright as the moon. When they saw each other for the first time, she and Tu had simply bowed to one another before hurrying together up the stairs to gather Linh from her bed and carry her down to the car. My contact is waiting for us in Vientiane, Tu had said breathlessly as if there were nothing else to explain. I don't know how long he'll wait. Qui's face remained smooth and untroubled, as if she'd always known that one day he would arrive on their doorstep and whisk them away.

The first hour on the road he told them everything about his years in a relocation camp on the Bataan Peninsula and how the Philippine government was in the process of closing the camp and sending the refugees home, repatriating people in, of all places, Cambodia, where the new cease-fire was holding.

Through the years he had moved all throughout Asia. Always east. After the boat hit the mine, he and some of the others had drifted on the wreckage to an island where the people robbed them before calling the authorities. He spent the first four years in a UN refugee camp in Thailand, then another three in Malaysia before being moved to Morong. I thought you were dead, he said. He looked over at Rabbit and tried to smile. An, Phuong, and Sang went straight from Thailand to the U.S. because An had a cousin in Orange County, he said. In the early morning light Rabbit could see what the effort to smile was costing him. Me, I'm former Vietcong, he said. The Americans will never let me in.

Rabbit could sense Qui in the backseat hanging on Tu's every word. Qui was even more beautiful than the night she had taken Tu in her arms on the floor of the floating house in Ba Nuoc. Behind the wheel Tu looked straight out the window, but somehow his eyes weren't on the road. For the moment the rising sun and the setting moon were both in the sky at once. There were thousands of people in the camps waiting for a slip of paper, Tu whispered, the birthmark on the edge of his hair shining like a ruby. Almost twenty years, half my life. He glanced at Rabbit. I still get letters from An in California. He sends money. Tu took a deep breath. All these years so many of us trying to get out of Vietnam, he said. An says the American people don't even know.

With Tu just an arm's length away, Rabbit didn't need to ask what had happened to the others. If she closed her eyes and let herself drift off into the light, her ears softly throbbing, she could see Hai floating in the water with one of his legs blown off. Phuong screaming uncontrollably. The doctor's wife and the little girl slipping under the surface without a sound, the wife still working her necklace of beads. Pieces of the boat burning in the fog. In the vision Rabbit couldn't see Duc anywhere. Just the boat's steering wheel floating on the ocean, Arun's body

drifting nearby, a smile fixed on his face. Three of the Cambodians were still alive and trying to lash together large pieces of
wreckage. Rabbit scanned the vision for Huyen, but she knew
that was how the old woman would have wanted it. The instant
erasure. No fuss.

Then the days dragging on for those left living. The sun burning them all until their skin bubbled. Phuong and Sang clinging
to each other. Phuong moaning I want to die and Sang holding
tighter to her mother all the while in the rags of her red *ao dai*.
An with a look of madness, grieving for his lost son. None of
the remaining Cambodians able to speak Vietnamese. Everyone
growing quiet and quieter. Qui and I spent a year in a reeducation camp, said Rabbit. Did it work, said Tu lightly. Were you
reeducated? Rabbit snickered. We spent the year weaving baskets.

Then Rabbit had a vision of Tu's life in the camps. She saw
an endless series of threadbare tents like a maze, the smell of
human excrement burning in metal drums, the clamor of ten
thousand people living in a few acres. During the day some of
the men were let out to try and find work. Some of the local
people cheated them. Some of the local people were generous.
There were two faces Rabbit didn't recognize, a woman with
the trademark pink cheeks of someone from the mountains of
Sapa, the capillaries in her skin broken from years of living at ten
thousand feet above sea level. A girl stood by the woman with
the same thick smile as Tu. There was something else about the
girl's face, an intensity in the eyes, a smattering of freckles. They
were carried away by one of the epidemics, said Tu, as if sens-
ing her vision. There were epidemics all the time. His voice was
calm, but Rabbit could tell it was hard-earned. Thuy was my
wife for eight years. Rabbit glanced in the rearview, but Qui's
marble-white face was inscrutable as ever. Tu continued. Chi
was six when they both died.

In the backseat Linh opened her eyes. They were only a few minutes from the border. Are we home yet, she said sleepily. Qui put her arm around her. The front of Qui's shirt was strangely dry considering she hadn't had time to nurse an orphaned baby. All they had brought with them was the pale blue rice bowl and the sack of bones.

From the backseat the male parakeet began to flap his wings. Lady. There was an urgency in his voice. Lady, I have something to tell you. Rabbit hadn't wanted to bring them along, but Qui had insisted in her own silent way. Rabbit remembered being a little girl and watching Binh grow smaller as Huyen paddled away to the floating market to trade the bird for the red *ao dai*. Okay, Rabbit had said. The birds can come.

The parakeet fluttered into the front seat and landed on Rabbit's shoulder. Lady, he said. I may never have the chance to speak with you again. The scent of lemon was almost gone from his wings. Hush, said Rabbit, not here. What, said Tu. The border was just up the road. What's not here, Tu said.

Most of what little traffic there was was coming from the other side into Vietnam. People herded animals and carried goods to sell in Nam Xoi. A few pulled carts loaded with produce. Occasionally the guard would stop one of the large carts and poke around. A few battered trucks were driving into Laos. The guard waved each truck through without stopping them.

When their turn came, Tu rolled down the window. Over the sound of a passing truck Rabbit didn't hear what Tu said, but she saw him slip some bills into the guard's hand. For a moment the guard turned and walked away openly counting the money. He stopped and came back a second time. Rabbit heard the guard ask something about the parakeets. If they were the endangered red-breasted variety. They're green, Linh said, her dimples blazing full force. Her charm didn't faze the guard. Maybe they're females, he said. Only the males of that species are red. Brother, I never thought of it that way, said Tu, handing the guard some more money. But they talk just like people, said Linh. Say something, said the guard to the male bird. *Xin chao,* said the bird. *Xin chao,* said the guard, and waved them through.

Nobody was standing in the gatehouse on the Laotian side. Tu breathed a sigh of relief. He hadn't budgeted for a third bribe.

Looking back to the Vietnamese side Rabbit could see a small figure standing all alone by the guardhouse. Even from where she sat on her way into another country, she could see the scratch running the length of his face.

Twenty minutes later they got out of the car to stretch and get their bearings. The landscape was otherworldly. Towering green hills shot dramatically up out of the ground, a dragon's back undulating out of the earth, the road winding among the limestone karsts. Rabbit reached out and took the male parakeet off Linh's shoulder. She walked a little ways up the road. What is it, she said. The bird looked at her with its black eyes. There was no understanding in its face. *Xin chao,* it said. *Xin chao. Xin chao.* Then it began cawing.

Tu said they would drive all the way to Vientiane, the City of Sandalwood on the banks of the Mekong. Vientiane Avenue was said to be wide as a river. At the Temple of the Emerald Buddha they would meet his contact who would accompany them into Thailand. Somehow An had arranged everything from the States. Tu said he was the unofficial mayor of Little Saigon. An was the one who had sent Tu the newspaper article from the *Viet Herald Daily News* in Orange County, in it a story about a psychic in Hanoi who had helped the government discover where a busload of northern veterans had driven off a bridge near Dak

To as they were touring old battle sites. In the article one government official was quoted as saying, "Without her, the northern martyrs would forever walk the earth." An had written in the margins: Cô ta còn sống bao lâu trước khi chính phủ phản bội cô ta? *She lives.* And: *how long before the government turns on her?*

Rabbit had known this day was coming. In Vietnam there were voices everywhere she looked. Northern martyrs, southern soldiers. The ethnic tribes. Children. The French. The Americans. The Cambodians. The Chinese. She couldn't turn her back on them, but it would only be a matter of time before word spread of what she'd found at My Kan. Southerners would flock to the wooden doors on Hang Giay begging her to find their loved ones and tell them who was responsible. The government would put her under house arrest as they had done to a local poet who had penned a song about the southern dead. Rabbit closed her eyes. How could she leave? There will always be souls who need to be found, Tu had said. No matter where you go.

By the roadside she could see Laos stretching out before her. The country was less developed, the terraced hills a brighter shade of green. In the distance water buffalo lumbered through the landscape, everywhere the tops of palm trees like fireworks. Rabbit walked back to the others. This is because of those people in My Kan, isn't it, Linh said. Rabbit didn't say no. She knew that when the guard Tong arrived at the big wooden doors on Hang Giay this morning, he would tell his superiors she was missing. Maybe an official had already spoken with Viet. Maybe they already knew about Tao with her child-sized feet and the four hundred and twenty-eight bodies lying in the field by the ruined church. The government doesn't care about the southern dead, does it, Linh said. They want to pretend it never happened. Nobody said anything. The front of Qui's shirt remained dry. They got back in the car. The parakeet sat dumbly on Rabbit's shoulder. An hour later Rabbit felt something wet sliding down her arm. The bird had defecated on her.

Another hour passed before they saw the first of them. The sun was already strong in the east. Qui tapped Tu on the shoulder and pointed. What is that, said Linh. Rabbit could see a series of them off in the distance, each one monolithic like a sentinel. Tu looked surprised. I've only heard about them, he said. During the American war the Communist rebels used this area. He glanced at his watch but didn't slow the car down. The Americans fought a secret war here, he said. Today there are no Hmong left in Laos because of it.

Fifteen minutes later they came around a turn in the road. The hills were dotted with them as far as the eye could see. Tu couldn't hide the wonder in his face. Okay, he said. He began looking for a place to pull over.

It took twenty minutes to walk up into the heart of it. At one point Rabbit glanced over at Qui. Something about her seemed different. The front of her shirt was crisp and dry, her face slightly animated, not as stony as usual. It took Rabbit a while to figure out exactly what it was. One of Qui's arms, the one closest to the window where she'd been sitting, was slightly pink from the sun.

When they got to the first one, Rabbit could see that it was taller than a man, the stone gray and weathered. There were hundreds of them. Some of them looked broken but many were intact. Some lay on their sides so that you could peer into the musty darkness. We're on the Plain of Jars, said Tu. Jars, repeated Linh incredulously. Tu nodded. Nobody knows who put them here, but they're thousands of years old. Rabbit brushed one with her hand. It was the size of a small boulder, a circular hole carved in the top. Each one was lidless and cold to the touch.

Some say they were built to catch the monsoon rains, said Tu. Others say they form maps of the stars. Linh picked something off the ground and handed it to him. Yes, he said. The thing gleamed in his fingers as if it had been polished. The land here is littered with bones.

Linh tugged Qui's sleeve. I need a bathroom, she said. Qui nodded and the two of them walked off to find a spot. Whose bones, said Rabbit. Tu shook his head and handed her the fragment. The thing was small and tapered like it might have been part of a foot. It's probably from the war, said Tu. Rabbit ran her fingers along the tip. Usually direct contact gave her an instant image, the picture so clear, the voice as if screaming.

Rabbit closed her eyes. She stood holding the bone and waiting for its story to come. She could feel the sun moving through the sky. Whole universes being born and falling dead. I can't hear anything, she said. Maybe it's too old, said Tu. Rabbit squeezed the bone even tighter in her palm. She sniffed it, then put it to her lips and slipped it in her mouth. It was sour and gritty and silent.

Then the sound of someone crying. Rabbit opened her eyes. She could see Qui and Linh walking back down the ridge, Qui's face pink with sun as the two of them picked their way down the hill through the forest of jars. Rabbit spit the bone out into her palm. What's wrong, she said. Qui walked with her arm around a crying Linh. I'm bleeding, said Linh. In the growing light her face look aged. Qui nodded, the front of her shirt dry. Rabbit closed her eyes again.

Already the others are heading back to the car, the sounds of Linh's sobs traveling on the wind. Rabbit stands on and on in the shadow of a stone jar gripping the bone fragment. Sweat trickles down her forehead. The sound of insects chirring in the dry grass. Nothing comes to her but the smell of bird shit rising from her arm.

VIETNAM

⊕ HANOI
• Mountain of the
Fragrant Traces

Life is a Wheel [2001]

CHINA

LAOS

THAILAND

South China Sea

CAMBODIA

HO CHI MINH
⊕ CITY

She is the One Who Hears the Cries of the World. In Her male form She is sometimes referred to as the One Who Holds the Lotus or He Who Perceives the Lamentations of the Living, in Her female form She is depicted with eleven heads, a thousand arms, the orphaned parrot who became Her disciple often on Her shoulder. Her home is a small grotto on the side of Fragrant Mountain. She can produce Her own light, can incarnate as anything or anyone. She is the Goddess of Mercy who postpones Her own nirvana for the sake of us. She will not leave the earth until every being has been freed from the dark cycle of life.

IN HER PREVIOUS LIFE, SHE WOULD HAVE HEARD THE ROAR OF their engines miles away in among the clamor of the world, her ears prickling at the distant sound. Instead she heard the roar of engines just as Linh did, the noise of their motorcycles like small boats on rough seas.

Something was biting her on the shin. Rabbit opened her eyes. She could feel the late-evening breeze fluttering through the gaps in the sun-bleached planks of the one-room hut in the shadow of the Mountain of the Fragrant Traces. Already Linh was standing guard in the doorway, the female parakeet perched on her shoulder. Even in the gathering darkness Rabbit could see the bird glaring at her as if to say you have nothing to lose by trying. You're wrong, Rabbit thought, but she remained silent in her hammock, not wanting the bird to begin lecturing her after all these years.

It was another ten minutes before the strangers arrived. The sun was down, the moon on the edge of the trees. She wondered where they were coming from so late in the day. Through the woods she could hear a dog barking, the meditative waters of the Swallow Bird River surging a short distance away. The Mountain of the Fragrant Traces was said to be the home of Quan Am, the Bodhisattva of Compassion, the Lady's home a grotto no bigger than a coffin. According to legend the tiny grotto was lined with a thirty-foot snake, the Lady curled up tight in its coils.

Qui and Tu were late coming home from the river. Perhaps the two of them had stopped somewhere in among the trees. Evenings Tu checked the nets for fish while Qui tended the hives barehanded. They never coupled in the one room the four of them shared, Rabbit and Linh sleeping in hammocks and the two of them down on a mat on the floor, though Rabbit knew things were different when they were alone. The way Tu and Qui would float back into the house at the end of the day, faces luminous.

And now someone was making their way to the door. Rabbit wondered who would be desperate enough to brave the government edict. She heard the gate creak open on its rusty hinges. At the noise, the female parakeet winced. Anytime the gate swung open, Rabbit thought of bone grinding on bone. Outside the full moon was rising like a trophy over the tops of the trees.

When the man and woman stepped into the yard, Linh was already standing in the doorway with her arms akimbo, the female parakeet perched on her shoulder, the little girl's delicate features in sharp contrast to her iron bearing. *Xin chao, xin chao,* said the bird. Linh stuck her finger in its black beak and quickly motioned the visitors inside. After they were in, she peered up and down the road to see if anyone was watching. When she finally closed the door, she blew out the candle burning on the table, throwing the scene even further into darkness.

The room was small and cluttered. Two sleeping mats lay in the dirt, a pair of hammocks hanging by the window, pots and baskets stacked on either side of the door. An old fishing net was heaped in a corner, the netting full of holes chewed by rats. The only light was from the fire burning in the open pit. In the tight space the woman visitor stood behind the man as if trying to make herself smaller. The man smelled of cigarettes, his teeth stained from addiction. The skin around his eyes was lighter than the rest of his face. Little Sister, he said to Linh. He kept his eyes on the floor. His hands were shaking. The villagers who live along the Swallow Bird River say in this house there is one who speaks with the dead.

Linh began to stroke the parakeet on her shoulder. She looked the man right in the face. Child, she said. You are mistaken. Linh waved her hand around the empty room. I am the only one here. Then the door opened and Tu and Qui walked in. There was a smattering of stray twigs stuck in Qui's silvery hair. What's going on here, said Tu. He was holding a fish, the thing wriggling and iridescent in his arms. Who are you? When he and Qui walked in, the room grew a little brighter.

The man began to talk. He explained who he was and what he did. He introduced the woman standing just at his shoulder, the woman with a face like none of them had ever seen, a face at once like their own but at the same time darker and foreign, her long eyelashes curling back on themselves. Please, said the man. I just want to show her everything there is to see in Vietnam. He made a gesture of supplication with his hands. This is the country where she was born, he said. Tu sighed. The fish continued to wriggle in his arms. We are her people, the man added as if that would help.

Then the floor opened up at their feet. The woman gasped and jumped back. The man with the pale skin ringing his eyes fell to his knees. Rabbit came rising out of the earth, the male parakeet on her shoulder. The female parakeet flew across the room and perched next to its mate. I hear you, said Rabbit. More than two decades after the end of the war, the woman's kind were starting to come back. For the past few years, thousands of adults who had been given up as children during the war were returning to the country where they'd been born.

Something fat and gray went scurrying across the floor leaving a trail in the dirt, the tracks an indecipherable script. The dark woman looked to her guide. Is she talking to me, said the woman. Please, is this about me?

Sometimes a body is lifted from a chair and walks to where it sees a silent crowd. When you come rising up out of the earth from the secret place your father has once again hollowed in the floor, a strange man and woman are standing in the room, the woman dark in a way you have never seen before. The journey she has taken to arrive at your door is long and arduous and weirdly joyful. This unlikely combination of circumstances opens your ears again for the first time in what will be for you a new age. Everything is interconnected. How the young rice is carried by hand from field to flooded field. Transplantation. The green stalk putting down roots. What you want to say to her: "Wherever you go in the world, even if you find yourself in a strange land among strangers who love you, know that someone will always be listening who loved you first," but there is no need to say this as the woman already knows, a presence at her shoulder keeping watch as she has always suspected. When you take her hand in yours, a symphony of voices rises from her skin, ancestors multi-various like the branches of a tree. The world stirs in mysterious ways. For your own reasons you stopped listening to us in the years when you lost hope, but now our voices are calling you back with our stories like song. The woman is not looking for anything or anyone. She is not asking you to listen on her behalf. She knows she does not walk alone and never has. And now in the light of this room where she stands in the presence of one who might bring her face-to-face with her origins, she lets the awareness wash over her. Consequently please do as you have always done and say, "I hear you," and leave it at that.

THEY WERE ALMOST TO THE RIVER. IT WAS A SHORT WALK
through the dense woods that surrounded the mountain. The
hour of biting insects was long over. Moonlight poured through
the canopy and dappled the ground. They walked single file,
bats darting through the muggy night air, the parakeets resting
on Qui and Linh's shoulders. Rabbit could hear the slow waters
of the Swallow Bird River ambling through the darkness, the
water gurgling like a baby. She could see the mountain looming
over the trees. For a moment it seemed as though a tiny light
were burning on the mountainside. She imagined a figure sitting
in the light as if at a window, the figure like a star, invisible in the
daylight but nevertheless always there.

After the two strangers left, Rabbit told Tu what she'd seen.
He took a deep breath. The stain on the edge of his hairline
gleamed as if freshly bloodied. Okay, he said. He handed her the
fish he'd been holding and went out the door to see if he could
find a boat.

Despite the lateness of the hour Qui began to flit around the
room. Rabbit watched as she hefted a pot in her hand, then put
it back. In time Qui tested everything they owned only to leave
it all where it was.

Finally Qui took the burlap sack hanging from the altar
out into the yard. From the doorway Rabbit noticed a strange
shadow gliding independently along in the moonlight. She
rubbed her eyes. When Qui found the small spade they used
to plant vegetables, she got to work, her silvery hair sparkling.
There were no voices chattering, just the clatter of bones as she
lowered the sack in and buried it. The shadow stayed put where
it was in the yard even as Qui hustled back inside, the shadow
quivering as if weeping. It had been years since Rabbit had seen
him standing at the border in the shadow of the guardhouse. She
knew if she could see him now, the eternal scratch branching
down his face would not be healed.

An hour passed. Linh sat by the fire grooming the parakeets with her fingers. Qui took the pale blue rice bowl off the altar and wrapped it up tight in her shirt. When there was nothing left to do, she sat down and milked herself into the dirt, not even bothering to go outside.

Rabbit lay in her hammock still holding the fish. It seemed to shine in her arms. She was still startled by the suddenness of the two unexpected visitors. It had been years since she'd spoken with the parakeets or seen Son. Whole lifetimes had passed since the rustling of voices stirred inside her. But tonight how the voices wafted easily off the strange woman, the room crowded with their music, the foreign woman's face at once Vietnamese and at the same time something else. Rabbit had seen Amerasians before, but generally they were pale with big eyes, their noses often large and western. The woman was different, her skin a deep chocolate, eyes dark, her nose small and flat.

On the way out the door the woman had gripped Rabbit's hands. She nodded as her guide, his voice shaking, the skin pale around his eyes as if marked by coins, expressed the woman's gratitude. Then the woman let go and the man took Rabbit's hands in his own. Suddenly her ears itched in the old way. An unexpected sadness filled her heart. She closed her eyes. A light dawned in the room inside her head. Somewhere a pair of naked legs lay cooling in a pool of blood under the unblinking moon. The man let go and the vision receded. *Cam on,* the foreign woman said, *thank you,* and then she and the man turned and disappeared into the darkness.

And so Rabbit was making her way to the river, the others trailing along. Tu had returned to the house shaking his head. Their neighbors wouldn't even answer the door, scared of being seen talking to anyone who had anything to do with the one under house arrest. It was as Rabbit had expected. They would make their way on foot. On the way out of the yard, Tu grabbed the small shovel just in case, thinking of a night long ago and the things one unexpectedly finds in the earth.

Rabbit was still carrying the fish Tu had brought home for dinner. It seemed wrong to leave it behind. They hadn't had time to do anything else with it. The fish was still alive, its skin streaked with iridescence, its mouth gaping open rhythmically as its gills folded open and closed.

Ever since they had walked back down out of the Plain of Jars, the four of them had lived in exile in their own country. Through the years they had each slipped away into their own worlds—Rabbit staring at shadows, her freckles fading as she holed up indoors, Qui and Tu entwined down by the river, Linh with the parakeets. Watching the foreign woman and her guide walk away in the moonlight, the simplicity of it had become apparent. That one could open the door and keep going, the man and woman lost to the night. Through the trees Rabbit could hear the rumblings of frogs. An insect buzzed near her ear. The government had forgotten her. She felt the knowledge wash over her. She had stayed in the one-room house all these years without being guarded because she had come to think of herself as a prisoner.

Years ago the drive back from Laos had been uneventful. Within minutes of crossing the border the others had regained their wondrousness—Qui pale as marble, Linh once again in perennial childhood, even the birthmark on Tu's face seemed to shine like a star. Only Rabbit herself was changed. She had been the one to insist they turn around and drive back, the prospect of living in both exile and silence too much to bear. At the border, Tu's face looked ghostly, as if drained of blood at the knowledge of what awaited them. Even after they'd crossed back into Vietnam, the silence that had enveloped Rabbit on the Plain of Jars pressed like a weight on her chest. When they pulled up at the great wooden doors leading into the house on Hang Giay, the police were already waiting. Within days the government had found a new psychic, a young girl who had been bitten by a rabid dog and awakened from her coma with strange abilities. Rabbit remembered the shame of being led away from the grand house on Hang Giay. In the papers and on the TV the government claimed her powers had been a sham. The Old Quarter ground to a halt as Rabbit was put in a car and driven off, the music from a funeral wafting down the street. Then the endless list of charges brought against her. Article 87: "Undermining national solidarity, sowing divisions between religious and non-religious people." Article 88: "Conducting propaganda against the So-cialist Republic of Vietnam." Article 258: "Abusing democratic freedoms to encroach on the interests of the state." It went on and on. She sat in the tiny cell on Duong Roi and imagined a monk in his orange robes, by his side a plastic bucket heaped with shit. The trial took less than a day. She had to ask the driver what was happening in the moment before two policemen got in the car. The driver said you are to be put under house arrest. How long, she'd asked, but one of the policemen got in the front seat and the driver didn't answer. It took Tu eight months to find out where she'd been taken. Did the government even know the beauty of it? The Mountain of the Fragrant Traces was one of the sacred sites, the Lady like a star on the mountainside. Rabbit barely remembered how she had managed during those eight months on her own. Each morning she would walk down to the river and cast the bones of the fish she'd eaten the night before into the waters. In the evening she would walk back to the same spot and put her hand in. Within minutes, a fish would swim into her palm and allow itself to be lifted into the air, each day the same iridescent fish putting its life in her hands. Rabbit remembered nothing else about those days except the silence and the glittering fish who was her only friend.

Already that was another lifetime ago. Tonight as she walked in the shadow of the mountain she clutched the fish in her arms and thought of the long years of solitude she had endured. In some ways it felt as if no time had passed, and in other ways she was just beginning to realize exactly what had been lost.

At last the four of them staggered out of the trees. The river shimmered expectantly. Rabbit could see a series of wooden boxes tucked away in the treeline. She imagined the colony of bees asleep inside with their treasure, the queen like a beacon among the workers. It hadn't rained in months, yet the boxes gleamed white as snow. Linh walked over and put her hand on one. A deep thrumming buzzed inside as if a storm were brewing in the box. The male parakeet fluffed his chest. Qui reached over and lifted one of the lids. Light poured out into the darkness. Linh stood on tiptoe to get a better look, her baby face suffused with brilliance. Rabbit peered over her shoulder. It was as she'd always imagined. Inside, golden universes being born and falling dead.

Qui put her hand in and pulled out a comb. It blazed in the night air. With Linh's help she wrapped it up in a palm leaf, then lowered the lid and tucked the comb in her shirt alongside the pale blue rice bowl. It was all they needed. They could go anywhere. A bat swooped overhead. Maybe tonight they would go anywhere.

How many times had they been on the road? In the darkness the land looked like another world. The Swallow Bird River was like none of the other rivers Rabbit had ever known, the waters slow and dark, a mist rising off the surface. The landscape incandesced like a scene on an ancient scroll. Everywhere small green mountains rising straight up out of the earth.

She didn't hear it until it pulled up beside them. In the moon-light Rabbit could see two figures squatting on a simple raft. The taller figure gestured with his fingers. Pay him, said the male parakeet. The sound startled Rabbit. She hadn't heard the bird speak since Laos. Cautiously she leaned over and slipped the live fish into the old man's arms. He hefted it in his palm as if judging its value, then handed the fish to a little girl squatting beside him. The old man was completely bald, his long gray beard pouring all the way down to his feet.

The girl brought the fish to her face the way one would a puppy. She kissed it and stroked its belly before reaching over the edge of the raft and letting it go. As it swam away Rabbit could see a trail of light left behind in the water like a comet blazing through the sky. The little girl laughed and clapped her hands together, her uneven braids bouncing on her shoulders. When she smiled, Rabbit could see the child was missing one of her front teeth, the head of the new tooth just starting to break the skin.

Rabbit couldn't believe the raft would hold all of them, but it did. As they boarded, a white cormorant dove into the water as if to make room. All the way downriver the bird swam beside them under the light of the full moon. Rabbit sat watching the cormorant, the bird an icy white. Suddenly the bird swung its head toward her. She felt its red stare pricking her skin. They need you, a voice said. Rabbit closed her eyes. When she opened them again, the bird was still floating by the side of the raft, its eyes locked straight ahead into the night.

At the front of the raft Linh was holding the little girl's hand. What's it like, she whispered. She and the little girl with the uneven braids were sitting crossed-legged, a parakeet on each of their shoulders. The little girl shrugged. How would you describe this, the girl said, waving her hand at the landscape. Were you scared, asked Linh. The little girl looked off toward the mountain. There wasn't time, she said. Qui tapped Linh on the back and shook her head. But I want to know, Linh whined. Qui shook her head again.

They came around a bend in the river. The old man paddled them to shore, his gray beard almost touching the water. The little girl pointed toward a copse of trees, her new tooth flashing in the moonlight. A fish jumped, a streak of iridescence rippling outward. Tu stepped off the raft and helped pull it closer to land.

Rabbit was the last one off. She turned and bowed her head to the old man and the little girl, beside them the white bird floating in the water like a cloud. In the next life I will serve you, she said. The old man laughed. In the moonlight his head seemed to shine as if radiating its own brilliance. Sister, he said. It's all one life.

When she stepped onshore, Rabbit felt corporeal in a way she hadn't experienced in years. The old familiar freckles on her nose and cheeks began to shimmer. She could feel her heart beating in her chest, a spark trying to catch in the dark. It felt strange to be walking on land, as if all those years at the foot of the mountain she'd somehow only been floating.

Linh stumbled on her first. The woman was lying facedown in the tall grass along the riverbank. It was obvious she had crawled there. She had no pants on, a large swatch of earth black and sticky under her pelvis. Her body was twisted in an unnatural shape, her hips displaced from their sockets, the agony of her final moments apparent. Rabbit scanned the grass for clues as to what had happened. The blood trail ran up the bank and into the woods, though the thing that had killed her was nowhere in sight. Qui pulled Linh to her and buried Linh's face in her chest. What happened, asked Linh. Already Tu was moving off to find a suitable spot. Quickly Qui followed, taking Linh with her.

Rabbit picked up the woman's wrist. The arm was stiff and cold. In the light of the moon the skin looked ghostly. The stain on the earth still seemed to be spreading. Rabbit could smell the dark blood. Wandering Mother, she said. Speak. Carefully she wove the woman's fingers into her own. Rabbit sat by the body for the two hours it took Tu to dig the grave. From time to time a breeze rustled the grass, but the world remained silent.

It took another twenty minutes to put the body in the earth. Rabbit walked silently beside Tu as he carried the corpse to the spot he'd found upriver. Qui and Linh trailed behind. Together they stood watching until it was done. Tu patted the earth with his shovel. The parakeets stirred the muggy air with their wings.

At the sound of the shovel tamping the dirt, Rabbit felt dizzy. Her limbs filled with the sensation of lying on a stony breast in the dark. She held her hand out to steady herself. Qui reached over and slipped something in her mouth. It was a piece of the honey comb, the comb melting on her tongue, honey the first thing she had ever tasted long ago in a box in the earth.

The moon came out from behind a cloud. Rabbit turned to look at the Mountain of the Fragrant Traces, searching it for even the faintest pinprick of light. The blood began to pound in her ears, the rising wind tinged with voices. In the moonlight, shadows seemed to ebb and wane, each one suddenly unattached to its object.

He was standing on the other side of the river searching the ground at his feet as if he'd been always been standing there, his body still lithe as a sapling, the water like a country between them. Even after all this time Rabbit could see the scratch forking down his face, the mark as if a god had touched his cheek with a finger. He didn't look at her but kept on scouring the earth. Finally he picked up a small stone, palming it in his hand, and when he seemed satisfied it would do, he stepped up to the river's edge and skipped it across the water, the gesture simply the act of a young boy at play. Rabbit watched the stone skim the dark surface, kissing it three times before sinking. She could feel the rooms flooding in her heart. The taste of honey lingered in her mouth. After the ripples faded, the river once again glassy, she looked back across the water. The air shimmered as if distorted by heat, but there was no trace of him.

Then Rabbit's ears began to itch. How many years had it been? In the night she could hear something stirring from a long ways off. She let herself be drawn toward it, the sound pulling her along. The dead woman had crawled all that way, a quarter mile down to the river in search of help, and the treasure she'd left behind was inland, secured in a spot where the trees didn't grow. Rabbit began to run, Tu and the others following, the song floating through the woods. Our Lady of the Fragrant Traces, watch over us in the darkness.

It was lying in the moonlight in the middle of a clearing. Rabbit picked it up and took it in her arms. Every inch of its skin was free of the gore she had witnessed down by the river. She had never seen anything like it, the woman's agony now fully apparent, though how she had gotten it out of her body was a mystery. It was shaped like a T. It had two arms and two legs but at the top of its torso its body branched like a banyan tree into two distinct necks with two distinct heads, two sets of eyes shining in its faces, a single small sea horse lumped between its thighs.

Already Qui has lifted her shirt and taken the bifurcated creature in her arms, but both heads refuse. Then Rabbit feels the spark catch in her chest. Here, she says, and Qui hands her the being. Rabbit lifts her shirt and cradles a head to each breast. The clearing fills with the voices of the dead, tens of hundreds of thousands of millions. Through the gathering roar she can hear voices crying *listen* as the two tiny mouths pull the light from her body. Something shoots down the vault of the sky. I hear you, she whispers. Under the full moon in her thousand thousand arms Rabbit holds the new life closer to her chest.

Bibliography

Balaban, John. *Ca Dao Vietnam: Vietnamese Folk Poetry*. Port Townsend, WA: Copper Canyon Press, 2003.

Cargill, Mary Terrell, and Jade Quang Hunyh, eds. *Voices of Vietnamese Boat People: Nineteen Narratives of Escape and Survival*. Jefferson, NC: McFarland & Co., 2000.

Doan, Van Toai, and David Chanoff. *The Vietnamese Gulag*. New York: Simon and Schuster, 1986.

Fitzgerald, Frances. *Fire in the Lake: The Vietnamese and the Americans in Vietnam*. New York: Back Bay Books, 1972.

Le, Huu Tri. *Prisoner of the Word: A Memoir of the Vietnamese Reeducation Camps*. Seattle: Black Heron Press, 2001.

Tran, Tu Binh. *The Red Earth: A Vietnamese Memoir of Life on a Colonial Rubber Plantation*. Athens, OH: Ohio University, Center for International Studies, 1985.

The insights into life and death on page 33 are quotations from the Buddha.

The poem etched in Little Mother's conical straw hat on page 50 is taken from *Ca Dao Vietnam: Vietnamese Folk Poetry,* translated by John Balaban.

Much of the language in the interludes "Baby, sleep well" on page 54 and "Beloved, stay with me" on page 229 is taken from Vietnamese children's songs that can be found at http://www.mamalisa.com.

On page 78 the line "After life there must be life" is taken from Lucie Brock-Broido's poem "After the Grand Perhaps" from the book *A Hunger.*

Specific incidents in the chapter "And the Water Was Made as Glass" come from Hung Nguyen's escape narrative titled "Coffee Shop from Two Spoons" in *Voices of Vietnamese Boat People*. An's experiences in a reeducation camp draw heavily from Huu Tri Le's *Prisoner of the Word* and Van Toai Doan and David Chanoff's *The Vietnamese Gulag*.

The interlude "The old songs seem so foreign to us now" on page 211 is the Vietnamese national anthem.

On page 256 the opening line is taken from C. D. Wright's *One with Others*.

Some language, which occurs most often in interludes, originally appeared in Quan Barry's poetry collection titled *Water Puppets*, published by the University of Pittsburgh Press in 2011.

The language of governmental charges against Rabbit was taken from the 2011 International Federation for Human Rights (FIDH) report "Rule of Law or Rule *by* Law? Crime and Punishment in the Socialist Republic of Vietnam," which can be found at www.queme .net/eng/doc/Crime_and_Punishment_in_Vietnam.pdf.

A NOTE ON THE TYPE

This book was set in a version of the well-known Monotype face Bembo. This letter was cut for the celebrated Venetian printer Aldus Manutius by Francesco Griffo, and first used in Pietro Cardinal Bembo's *De Aetna* of 1495.

The companion italic is an adaptation of the chancery script type designed by the calligrapher and printer Lodovico degli Arrighi.

Composed by North Market Street Graphics, Lancaster, Pennsylvania

Printed and bound by Berryville Graphics, Berryville, Virginia

Designed by Betty Lew